NEW YORK TIMES BESTSELLER

USA TODAY BESTSELLER

REAL SIMPLE'S BEST BOOKS OF THE YEAR

BOOK OF THE MONTH CLUB SELECTION

GOODREADS CHOICE AWARD FINALIST

PUBLISHERS WEEKLY'S
TOP 10 MYSTERIES/THRILLERS OF FALL

PARADE'S BEST BOOKS OF FALL

———

"I loved it!"
—SARAH PINBOROUGH,
bestselling author of *Behind Her Eyes*

"Deliciously dark . . . An exquisitely constructed,
hugely entertaining thriller."
—CATHERINE RYAN HOWARD,
bestselling author of *56 Days*

"Marriage has never been so disturbing . . . or so compelling.
Alice Feeney has written a staggering novel filled with tension,
suspense, and an ending that will leave you flabbergasted. You
think you know where it's going, but you have no idea."
—SAMANTHA DOWNING,
bestselling author of *My Lovely Wife*

"Read it before it heads to the screen."
—CRIMEREADS

THE MILLION-COPY BESTSELLING AUTHOR

ROCK

PAPER

SCISSORS

ALSO BY ALICE FEENEY

His & Hers

I Know Who You Are

Sometimes I Lie

Daisy Darker

ROCK
PAPER
SCISSORS

ALICE FEENEY

FLATIRON
BOOKS
NEW YORK

ROCK PAPER SCISSORS. Copyright © 2021 by Diggi Books Ltd. All rights reserved. Printed in the United States of America. For information, address Flatiron Books, 120 Broadway, New York, NY 10271.

www.flatironbooks.com

Designed by Donna Sinisgalli Noetzel

Illustrations by Rhys Davies

The Library of Congress has cataloged the hardcover edition as follows:

Names: Feeney, Alice, author.
Title: Rock paper scissors / Alice Feeney.
Description: First Edition. | New York : Flatiron Books, 2021.
Identifiers: LCCN 2021024203 | ISBN 9781250266101 (hardcover) | ISBN 9781250838926 (international, sold outside the U.S., subject to rights availability) | ISBN 9781250266118 (ebook)
Subjects: GSAFD: Suspense fiction. | Mystery fiction.
Classification: LCC PR6106.E34427 R63 2021 | DDC 823/.92—dc23
LC record available at https://lccn.loc.gov/2021024203

ISBN 978-1-250-26612-5 (trade paperback)

Our books may be purchased in bulk for promotional, educational, or business use. Please contact your local bookseller or the Macmillan Corporate and Premium Sales Department at 1-800-221-7945, extension 5442, or by email at MacmillanSpecialMarkets@macmillan.com.

First published in the U.S. by Flatiron Books in 2021

First Flatiron Books Paperback Edition: 2022

10 9 8

For my Daniel, of course

ROCK

PAPER

SCISSORS

AMELIA

February 2020

My husband doesn't recognize my face.

I feel him staring at me as I drive, and wonder what he sees. Nobody else looks familiar to him either, but it is still strange to think that the man I married wouldn't be able to pick me out in a police lineup.

I know the expression his face is wearing without having to look. It's the sulky, petulant, "I told you so" version, so I concentrate on the road instead. I need to. The snow is falling faster now, it's like driving in a whiteout, and the windscreen wipers on my Morris Minor Traveller are struggling to cope. The car—like me—was made in 1978. If you look after things, they will last a lifetime, but I suspect my husband might like to trade us both in for a younger model. Adam has checked his seat belt a hundred times since we left home, and his hands are balled into conjoined fists on his lap. The journey from London up to Scotland should have taken no more than eight hours, but I daren't drive any faster in this storm.

Even though it's starting to get dark, and it seems we might be lost in more ways than one.

Can a weekend away save a marriage? That's what my husband said when the counselor suggested it. Every time his words replay in my mind, a new list of regrets writes itself inside my head. To have wasted so much of our lives by not really living them, makes me feel so sad. We weren't always the people we are now, but our memories of the past can make liars of us all. That's why I'm focusing on the future. Mine. Some days I still picture him in it, but there are moments when I imagine what it would be like to be on my own again. It isn't what I want, but I do wonder whether it might be best for both of us. Time can change relationships like the sea reshapes the sand.

He said we should postpone this trip when we saw the weather warnings, but I couldn't. We both know this weekend away is a last chance to fix things. Or at least to try. He hasn't forgotten *that*.

It's not my husband's fault that he forgets who I am.

Adam has a neurological glitch called prosopagnosia, which means he cannot see distinguishing features on faces, including his own. He has walked past me on the street on more than one occasion, as though I were a stranger. The social anxiety it inevitably causes affects us both. Adam can be surrounded by friends at a party and still feel like he doesn't know a single person in the room. So we spend a lot of time alone. Together but apart. Just us. Face blindness isn't the only way my husband makes me feel invisible. He did not want children—always said that he couldn't bear the thought of not recognizing their faces. He has lived with the condition his whole life, and I have lived with it since we met. Sometimes a curse can be a blessing.

My husband might not know my face, but there are other ways he has learned to recognize me: the smell of my perfume, the sound of my voice, the feel of my hand in his when he still used to hold it.

Marriages don't fail, people do.

I am not the woman he fell in love with all those years ago. I

wonder whether he can tell how much older I look now? Or if he notices the infiltration of gray in my long blond hair? Forty might be the new thirty, but my skin is creased with wrinkles that were rarely caused by laughter. We used to have so much in common, sharing our secrets and dreams, not just a bed. We still finish each other's sentences, but these days we get them wrong.

"I feel like we're going in circles," he mutters beneath his breath, and for a moment I'm not sure whether he's referring to our marriage or my navigational skills. The ominous-looking slate sky seems to reflect his mood, and it's the first time he's spoken for several miles. Snow has settled on the road ahead, and the wind is picking up, but it's still nothing compared with the storm brewing inside the car.

"Can you just find the directions I printed out and read them again?" I say, trying, but failing, to hide the irritation in my voice. "I'm sure we must be close."

Unlike me, my husband has aged impossibly well. His forty-plus years are cleverly disguised by a good haircut, tanned skin, and a body shaped by an overindulgence in half-marathons. He has always been very good at running away, especially from reality.

Adam is a screenwriter. He started far below the bottom rung of Hollywood's retractable ladder, not quite able to reach it on his own. He tells people that he went straight from school into the movie business, which is only an off-white lie. He got a job working at the Electric Cinema in Notting Hill when he was sixteen, selling snacks and film tickets. By the time he was twenty-one, he'd sold the rights to his first screenplay. Rock Paper Scissors has never made it beyond development, but Adam got an agent out of the deal, and the agent got him work, writing an adaptation of a novel. The book wasn't a bestseller, but the film version—a low-budget British affair—won a Bafta, and a writer was born. It wasn't the same as seeing his own characters come to life on-screen—the roads to our dreams are rarely direct—but it did mean that Adam could quit selling popcorn and write full-time.

Screenwriters don't tend to be household names, so some people might not know his, but I'd be willing to bet money they've seen at least one of the films he's written. Despite our problems, I'm so proud of everything he has achieved. Adam Wright built a reputation in the business for turning undiscovered novels into blockbuster movies, and he's still always on the lookout for the next. I'll admit that I sometimes feel jealous, but I think that's only natural given the number of nights when he would rather take a book to bed. My husband doesn't cheat on me with other women, or men, he has love affairs with their words.

Human beings are a strange and unpredictable species. I prefer the company of animals, which is one of the many reasons why I work at Battersea Dogs Home. Four-legged creatures tend to make better companions than those with two, and dogs don't hold grudges or know how to hate. I'd rather not think about the other reasons why I work there; sometimes the dust of our memories is best left unswept.

The view beyond the windscreen has offered an ever-changing dramatic landscape during our journey. There have been trees in every shade of green, giant glistening lochs, snowcapped mountains, and an infinite amount of perfect, unspoiled space. I am in love with the Scottish Highlands. If there is a more beautiful place on Earth, I have yet to find it. The world seems so much bigger up here than in London. Or perhaps I am smaller. I find peace in the quiet stillness and the remoteness of it all. We haven't seen another soul for more than an hour, which makes this the perfect location for what I have planned.

We pass a stormy sea on our left and carry on north, the sound of crashing waves serenading us. As the winding road shrinks into a narrow lane, the sky—which has changed from blue, to pink, to purple, and now black—is reflected in each of the partially frozen lochs we pass. Farther inland, a forest engulfs us. Ancient pine trees, dusted with snow, and taller than our house, are being bent out of shape by the storm as though they are matchsticks. The wind wails

like a ghost outside the car, constantly trying to blow us off course, and when we slide a little on the icy road, I grip the steering wheel so tight that the bones in my fingers seem to protrude through my skin. I notice my wedding ring. A solid reminder that we are still together, despite all the reasons we should perhaps be apart. Nostalgia is a dangerous drug, but I enjoy the sensation of happier memories flooding my mind. Maybe we're not as lost as we feel. I steal a glance at the man sitting beside me, wondering whether we could still find our way back to us. Then I do something I haven't done for a long time, and reach to hold his hand.

"Stop!" he yells.

It all happens so fast. The blurred, snowy image of a stag standing in the middle of the road ahead, my foot slamming on the brake, the car swerving and spinning before finally skidding to a halt just in front of the deer's huge horns. It blinks twice in our direction before calmly walking away as if nothing happened, disappearing into the woods. Even the trees look cold.

My heart is thudding inside my chest as I reach for my handbag. My trembling fingers find my purse and keys and almost all other contents before locating my inhaler. I shake it and take a puff.

"Are you okay?" I ask, before taking another.

"I told you this was a bad idea," Adam replies.

I have bitten my tongue so many times already on this trip, it must be full of holes.

"I don't remember you having a better one," I snap.

"An eight-hour drive for a weekend away . . ."

"We've been saying for ages that it might be nice to visit the Highlands."

"It might be nice to visit the moon, too, but I'd rather we talked about it before you booked us on a rocket. You know how busy things are for me right now."

"Busy" has become a trigger word in our marriage. Adam wears his busyness like a badge. Like a Boy Scout. It is something he is proud of: a status symbol of his success. It makes him feel

important, and makes me want to throw the novels he adapts at his head.

"We are where we are because you're always too busy," I say through gritted, chattering teeth. It's so cold in the car now, I can see my own breath.

"I'm sorry, are you suggesting it's *my* fault that we're in Scotland? In February? In the middle of a storm? This was your idea. At least I won't have to listen to your incessant nagging once we've been crushed to death by a falling tree, or died from hypothermia in this shit-can car you insist on driving."

We never bicker like this in public, only in private. We're both pretty good at keeping up appearances and I find people see what they want to see. But behind closed doors, things have been wrong with Mr. and Mrs. Wright for a long time.

"If I'd had my phone, we'd be there by now," he says, rummaging around in the glove compartment for his beloved mobile, which he can't find. My husband thinks gadgets and gizmos are the answer to all of life's problems.

"I asked if you had everything you needed before we left the house," I say.

"I *did* have everything. My phone was in the glove compartment."

"Then it would still be there. It's not my job to pack your things for you. I'm not your mother."

I immediately regret saying it, but words don't come with gift receipts and you can't take them back. Adam's mother is at the top of the long list of things he doesn't like to talk about. I try to be patient while he continues searching for his phone, despite knowing he'll never find it. He's right. He *did* put it in the glove compartment. But I took it out before we left home this morning and hid it in the house. I plan to teach my husband an important lesson this weekend and he doesn't need his phone for that.

Fifteen minutes later, we're back on the road and seem to be

making progress. Adam squints in the darkness as he studies the directions I printed off—unless it's a book or a manuscript, anything written on paper instead of a screen seems to baffle him.

"You need to take the first right at the next roundabout," he says, sounding more confident than I would have expected.

We are soon reliant on the moon to light our way and hint at the rise and fall of the snowy landscape ahead. There are no streetlights, and the headlights on the Morris Minor barely light the road in front of us. I notice that we are low on petrol again, but haven't seen anywhere to fill up for almost an hour. The snow is relentless now, and there has been nothing but the dark outlines of mountains and lochs for miles.

When we finally see a snow-covered old sign for Blackwater, the relief in the car is palpable. Adam reads the last set of directions with something bordering on enthusiasm.

"Cross the bridge, turn right when you pass a bench overlooking the loch. The road will bend to the right, leading into the valley. If you pass the pub, you've gone too far and missed the turning for the property."

"A pub dinner might be nice later," I suggest.

Neither of us says anything when the Blackwater Inn comes into view in the distance. I turn off before we reach the pub, but we still get close enough to see that its windows are boarded up. The ghostly building looks as though it has been derelict for a long time.

The winding road down into the valley is both spectacular and terrifying. It looks like it has been chiseled out of the mountain by hand. The track is barely wide enough for our little car, and there's a steep drop on one side with not a single crash barrier.

"I think I can see something," Adam says, leaning closer to the windscreen and peering into the darkness. All I can see is a black sky and a blanket of white covering everything beneath it.

"Where?"

"There. Just beyond those trees."

I slow down a little as he points at nothing. But then I notice what looks like a large white building all on its own in the distance.

"It's just a church," he says, sounding defeated.

"That's it!" I say, reading an old wooden sign up ahead. "Blackwater Chapel is what we're looking for. We must be here!"

"We've driven all this way to stay in . . . an old church?"

"A converted chapel, yes, and I did all the driving."

I slow right down, and follow the snow-covered dirt track that leads away from the single-lane road and into the floor of the valley. We pass a tiny thatched cottage on the right—the only other building I can see for miles—then we cross a small bridge and are immediately confronted by a flock of sheep. They are huddled together, eerily illuminated by our headlights, and blocking our path. I gently rev the engine, and try tapping the car horn, but they don't move. With their eyes glowing in the darkness they look a little supernatural. Then I hear the sound of growling in the back of the car.

Bob—our giant black Labrador—has been quiet for most of the journey. At his age he mostly likes to sleep and eat, but he is afraid of sheep. And feathers. I'm scared of silly things too, but I am right to be. Bob's growling does nothing to scare the herd. Adam opens the car door without warning, and a flurry of snow immediately blows inside, blasting us from all directions. I watch as he climbs out, shields his face, then shoos the sheep, before opening a gate that had been hidden from view behind them. I don't know how Adam saw it in the dark.

He climbs back into the car without a word, and I take my time as we trundle the rest of the way. The track is dangerously close to the edge of the loch and I can see why they named this place Blackwater. As I pull up outside the old white chapel, I start to feel better. It's been an exhausting journey, but we made it, and I tell myself that everything will be okay as soon as we get inside.

Stepping out into a blizzard is a shock to the system. I wrap my coat around me, but the icy cold wind still knocks the air out of my lungs and the snow pummels my face. I get Bob from the boot, and

the three of us trudge through the snow toward two large gothic-looking wooden doors. A converted chapel seemed romantic at first. Quirky and fun. But now that we're here, it does feel a bit like the opening of our own horror film.

The chapel doors are locked.

"Did the owners mention anything about a key box?" Adam asks.

"No, they just said that the doors would be open," I say.

I stare up at the imposing white building, shielding my eyes from the unrelenting snow, and take in the sight of the thick white stone walls, bell tower, and stained-glass windows. Bob starts to growl again, which is unlike him, but perhaps there are more sheep or other animals in the distance? Something that Adam and I just can't see?

"Maybe there is another door around the back?" Adam suggests.

"I hope you're right. The car already looks like it might need digging out of the snow."

We traipse toward the side of the chapel, with Bob leading the way, straining on his lead as though tracking something. Although there are endless stained-glass windows, we don't find any more doors. And despite the front of the building being illuminated by exterior lights—the ones we could see from a distance—inside, it's completely dark. We carry on, heads bowed against the relentless weather until we have come full circle.

"What now?" I ask.

But Adam doesn't answer.

I look up, shielding my eyes from the snow, and see that he is staring at the front of the chapel. The huge wooden doors are now wide open.

ADAM

If every story had a happy ending, then we'd have no reason to start again. Life is all about choices, and learning how to put ourselves back together when we fall apart. Which we all do. Even the people who pretend they don't. Just because I can't recognize my wife's face, it doesn't mean I don't know who she is.

"The doors were closed before, right?" I ask, but Amelia doesn't answer.

We stand side by side outside the chapel, both shivering, with snow blowing around us in all directions. Even Bob looks miserable, and he's always happy. It's been a long and tedious journey, made worse by the steady drumbeat of a headache at the base of my skull. I drank more than I should with someone I shouldn't have last night. Again. In alcohol's defense, I've done some equally stupid things while completely sober.

"Let's not jump to conclusions," my wife says eventually, but I think we've both already hurdled over several.

"The doors didn't just open by themselves—"

"Maybe the housekeeper heard us knocking?" she interrupts.

"The housekeeper? Which website did you use to book this place again?"

"It wasn't on a website. I won a weekend away in the staff Christmas raffle."

I don't reply for a few seconds, but silence can stretch time so it feels longer. Plus, my face feels so cold now, I'm not sure I can move my mouth. But it turns out that I can.

"Just so I've got this clear . . . you won a weekend away, to stay in an old Scottish church, in a staff raffle at Battersea Dogs Home?"

"It's a chapel, but yes. What's wrong with that? We have a raffle every year. People donate gifts, I won something good for a change."

"Great," I reply. "This has definitely been 'good' so far."

She knows I detest long journeys. I hate cars and driving full stop—never even took a test—so eight hours trapped in her tin-can antique on four wheels, during a storm, isn't my idea of fun. I look at the dog for moral support, but Bob is too busy trying to eat snowflakes as they fall from the sky. Amelia, sensing defeat, uses that passive-aggressive singsong tone that used to amuse me. These days it makes me wish I was deaf.

"Shall we go inside? Make the best of it? If it's really bad we'll just leave, find a hotel, or sleep in the car if we have to."

I'd rather eat my own liver than get back in her car.

My wife says the same things lately, over and over, and her words always feel like a pinch or a slap. "I don't understand you" irritates me the most, because what's to understand? She likes animals more than she likes people; I prefer fiction. I suppose the real problems began when we started preferring those things to each other. It feels like the terms and conditions of our relationship have either been forgotten, or were never properly read in the first place. It isn't as though I wasn't a workaholic when we first met. Or "writeraholic" as she likes to call it. All people are addicts, and all addicts desire the same thing: an escape from reality. My job just happens to be my favorite drug.

Same but different, that's what I tell myself when I start a new screenplay. That's what I think people want, and why change the ingredients of a winning formula? I can tell within the first few pages of a book whether it will work for the screen or not—which is a good thing, because I get sent far too many to read them all. But just because I'm good at what I do, doesn't mean I want to do it for the rest of my life. I've got my own stories to tell. But Hollywood isn't interested in originality anymore, they just want to turn novels into films or TV shows, like wine into water. Different but same. But does that rule also apply to relationships? If we play the same characters for too long in a marriage, isn't it inevitable that we'll get bored of the story and give up, or switch off before we reach the end?

"Shall we?" Amelia says, interrupting my thoughts and staring up at the bell tower on top of the creepy chapel.

"Ladies first." Can't say I'm not a gentleman. "I'll grab the bags from the car," I add, keen to snatch my last few seconds of solitude before we go inside.

I spend a lot of time trying not to offend people: producers, executives, actors, agents, authors. Throw face blindness into that mix, and I think it's fair to say I'm Olympian level when it comes to walking on eggshells. I once spoke to a couple at a wedding for ten minutes before realizing they were the bride and groom. *She* didn't wear a traditional dress, and *he* looked like a clone of his many groomsmen. But I got away with it because charming people is part of my job. Getting an author to trust me with the screenplay of their novel can be harder than persuading a mother to let a stranger look after their firstborn child. But I'm good at it. Sadly, charming my wife seems to be something I've forgotten how to do.

I never tell people about having prosopagnosia. Firstly, I don't want that to define me, and honestly, once someone knows, it's all they want to talk about. I don't need or want pity from anyone, and I don't like being made to feel like a freak. What people don't ever seem to understand, is that for me, it's normal not to be able to

recognize faces. It's just a glitch in my programming; one that can't be fixed. I'm not saying I'm okay with it. Imagine not being able to recognize your own friends or family? Or not knowing what your wife's face looks like? I *hate* meeting Amelia in restaurants in case I sit down at the wrong table. I'd choose takeout every time were it up to me. Sometimes I don't even recognize my own face when I look in the mirror. But I've learned to live with it. Like we all do when life deals us a less than perfect hand.

I think I've learned to live with a less than perfect marriage, too. But doesn't everyone? I'm not being defeatist, just honest. Isn't that what successful relationships are really about? Compromise? Is any marriage really *perfect*?

I love my wife. I just don't think we like each other as much as we used to.

"That's nearly all of it," I say, rejoining her on the chapel steps, saddled with more bags than we can possibly need for a few nights away. She glares at my shoulder as if it has offended her.

"Is that your laptop satchel?" she asks, knowing full well that it is.

I'm hardly a rookie so I can't explain or excuse my mistake. I imagine Amelia pulling a Go to Jail–card face. This is not a good start. I will not be allowed to write this weekend or pass Go. If our marriage were a game of Monopoly, my wife would charge me double every time I accidentally landed on one of her hotels.

"You promised *no* work," she says in that disappointed, whiney tone that has become so familiar. My work paid for our house and our holidays; she didn't complain about that.

When I think about everything we have—a nice home in London, a good life, money in the bank—I think the same thing as always: we *should* be happy. But all the things we don't have are harder to see. Most friends our age have elderly parents or young children to worry about, but we only have each other. No parents, no siblings, no children, just us. A lack of people to love is something we've always had in common. My father left when I was too young

to remember anything about him, and my mother died when I was still in school. My wife's childhood was no less *Oliver Twist*, she was an orphan before she was born.

Bob saves us from ourselves by growling at the chapel doors again. It's strange, because he *never* does that, but I'm grateful for the distraction. It's hard to believe he used to be a tiny puppy, abandoned in a shoe box and dumped in the trash. Since then he has grown into the biggest black Labrador I have ever seen. He has a collection of gray hairs on his chin these days, and walks more slowly than he used to, but the dog is the only one still capable of unconditional love in our family of three. I'm sure everyone thinks we treat him like a surrogate child, even if they are too polite to say so. I always said I didn't mind not having a real one. People who don't get to name their children get to name a different future. Besides, what's the point in wanting something you know you can't have? Too late for that now.

I don't normally feel forty. I sometimes struggle to understand where the years went and when I transitioned from boy to man. Maybe doing a job that I love has something to do with that. My work makes me feel young, but my wife makes me feel old. The marriage counselor was Amelia's idea, and this trip was theirs. "Call me Pamela," the so-called expert, thought a weekend *away* might fix us. I guess all the weekends and evenings spent together at *home* were null and void. Weekly visits to share the most private corners of our lives with a complete stranger cost more than just the extortionate fee. For that money, and several other reasons, I repeatedly called the woman Pammy or Pam every time we met. "Call me Pamela" didn't like that, but I didn't like her much so it helped make things even. My wife didn't want anyone else to know that we were having problems, but I suspect some might have noticed. Most people can see the writing on the wall, even if they can't always read what it says.

Can a weekend away really save a marriage? That's what Amelia said when "Call me Pamela" suggested it. I don't think so. Which

is why I came up with my own plan for us long before I agreed to hers. But now we're here . . . climbing the chapel steps . . . and I don't know if I can go through with it.

"Are you sure you want to do this?" I say, stopping just before going inside.

"Yes. Why?" she asks, as though she can't hear the dog growling and the wind howling.

"I don't know. Something doesn't feel right—"

"This isn't a horror story written by one of your favorite authors, Adam. This is real life. Maybe the wind blew the doors open?"

She can say what she likes, but the doors weren't just closed before. They were locked and we both know it.

We find ourselves in what posh people call a boot room and I put the bags down. A puddle of melting snow forms around my feet. The flagstone floor looks ancient, and there is built-in storage along the back wall with rustic wooden cubbyholes designed for boots. There are also rows of hooks for coats, all of which are empty. We don't remove our snow-covered shoes or jackets. Partly because it is just as cold in here as it was outside, but also perhaps because it still seems uncertain whether we are staying.

One wall is covered in mirrors, small ones, no bigger than my hand. They are all odd shapes and sizes with intricate metal frames, and have been hung haphazardly in place with rusty nails and rustic twine. There must be fifty sets of our faces reflected back at us. Almost as though all the versions of ourselves we became to try and make our marriage work, have gathered together to look down on who we've become. Part of me is glad I can't recognize them. I'm not sure I'd like what I saw if I could.

That isn't the only interesting feature of interior design. The skulls and antlers of two stags have been mounted like trophies on the farthest whitewashed wall, with four white feathers protruding from the holes where their eyes must once have been. It's a little strange, but my wife takes a closer look and stares in fascination, like she's visiting an art gallery. There is an old church bench in the

corner that attracts my attention. It looks antique and is covered in dust, as if nobody has been here for a very long time. As first impressions go, this isn't a great one.

I remember the way Amelia and I used to be together, in the beginning. Back then, we just clicked—we loved the same food, the same books, and the sex was the best I'd ever had. Everything I could and couldn't see about her was beautiful. We had so much in common and we wanted the same things in life. Or at least, I thought we did. These days she seems to want something else. Maybe *someone* else. Because I'm not the one who changed.

"You don't need to draw in the dust to make a point," Amelia says. I stare at the small, childish, smiley face she is referring to on the church bench. I hadn't noticed it before.

I didn't draw it.

The large wooden outside doors slam closed behind us before I can defend myself.

We both spin around, but there is nobody here except us. The whole building seems to tremble, the tiny mirrors on the wall swing a little on their rusty nails, and the dog whimpers. Amelia looks at me, her eyes wide, and her mouth forming a perfect O. My mind tries to offer a rational explanation, because that's what it always does.

"You thought the wind might have blown the doors open . . . maybe it blew them shut," I say, and Amelia nods.

The woman I married more than ten years ago would never believe that. But these days, my wife only ever hears what she wants to hear, and sees what she wants to see.

ROCK

Word of the year:
limerence *noun*. An involuntary state of mind
caused by a romantic attraction to another
person combined with an overwhelming,
obsessive need to have one's feelings
reciprocated.

October 2007

Dear Adam,
It was something at first sight when we met.

I wasn't sure what, but I know you felt it too.

The Electric Cinema was a first date with a difference.
We'd both gone to see a film alone but I sat in your seat by
mistake, we got talking, and left together after the movie.
Everyone thought we were crazy and that the whirlwind romance wouldn't last, but I've always got great satisfaction

from proving people wrong. As have you. It's one of the many things we have in common.

I confess that moving in together wasn't exactly how I imagined. It's harder to hide the ~~darker side~~ real you from someone you live with, and you did a better job of concealing all the clutter when I only came to visit. I have renamed the hallway Story Street, because it is lined with so many teetering piles of manuscripts and books, we have to sidestep to pass through it. I knew that reading and writing were a big part of your life, but we might need to find something bigger than a basement studio in an old Notting Hill town house now that I live here too. I am so happy though. I've gotten used to playing second fiddle in the orchestra of us, and I accept that there will always be three of us in this relationship: you, me, and your writing.

It was the cause of our first big argument, do you remember? I suppose I should have known better than to search through the drawers in your desk, but I was only looking for matches. That's when I found the manuscript for *Rock Paper Scissors*, with your name neatly typed in Times New Roman on the front page. I had the flat to myself, and a decent bottle of wine, so I read the whole thing that night. From the look on your face when you came home, anyone would have thought I'd read your diary.

But I think I understand now. That manuscript wasn't just an unsold story; it was like an abandoned child. *Rock Paper Scissors* was your first ever screenplay but it's never made it to screen. You've collaborated with three producers, two directors, and one A-list actor. You spent so many years writing draft after draft, but it still never got beyond development. It must be upsetting that your favorite story has been forgotten about, left to die in a desk drawer, but I'm sure it won't stay that way forever. I've become your official first reader since

then—a role I am very proud of—and your writing just gets better and better.

I know you'd rather see your own tales turned into films, but for now it's all about other people's. I still haven't quite gotten used to the amount of time you spend reading their novels, because someone somewhere thinks they might work on screen. But I've watched you disappear inside a book like a rabbit inside a magician's hat, and I've learned to accept that sometimes you ~~are a bit self involved~~ don't resurface for days.

Luckily, books are something else we have in common, though I think it's fair to say we have different taste. You like horror stories, thrillers, and crime novels, which are not my cup of tea at all. I've always thought there must be something seriously wrong with people who write dark and twisted fiction. I prefer a good love story. But I've tried to be understanding about your work—even though it sometimes hurts when you choose to spend your time in a world of fantasy, instead of here in the real one, with me.

I think that's why I got so upset when you said we couldn't get a dog. I've been nothing but supportive of you and your career since we met, but sometimes I worried that our future was really only about yours. I know working for Battersea Dogs Home isn't as glamorous as being a screenwriter, but I like my job, it makes me happy. Your reasons for not getting a dog were rational (you always are). The flat is ridiculously small, and we do both work long hours, but I'd always said I could take the dog to work with me. You bring your work home after all.

I see abandoned puppies every day, but this one was different. As soon as I saw that beautiful ball of black fur, I knew he was the one. What kind of monster puts a tiny Labrador puppy in a shoe box, throws him in a dumpster, and leaves him there to die? The vet said he was no more than six weeks

old, and the rage I felt was all-consuming. I know what it is like to be abandoned by someone who is supposed to love you. There is nothing worse.

I wanted to bring the puppy home the next day, but you said no, and I was heartbroken for the first time since we met. I thought I still had time to persuade you, but the following afternoon, one of the receptionists at Battersea came into my office and said that someone had come to adopt the dog. It's my job to assess all would-be pet owners, so as I walked down the corridor to meet them, I secretly hoped they would be unsuitable. Nobody goes to a home where they won't really be loved on my watch.

The first thing I saw when I stepped into the waiting room was the puppy. All alone, sitting in the middle of the cold stone floor. He was such a tiny smudge of a thing. Then I noticed the little red collar he was wearing, and the silver, bone-shaped name tag. It didn't make sense. I hadn't even met the prospective owners yet, so they had no business behaving as though the dog was theirs already. I scooped the puppy up off the floor to take a closer look at the inscription on the shiny metal:

WILL YOU MARRY ME?

I nearly dropped him.

I don't know what my face did when you stepped out from behind the door. I know I cried. I remember half my team seemed to be watching us through the observation window. They had tears in their eyes too, and big smiles on their faces. Everyone was in on it apart from me! Who knew you were so good at keeping secrets?

I'm sorry I didn't say yes straight away. I think I went into shock when you went down on one knee. When I saw the sapphire engagement ring—which I knew had been your mother's—I was overcome with a wave of emotions that I

couldn't quite process. And with everyone staring at us, I felt completely overwhelmed.

"I think it's best to make all important life decisions with a game of rock paper scissors," I teased, because I believe in your writing just as much as I believe in us, and I don't think we should ever give up on either.

You smiled. "So, just to clarify, if I lose, it's a yes?"

I nodded and formed a fist.

My scissors cut your paper, just like they always do when we play that game, so it wasn't really that much of a gamble. Whenever I win at anything you always like to think you let me.

For the first few months of our relationship, I mocked you for using too many long words, and you teased me back for not knowing what they meant.

"I don't know whether this is limerence or love," is what you said after kissing me for the first time. I had to look it up when I got home. The odd things you sometimes came out with, along with the disparity in our vocabulary, started our tradition of "word of the day" before bedtime. Yours are often better than mine because I let you win too sometimes. Perhaps we could start having a word of the year? This year's should be "limerence," I still have a soft spot for that one.

I know you think words are important—which makes sense given your chosen career—but I have realized recently that words are just words, a series of letters, arranged in a certain order, most likely in the language we were assigned at birth. People are careless with their words nowadays. They throw them away in a text or a tweet, they write them, pretend to read them, twist them, misquote them, lie with, without, and about them. They steal them, then they give them away. Worst of all, they forget them. Words are only of value if we remember how to feel what they mean. We won't

forget, will we? I like to think that what we have is more than just words.

I'm glad I found your secret screenplay hidden away in your desk, and I understand why it means more to you than anything else you have written. Reading *Rock Paper Scissors* was like getting a little glimpse of your soul; a part of you that you weren't quite ready to show me, but we shouldn't hide secrets from each other or ourselves. Your dark and twisted love story, about a man who writes a letter to his wife every year on their anniversary, even after she dies, has inspired me to start writing some letters of my own. To you. Once a year. I don't know whether I'll share them with you yet, but maybe one day our children can read how we wrote our own love story, and lived happily ever after.

Your future wife

xx

ADAM

I slammed the chapel doors closed. I didn't mean to do it that hard, or realize it was going to make such a loud bang. And I don't know why I didn't just confess to it rather than blaming the wind. Maybe because I'm tired of being told off by my wife every five minutes.

There is another door in the boot room, right in the middle of the wall of miniature mirrors. Bob starts scratching at it, leaving marks on the wood. Along with the growling earlier, it's something else he's never done before.

I hesitate before turning the handle, but when I do, the door opens revealing a long, dark hallway. The sound of our footsteps on the stone floor seems to echo off the white walls, as the three of us walk toward the next door in the distance. When we step through that, all I can see is darkness. But when my fingers find a light switch, I see that we are in a very normal-looking kitchen. It's enormous, but still looks cozy and homely. If it weren't for the vaulted ceiling, exposed beams, and stained-glass windows, you would never know that the room used to be part of a chapel.

A large cream-colored stove takes center stage, surrounded by expensive-looking cabinets. There is a solid-looking wooden table

in the middle of the room, surrounded by restored church pews. It's the kind of kitchen you see in magazines, except for the thick layer of dust covering every single surface.

Something on the table catches my eye. I take a step closer and see that it is a typed note, addressed to us.

Dear Amelia, Adam, and Bob,
Please make yourselves at home.
The bedroom at the end of the landing has been made up for you. There is food in the freezer, wine in the crypt, and you'll find extra firewood in the log store out back should you need it.
We hope you enjoy your stay.

"Well, at least we know we're in the right place," Amelia says, twisting her engagement ring around her finger. It's something she always does when she's nervous. One of those little quirks I used to find endearing.

"Who is the 'we' in the note?" I ask.

"What?"

"'*We* hope you enjoy your stay.' You said you won this weekend away in a raffle, but who owns the place?"

"I don't know . . . I just got an email saying that I'd won."

"From who?"

Amelia shrugs. "The housekeeper. She sent the directions and a picture of the chapel with Blackwater Loch in the background. It looked amazing. I can't wait for you to see it in daylight—"

"Okay, but what was her name?"

She shrugs. "I don't know. What makes you think it's a woman? Men are also capable of cleaning, even if you never do."

I ignore the snipe, I've learned it's best to, but even my wife can't deny that there is something very strange about all of this.

"We're here now," she says, wrapping her arms around me. The hug feels awkward, like we're out of practice. "Let's try to make the

most of it. It's only for a couple of nights and it will be one of those funny stories we can tell our friends afterwards."

I can't see expressions on faces, but she can, so I try to keep mine neutral and resist pointing out that we don't really have any friends anymore. Not ones that we see together. Our social circle has become a bit square. She has her life and I have mine.

We explore the rest of the ground floor, which has basically been divided into two huge rooms: the kitchen, and a large lounge, which looks more like a library. Bespoke wooden bookcases line the walls from floor to ceiling—except for the occasional stained-glass window—and all the shelves are crammed full with books. They're neatly arranged and color coordinated, possibly organized by someone with a bit too much time on their hands.

An intricately designed wooden spiral staircase dominates the middle of the room on one side. On the other, there is an enormous stone fireplace, blackened with soot and age, and literally big enough to sit in. The grate has already been prepared with paper, kindling, and logs, and there is a box of matches beside it. I light it straightaway—the place is freezing and so are we. Amelia takes the matchbox from my hand, and lights the church candles on the gothic-looking mantelpiece, as well as a few others she finds in hurricane lanterns dotted around the room. It looks and feels a lot cozier already.

The uneven stone floor—which must have been the same when the chapel was still a chapel—is covered in ancient-looking rugs, and the two tartan sofas either side of the fireplace look well-loved and worn. There are indentations on the seat and cushions, as though someone might have been sitting there moments before we arrived.

Just as I'm starting to relax, there is an eerie tapping and scraping sound at one of the windows. Bob barks, and my own heart starts to race a little when I see what looks like a skeletal hand banging on the glass. But it's just a tree. Its bare, bonelike branches, being blown against the building by the gale outside.

"Why don't you put some music on? Maybe we can drown out

the sound of the storm?" Amelia says, and I obediently find the bag where I packed the travel speakers. I have a much better selection of music on my phone than she does, but then I remember it not being in the car. I stare at my wife and wonder if this was a test.

"I don't have my mobile," I say, wishing I could see her expression.

I don't like to talk about face blindness, not even with her. The things that define us are rarely what we might choose. But sometimes, when I look at other people's faces, the features on them start to swirl like a van Gogh painting.

"I think a surgeon would struggle to separate you from your phone most of the time. It's probably a blessing in disguise that you left it at home by mistake. There are some albums you like on mine, and a break from staring at screens all day will do you good," she says.

But it's a bad and wrong answer.

I saw her remove my mobile from the glove compartment before we left home this morning. I always put it in there for long journeys—I feel nauseous if I look at screens in cars or taxis—and she knows that. I watched her take it out and put it back in the house. Then I listened to her lie about it all the way here.

Having been married for so long, I know better than to think that my wife doesn't have some secrets—I certainly do—but I have never known her to behave like this. I don't have to see her face to know when she isn't telling me the truth. You can feel it when someone you love is lying. What I don't know, yet, is why.

AMELIA

I watch Adam as he adds another log to the fire. He's behaving even more strangely than normal and looks tired. Bob seems equally unimpressed, stretched out on the rug. They are both prone to grumpiness when hungry. We have plenty of dog food—Adam always says that I take better care of the dog than I do of him—but that doesn't help solve the problem of what *we* can eat. I should have packed more than just biscuits and snacks for the journey. The shop I intended to stop at closed early due to the storm, and my backup plan of dinner at the Blackwater Inn was an epic fail—the derelict pub looked like it had been abandoned for years.

"The note in the kitchen said something about there being food in the freezer. Why don't we see what we can find?" I suggest, walking back toward the kitchen without waiting for an answer.

The cupboards are empty and I can't find a freezer.

The fridge is also bare and not even plugged in. There is a coffee machine, but no coffee, or tea. There aren't even any pots and pans. I do find two plates, two bowls, two wineglasses, and two knives and forks, but that's it. The property is so big, it seems odd to only have two of everything.

I can hear Adam in the other room. He's put on one of the albums we loved listening to when we first met, and I feel myself soften a little. That version of us was a good one. Sometimes my husband reminds me of the stray dogs at work—someone who needs protecting from the real world. It's probably why he spends so much of his life disappearing inside stories. Believing in someone is one of greatest gifts you can give them, it's free and the results can be priceless. I try to apply that rule to my personal life as well as my work.

Last week, I interviewed three prospective owners at Battersea for a cockapoo called Bertie. The first was a blond woman in her late forties. Stable home environment, good job, great on paper. Considerably less so in person. Donna was late for her appointment, but sat down in my little office without even the hint of an apology, dressed in bubble gum pink running gear, and stabbing her phone with a matching fake nail.

"Is this going to take long? I have a lunch date," she said, barely looking up.

"Well, we always like to meet potential new owners. I wonder if you could tell me what it was about Bertie that made you interested in adopting him?"

Her face folded in on itself, as if I'd asked her to solve a complex equation.

"Bertie?" She pouted.

"The dog . . ."

She cackled. "Of course, sorry, I'm going to change his name to Lola once I get him home. Everyone has a cockapoo now, don't they? I've seen them all over Insta."

"We don't recommend changing a dog's name when they're a bit older, Donna. And Bertie is a boy. Changing his name to Lola would be like me calling you Fred. Once we've had a chat, I'll take you to meet Bertie and see how the two of you get along. But you won't be able to take him home today, I'm afraid. There are several steps to this process. So that we can be sure it's the right fit."

"I'm sure I'll be fine."

"The right fit for the dog."

"But . . . I've bought the matching outfits already."

"Outfits?"

"Yes, off eBay. Ghostbusters costumes. One for me, and a mini dog version for Lola. My Insta followers are gonna love it! Does it do tricks?"

I rejected Donna's application. I rejected the next two people who came to see Bertie too—even though one threatened to "speak to my manager" and the other called me a "see you next Tuesday." Nobody goes to a home where they won't really be loved on my watch.

There are as many varieties of heartbreak as there are love, but fear is always the same, and I'm not ashamed to admit that I'm afraid of so many things right now. I think perhaps the real reason I am so scared of losing—or leaving—my husband, is because I don't have anyone else. I've never known what it is like to have a real family, and I've always been better at collecting acquaintances than making friends. On the rare occasions when I feel like I have met someone I can trust, I hold on. Tight. But my judgment can be faulty. There are some people in my life I shouldn't have walked away from: I should have run.

I never met my parents. I know that my dad liked old cars, perhaps that's why I do too, and why I can't let go of my ancient Morris Minor despite Adam's constant complaints. I find it hard to trust new things, or places, or people. My dad swapped his vintage MG Midget for a brand-new family car just before I was born. New doesn't always mean better. The brakes failed on the way to the hospital when my mum was in labor, a truck smashed into the driver's side of their car and they both died instantly. The doctor—who had been driving in the other direction—somehow delivered me into the world on the side of the street. He called me a miracle baby, and named me Amelia because of his obsession with the aviator. She liked to fly away too. I flew from one foster home to the other until I was eighteen.

"I'm guessing people don't stay here very often. It's freezing cold and everything is covered in dust," Adam says, appearing behind me and making me jump. "Sorry, didn't mean to scare you."

He did.

"I wasn't scared . . ."

I was.

"I'm just tired from the drive and I can't find anything to eat."

"Did you try in here?" he asks, heading for an arched door in the corner of the kitchen.

"Yes, but it's locked," I reply, without looking up. Adam always thinks he knows better than me.

"Perhaps the handle was just a bit stiff," he says, as the door creaks open.

He flicks a switch, and when I catch up, I see that the door leads to what looks like a walk-in larder. But the shelves are filled with tools instead of food. There are neatly stacked boxes of nails and screws, nuts and bolts, different-sized spanners and hammers, and a selection of saws and axes hanging on the back wall. There are also a series of strange-looking smaller tools I don't recognize, like miniature chisels, curved knives, and round blades all with matching wooden handles. The damp, dark space is lit by a single lightbulb dangling down from the ceiling. It struggles to illuminate everything below, but it's impossible to miss the large chest freezer in the corner of the room. It's bigger than me—the kind you might find in a supermarket—and, unlike the fridge, I already know it is plugged in from the humming sound it makes.

I hesitate before lifting the lid but needn't have worried.

The freezer is stocked full of what look like individual homemade frozen meals. Each foil container and cardboard lid is carefully labeled with elaborate joined-up writing. There must be over a hundred dinners for one in here, and quite the selection: lasagna, spaghetti bolognese, roast beef, steak pie, toad in the hole . . .

"Chicken curry?" I suggest.

"Sounds good. Now we just need some wine. Luckily, I think I might have found the crypt," Adam says.

He has discovered a torch among all the other tools, and is shining it on the stone floor. It's only then that I realize some of the giant slabs we are standing on are old headstones, the names engraved on them worn away after years of being walked over.

"Down here," Adam says, shining the torch on an ancient-looking wooden trapdoor.

I shiver, and not just because this room is inexplicably cold.

PAPER

Word of the year:
shenanigans *plural noun.* Secret or dishonest
activity or maneuvering. Silly or high-spirited
behavior; mischief.

28th February 2009—our first anniversary

Dear Adam,

It's our first wedding anniversary and, as promised, I am writing my annual secret letter to you, just like the characters in your favorite screenplay. I'm convinced *Rock Paper Scissors* will be a big hit in Hollywood one day, and even if I never let you read the letters I write, I still love the idea of being able to look back at the true story of you and me when we are older.

The past twelve months have been quite the roller coaster for us. Getting married on a leap day was my idea, going to Scotland for our honeymoon was yours. If there is a more

beautiful corner of the world, I have yet to find it. I hope we'll visit there often. I got promoted at work, and you were asked to write a modern adaptation of *A Christmas Carol* for a BBC special. I know it isn't what you really want to be doing, but the commission was a relief. After two failed pilots, your writing work was drying up. You kept saying that it happens to everyone, but it's obvious you never thought it would happen to you.

I've been trying to help—reading books about writing and screenplays, teaching myself about storytelling—and you always ask me to read what you've written. I enjoy feeling like part of the process, and as well as being your first reader, I've started editing some of your work. Just a few notes on the manuscript here and there, which you ~~often mostly sometimes~~ seem to appreciate. I just wish there was something more I could do to help. I believe in you and your stories.

Being married to a screenwriter isn't as glamorous as people think, neither is living in a studio flat in Notting Hill. Our morning routine as husband and wife is almost always the same. If this were a normal day, you would have kissed me on the cheek, got up, put on your dressing gown, made some coffee and toast, then sat down at your tiny little desk in the corner of the studio to start work. Your job seems to involve a lot of time ~~daydreaming~~ staring at your laptop and occasionally tapping the keyboard. You like to start early, but that doesn't always prevent you from still writing late at night. Sometimes you only seem to stop to sleep or eat. But I don't mind. I've learned that you have a low threshold for boredom and that work is your favorite cure.

If this were a normal day, I would have ironed my uniform on the bed—we don't own a board and there's no room or real need for one—then I'd have dressed myself while the fabric was still warm. I would have put some of your left-over coffee in my flask, grabbed Bob, and jumped in my old

banger of a car for my commute. Every day is bring your pet to work day at Battersea Dogs Home.

But today was not a normal day.

It's our first anniversary, it's the weekend, and I read something very exciting as soon as I woke up.

"He's dead!"

"Who is dead?" you asked, rubbing the sleep from your eyes.

Your voice was an octave lower than normal, as it always is after too much red wine the night before. You've started drinking more than you used to, and the cheap alcohol only seems to oil the hamster wheel of late-night writing you're currently trapped in. But we can't afford the good stuff. The shoestring we're living on is looking a little frayed, and that keeps us both awake.

I held my phone right in front of your face, so that you could read the headline.

"Henry Winter."

"Henry Winter died?" you said, sitting up and giving me your half-full attention.

I already knew that Henry Winter was your favorite author, you talked about him and his books often enough, and how you would love to see them on screen. The elderly writer is famous for not being famous, rarely gives interviews, and has looked the same for more than twenty years: an unsmiling old man with an overgrown mop of white hair and the bluest eyes I've ever seen. In the rare photos of him online, he always wears tweed jackets and bow ties. I think it's a disguise: a persona he hides behind. I do not share your enthusiasm for the man or his work, but that doesn't change the fact that he is one of the most successful authors of all time. More than a hundred million copies of his murder mysteries and creepy thrillers have been sold in countries around the globe, and he is a giant in the literary world. Albeit an unfriendly one.

"No, Henry Winter is alive and well." I resisted the urge to add the word "sadly." "That man will live to be a hundred. It's his agent who is dead."

I waited for you to react the way I hoped you would, but instead you just yawned.

"Why are you waking me up with this news?" you asked, closing your eyes and burrowing back down under the bed-covers. Your thirties suit you. You are growing into your good looks.

"You know why," I said.

You stopped pretending that you didn't, but shook your head. "He has never said yes to any TV or film adaptations of his books. Ever. His agent dying isn't going to change that, and even if it does, Henry Winter is never going to agree to *me* writing a screenplay of his work, when he has spent a lifetime saying no to everybody else."

"Well, I agree that you don't stand a chance with that attitude. But with the gatekeeper removed from play, isn't it worth a shot? Maybe his agent was the one who didn't like the idea? Some authors do everything their agents tell them to do. Just imagine if he said yes."

Your hair fell over your eyes—always too busy writing to visit the barbers—so I couldn't see what you were thinking. But I didn't need to. We both knew that if you could get Henry Winter to let you adapt one of his novels, it would be a game changer for your career.

"I think you should get your agent to set up a meeting," I said.

"My agent is bored of me. I don't make him enough money."

"That isn't true. Writing is a fickle business, but you're a BAFTA Award–winning screenwriter—"

"The Bafta was years ago—"

"With a star-studded CV—"

"I haven't been nominated for a single prize since—"

"And a string of successful adaptations. What harm could it do?"

"What good could it do? Besides, if Henry Winter's agent just died, the poor man is probably grieving. It would be inappropriate."

"So is not paying this month's rent."

Your naïveté about some of the authors you admire so much baffles me. You're one of the most intelligent people I've ever met, but you ~~are easily fooled~~ see all authors through rose-tinted reading glasses. The ability to write a good book doesn't make someone a good person.

I could tell this wasn't a battle I was going to win without changing strategy, so I opened the drawer in my bedside cabinet, and took out a small brown paper parcel.

"What is this?" you asked as I put it on the bed.

"Open it and see."

You untied the string with such care, as though you might want to keep the wrapping. We both didn't have much to call our own as children, and I think a little of that "make do and mend" mind-set follows people like us into adulthood. Finding the money to pay for our wedding was another challenge this year. It wasn't the venue—the rows of chairs in the registry office were mostly empty with no family on either side, and only a handful of close friends living in London. I adore your mother's sapphire engagement ring. It fits perfectly—as though it were always mine—and I never take it off, but there were still wedding rings to buy, and a suit, and a dress. Getting married costs a pretty penny, and pennies are prettiest when you don't have many of them.

"It's a crane," I explained, saving you from having to ask what the gift was when you held it up to the light. "Paper is the traditional gift for a first wedding anniversary, so when an abandoned poodle called Origami was dumped on the

doorstep of Battersea Dogs Home overnight last week, it gave me the idea. I taught myself to make it by watching a YouTube video, and chose the crane because it is a symbol of happiness and good fortune."

"It's . . . lovely," you said.

"It's meant to bring good luck."

I knew you would like it more once you knew that. You're the most superstitious man I've ever met. I'm actually very fond of the way you salute magpies, avoid walking under ladders, and are appalled by people who open umbrellas indoors. I find it endearing. Luck, whether it is the good or bad variety, is something you take very seriously.

I smiled as you slipped the little paper crane inside your wallet. I wonder if you'll keep it in there forever? I hope so, I like the idea of that. Unless something luckier comes along.

"I didn't forget," you said. "I just didn't know we were doing this today. Technically it isn't our anniversary until 2012."

"Is that so?"

"Well, we got married on February twenty-ninth 2008. Today is the twenty-eighth. It won't be a leap year again for another three years."

"We might be dead by then."

"Or divorced."

"Don't say that."

"Sorry."

You've been so busy lately. I'm not surprised you forgot. Besides, you're only a man, forgetting anniversaries is something you're preprogrammed to do.

"You'll just have to make it up to me," I said.

Then you slipped your hand inside my pajama bottoms. I think you'll remember what we did after that without me writing it down. I didn't tell you, but I made a wish. If we have a baby this time next year, you'll know it came true.

I knew you needed to work this weekend—despite it

being our anniversary—and the studio is barely big enough for three at the best of times, so I left you to write, and Bob to sleep, and went out to spend an afternoon in town. I quite enjoy my own company, so I've never minded that you need to be alone too. I wandered around Covent Garden for a while, then spent a couple of hours at the National Portrait Gallery. I love looking at all those faces, and it's somewhere we can never go together. Not being able to recognize anyone makes it a bit of a dull day out for you.

When I got home, our little basement flat was so full of candles that you had to remove the batteries from the smoke alarm. The coffee table—we don't have room for a dining one—had been set with two plates, two sets of cutlery, two glasses, and a bottle of champagne. The menu for our favorite Indian takeaway was leaning against it, along with an envelope with my name on. You and Bob watched as I opened it.

HAPPY ANNIVERSARY!

It read on the outside. The three words on the inside were less predictable:

He said yes.

"What does this mean?" I asked. The smile on your face and the look in your eyes already told me the answer. I just couldn't believe it.

"You are looking at the first screenwriter in history to ever be trusted to adapt one of Henry Winter's novels," you said, beaming like a schoolboy who just scored the winning goal.

"Are you serious?"

"Almost always."

"Then let's open the champagne!"

"I think your lucky paper crane got me the gig," you said, popping the cork and filling the tumblers—we don't have flutes. "My agent called me, completely out of the blue, to say that Henry Winter wanted to meet me. I thought I was

dreaming at first—what with you suggesting the idea only this morning—but I wasn't, it was real! I met him this afternoon."

We clinked glasses. You took a sip and I took a large gulp.

"And?"

"My agent gave me an address in North London, said I had to be there at one o'clock on the dot. There was a massive gate outside, I had to be buzzed in, and then this woman—who I presume was some kind of housekeeper—led me through to a library. It was like being in a Henry Winter crime novel, and I half expected the lights to go out and someone to attack me with a candlestick. But then in he walks, a little shorter in real life than I was expecting, but wearing a tweed jacket and blue bow tie. He poured two glasses of whiskey—the first of many—and then we just talked."

"And he asked you to write a screenplay of one of his books?"

You shook your head. "No, he didn't mention it once."

My excitement started to fade a little around the edges when you said that.

"We just talked about his novels, all of them, and he asked lots of questions about me . . . and you. I showed him the crane you made for me and it was the only time he smiled. The whole afternoon felt so surreal, as if I had made it up, but then my agent called again half an hour after I left, and said that Henry would like me to write an adaptation of his first novel, *The Doppelgänger*. If Henry likes it, he says I can sell it! Such shenanigans!"

"Nobody has used the word 'shenanigans' since the war," I teased. "Maybe that could be word of the day, or even the year?"

Then I cried.

You presumed they were tears of happiness and at least some of them were.

"I'm so proud of you," I said. "Everything will change now, you'll see. Once you've written the first adaptation of Henry Winter's work, there will be studios banging on the door begging you to write for them," I added, knowing it was true. Then we clinked glasses again and I downed my champagne.

We finished the bottle and then celebrated my favorite way—twice in one day! Several manuscripts were hurt as a result, but there isn't a lot of space in our flat and we couldn't quite make it to the bedroom. In some ways, tonight felt like the best night of our lives. But now you're fast asleep and I'm wide awake—as usual—and for the first time since we got married, I have a new secret that I have to keep from you. One I'm not sure I can ever share. We weave our lives out of threads of opportunity and stitches of chance, nobody wants a future full of holes. But I worry that if you knew Henry Winter only trusted you with his book because of me, it might be the end of us.

I suppose I can't share this letter with you now either. Maybe one day.

All my love,
Your wife

xx

AMELIA

Adam heaves the rickety trapdoor open. A set of stone steps lead down, and he doesn't hesitate.

"Be careful," I call after him, and he laughs.

"Don't worry, I think a lot of old chapels have crypts. Besides, what's the worst that can happen? Unless it is a secret dungeon, containing the rotting corpses of the last people who stayed here. That would at least explain the smell."

I stay where I am, but listen to the sound of his footsteps until he disappears from view. The torchlight flickers, then goes out.

Everything is silent.

I realize that I'm holding my breath.

But then Adam swears, and a light comes on down below.

"Are you okay?" I ask.

"Yes, just bumped my head on the low ceiling when the torch died. Probably needs new batteries. But I've found a light switch, and I'm pleased to report that there are no ghosts or gargoyles down here, just racks full of wine!"

Adam emerges like a triumphant explorer, with a smile and

a dusty bottle of red. I manage to find a corkscrew and—even though neither of us are wine snobs—we take a sip and conclude that 2008 was an excellent year for Ribera del Duero. Some people say that marriage is like wine and gets better with age, but I guess it all depends on the grapes. There are definitely years that were more pleasurable than others, and I'd have bottled them if I could.

I start to relax once I've had a glass and we have eaten. The frozen chicken curry was surprisingly tasty after being blasted in the microwave, and I can feel myself begin to unwind as we drink our wine in front of the fire, in the lounge that is more like a library. The comforting hiss and crackle is hypnotic, and the flames seem to skip and sway, casting shadowy patterns all around the room full of books.

The storm outside has stepped up another gear. The snow is still falling and the wind is now wailing, but it's warm enough on the sofa in front of the fire. Bob is gently snoring on the rug at our feet and, maybe it's the tiredness from the journey, or the wine, but I feel strangely . . . content. My fingers walk toward Adam's—I can't remember the last time we touched each other—but my hand stops short, as if scared of getting burned. Affection is like playing the piano and you can forget how to do it without practice.

I can feel him staring but continue to look down at my hands. I wonder what he sees when he looks at me? Blurred features? A familiar but undefinable outline of a person? Do I just look the same as everyone else to him?

Ten years is a long time to be married to someone you forget.

I haven't been completely honest with him about this weekend away. I haven't been completely honest about a lot of things, and sometimes I think *he knows*. But I tell myself that isn't possible. We've tried date nights, and marriage counseling, but spending more time together isn't always the same as spending less time apart. You can't get this close to a cliff edge without seeing the

rocks at the bottom, and even if my husband doesn't know the full story, he knows that this weekend is a last attempt to mend what got broken.

What he doesn't know, is that if things don't go according to plan, only one of us will be going home.

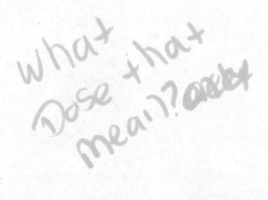

ADAM

We sit in silence after dinner. The frozen curry wasn't as grim as I expected, and the wine was considerably better. I could do with another glass. I notice Amelia's hand close to mine on the sofa. I have an overwhelming urge to hold it and don't know what's come over me—affection has been absent without leave for a long time in our marriage. Just as I am about to reach for her hand, she withdraws it to her lap. Probably for the best, given what this weekend is really about, and what I plan to do.

Staring at the flames dancing in the enormous fireplace, my mind wanders down other paths to other things. Work, mostly. I've adapted three of Henry Winter's novels for film over the past decade and I'm proud of each one. Getting those screenplays greenlighted was a real turning point in my career, but I haven't spoken to the man for a long time. I don't know why I'm thinking of him now. This room probably, it's more like a library than a lounge, he would have loved it.

I'm between projects at the moment. I can't seem to get excited about anything my agent sends my way, and I wonder whether it is time to start working on something of my own again. I've been

meaning to do that for a while, but I guess I had the confidence kicked out of me. Maybe this *is* the right time to—

"Maybe you could revisit one of your own screenplays, if you're not working on anything else for a while," Amelia says, interrupting my thoughts as though she can hear them. I hate that she can always read my mind; how *do* women do that?

"It isn't the right time," I reply.

"What about that one you spent *years* working on, might that be worth another look?"

She can't even remember the name of my favorite screenplay. I don't know why it bothers me, but it does. She used to be far more interested in my work, and seemed to really care about my writing. Her indifference these days hurts more than it should.

"My agent said there was a new eight-part thriller I might be up for. Another novel adaptation. But an old one . . ." I look over my shoulder at all the bookcases ". . . there might even be a copy of it on one of these shelves."

"We agreed no work this weekend," she snaps, suffering a sense of humor bypass.

"I was joking, and *you* brought it up!"

"Only because I could hear you thinking about it. And you were pulling that vacant face you pull when you're not really here, even when you're sitting by my side."

I can't see what face *she's* pulling, but I resent her tone. Amelia doesn't understand. I always need to be working on a story or the real world gets too loud. I can't seem to talk about *anything* lately without her getting upset. She sulks if I'm *too quiet*, but opening my mouth feels like navigating a minefield. I can't win. I haven't told her about what happened with Henry Winter because that's something else she wouldn't understand. Henry and his books weren't just work for me, he became a surrogate father figure. I doubt he felt the same way, but feelings don't have to be mutual to be real.

The wind rattles the stained-glass windows, and I'm grateful for anything that might drown out the loudest thoughts inside my

head. I wouldn't want her to hear those. My hands still need something to do—I no longer want to hold hers and my fingers feel redundant without my phone. I take my wallet from my pocket and find the crumpled paper crane between the leather folds. The silly old origami bird has always brought me luck, and comfort. I hold it for a while, and don't care that Amelia sees me doing it.

"I've been carrying this paper bird around with me for such a long time," I say.

She sighs. "I know."

"I showed it to Henry Winter the first time I met him at his fancy London house."

"I remember the story."

She sounds bored and miserable and it makes me feel the same. I've heard all of her stories before too, and none of them are particularly thrilling.

I wish people were more like books.

If you realize halfway through a novel that you aren't enjoying it anymore, you can just stop and find something new to read. Same with films and TV dramas. There is no judgment, no guilt, nobody even needs to know unless you choose to tell them. But with people, you tend to have to see it through to the end, and sadly not everyone gets to live happily ever after.

The snow has turned to sleet. Large, angry droplets pelt the windows before crying down the glass like tears. Sometimes I want to cry but I can't. Because that wouldn't fit with who my wife thinks I am. We're all responsible for casting the stars in the stories of our own lives, and she cast me in the role of her husband. Our marriage was an open audition, and I'm not sure either of us got the parts we deserved.

Her face is an unrecognizable blur, her features swirling like an angry sea. It feels like I am sitting next to a stranger, not my wife. We've been together *all* day and I feel claustrophobic. I'm someone who needs space, a little time on my own. I don't know why she has to be so . . . suffocating.

Amelia snatches the paper crane from my fingertips.

"You spend too long living in the past instead of focusing on the future," she says.

"Wait, no!" I cry, as she throws my lucky charm into the fire.

I'm up and off the tartan sofa in a flash, and almost burn my hand retrieving the bird. One edge is singed, but otherwise undamaged. That's it. The final act. If I wasn't sure before I am now, and I'm counting down the hours until this is over once and for all.

COTTON

Word of the year:
growlery *noun*. A place of refuge or sanctuary
for use while one is feeling out of sorts. A
private room, or den, to growl in.

28th February 2010—our second anniversary

Dear Adam,

Another year, another anniversary, and it was a great one!
Since you sold the first Henry Winter adaptation, you have
been busier with work than ever before. The Hollywood studio who bought it at auction paid more for those 120 pages
than I could earn in ten years. It was amazing, and I'm so
happy for you, but so sad for us because now we see even
less of each other than we used to. You don't seem to need
me or my input into your work ~~as much~~ at all now. But I
understand. I really do.

A lot has changed for you during the last twelve months,

but sadly not for me. We still don't have a baby. You kept your word about taking some time off for our anniversary though—something which had become inconceivable in recent months—so that we could go away for the weekend. You arranged for a neighbor to look after Bob, told me to pack a bag, and my passport, but wouldn't tell me where we were going. I swapped my dog hair–covered jeans for a designer dress I'd found in a Notting Hill charity shop, and even splashed out on a new lipstick.

You hailed a black cab as soon as we left the flat for our anniversary weekend away. I thought the taxi might take us to St. Pancras . . . or the airport. But after thirty minutes of negotiating London's all-day rush hour, we stopped on a residential street in Hampstead Village, one of your favorite parts of London. Probably because Henry Winter owns a house there. It's super posh, but I didn't think people like us needed a passport to visit, so I wondered why you had told me to bring mine.

After paying the driver, including a generous tip, we clambered out onto the pavement with our bags and you reached inside your pocket.

"What's that?" I asked, eyeing up the small but perfectly wrapped gift in your hand. The ribbon was tied in such a pretty bow, I wondered if someone had done it for you.

"Happy anniversary," you replied with a grin.

"We weren't meant to exchange presents until Sunday—"

"Oh, really? I'll take it back then."

I grabbed the pretty parcel. "I've seen it now, so may as well open it. I hope it's cotton. That's the traditional gift for surviving two years of marriage."

"I think it's about celebrating, not surviving, and I didn't know I'd married someone so demanding."

"Yes, you did," I said, carefully removing the paper.

It revealed a small velvet box—the kind that might contain

jewelry—and was turquoise; my favorite color. I think I was half expecting earrings, but when I opened the lid, I found a key.

"If you could live in any house on this street, which one would you choose?" you asked.

I stared up at the old, detached, double-fronted Victorian house we were standing outside. Its redbrick walls were overgrown with what looked like a mix of wisteria branches and ivy. Some of the glass in the bay windows was smashed, others were boarded up. It was the definition of a fixer-upper—broken but beautiful—and I couldn't help noticing the SOLD sign outside.

"Are you serious?" I asked.

"Almost always."

I felt like a kid who had been given the key to a chocolate factory.

The front door was the same turquoise color as the velvet box and had been recently painted, unlike any other part of the building. When the key opened the door, I cried—I couldn't believe that we owned an actual house, having struggled to pay the rent for a ~~shitty~~ tiny studio flat for so long.

The scene inside was just as derelict as the view from the street. The whole place smelled of damp, there were missing floorboards, peeling wallpaper, and ancient fixtures and fittings covered in dust and cobwebs. Loose wires hung from holes in the ceiling where I presumed lights must once have been, and there was graffiti on some of the walls. But I was already in love. I wandered around the large, bright rooms, all of which were empty but filled with possibilities and potential.

"Did you decorate it yourself?" I asked and you laughed.

"No, I thought maybe you could. I know it needs a bit of work—"

"A bit?"

"But we never would have been able to afford it otherwise."

"I love it."

"Do you?" you asked.

"Yes. All I got you was a pair of socks."

"Well, that's ruined the surprise . . ."

"At least my gift was made of cotton."

"Which year is bricks? We could wait until then . . ."

My anxiety rose to the surface and spoiled our fun. "Can we really afford it?"

You smiled to cover your ~~lie~~ hesitation, but I still saw it. You've always liked to measure out your answers before giving them, never offering too much or too little.

"Yes, it's been a very good year. I've been a bit too busy to enjoy it, but I think it's time we started living the life we always dreamed of. Don't you? I thought we could take our time renovating . . . do some of the work ourselves. Turn it into our very own growlery and make this our forever home." I made a mental note to look up the word "growlery." "If you think the ground floor is good, you should see upstairs," you said.

My hands felt their way up the old wooden banister, and my feet were cautious—careful not to twist an ankle on any of the broken steps in the gloom. There were more cobwebs, dust, and dirt covering almost every surface, but I could already see how beautiful things might be one day. And I've never been scared of hard work.

I followed you along the landing, until we reached a large bedroom. I gasped out loud when I saw the beautifully made-up bed—it was the only furniture in the house—and there was a bottle of champagne in an ice bucket on the floor.

"The sheets are a hundred percent Egyptian cotton. See, I didn't forget. Happy anniversary, Mrs. Wright," you said, wrapping your arms around me.

"What about the other bedrooms?" I asked.

"Well, I think we should get to work on filling them, don't you?"

We've been here for three days, only leaving to go for walks and to get food. Thank you for a wonderful weekend, a very happy anniversary, and for being the love of my life. I plan to spend all my spare time renovating this house and decorating every room until it's the forever home we both dreamed of. It's hard to imagine feeling luckier than I do right now.

All my love,
Your wife
xx

AMELIA

It's hard to imagine feeling unhappier than I do right now.

I didn't mean to throw the paper crane on the fire, I just . . . snapped. It wasn't my fault; it was his for making me feel this crazy in the first place. I watch as he slips it back inside his wallet before looking up at me with nothing but hate in his eyes.

"I'm sorry. I don't know why I did that," I say, but Adam doesn't answer.

Sometimes I feel like one of the abandoned pets I see at work every day, the way my husband disappears inside his writing all the time. Leaving me behind. Forgotten. This is always a difficult time of year in my job. All the people who bought puppies for Christmas, often discover they don't want them for life around Valentine's Day. A German shepherd called Lucky was brought in this week, sadly his name tag had no address. I would've liked to have been able to track down his owners and have them arrested. Lucky had been left tied to a lamppost in the rain, severely malnourished, starving, covered in fleas and filth, and soaked to the skin. The vet said his wounds could only be a result of regular beatings over a long period of time. That poor old dog wasn't "lucky" at all, and

neither is the paper crane Adam keeps in his wallet. It's just superstitious nonsense.

"I don't know why you are so angry all the time," he says.

His words make me angrier.

"I'm not *angry*," I say, sounding it. "I'm just tired of being the only one making an effort in this relationship. We never talk anymore. It's like living with a housemate, not a husband. You never ask about *my* day, or *my* work, or how *I'm* feeling. Just 'what's for dinner?' or 'where is my blue shirt?' or 'have you seen my keys?' I'm not a housewife. I have a life and a job of my own. You make me feel so unlikable, and unloved, and *invisible*, and . . ."

I rarely cry, but I can't stop myself.

Adam hardly ever shows affection these days, as though he can't remember how, but he does the strangest thing then. He holds me.

"I'm sorry," he whispers, and before I can ask which part he is specifically apologizing for, he kisses me. Properly. Holding my face in his hands, the way we used to kiss when we first got together, before life pushed us apart.

I feel my cheeks blush, as though I've been kissed by a stranger, not my husband.

I've gotten good at feeling guilty for doing what is best for me. And guilt is one of those emotions that rarely comes with an off switch. Sometimes I feel like I need to check out of life the way other people check out of hotels. Sign whatever I need to sign, hand back the keys to the life I am living, and find somewhere new. Somewhere safe. But maybe there is still something worth staying for?

"It's been a long day, I think we're both just a bit tired," Adam says.

"We could head upstairs, find the bedroom, have an early night?" I suggest.

"How about another glass of wine first?"

"Good idea. I'll take the plates out and grab the bottle."

I don't know why he left it in the kitchen if he wanted more, but don't mind going to fetch it. This is the most intimate things have

been between us for months. The music has stopped, and I can hear the wind whistling through any cracks and crevices it can find in the chapel walls. The stone floor is so cold it seems to bite my socked feet. I'm in a hurry to get back to the warmth of the other room, but something about the stained-glass windows catches my eye. When I take a closer look, they do seem very unusual. There are no religious scenes, only a series of different colored faces.

I freeze when one of them moves.

And then I scream, because the white face in the window is real. Someone is outside and they are staring right at me.

What the hell?
who is in the window

ADAM

"What's wrong?" I ask, running into the kitchen.

I heard something smash before Amelia started screaming, and I can see that she has dropped the bottle of red wine. There are pieces of glass all over the stone floor, and I grab Bob's collar to stop him from walking on them. "What happened? Are you okay?"

"No. There's someone outside!"

"What? Where?"

"The window," she says, pointing.

I walk over and peer out into the darkness. "I can't see anything—"

"Well, they've gone now. They ran as soon as I screamed," she says, and starts to pick up the broken pieces of glass.

"I'll go outside, take a look."

"No! Are you crazy? We're in the middle of nowhere, who knows who could be out there? Shit!"

She's cut her finger on a sharp piece of bottle, and the sight of blood makes me queasy. I can write about all kinds of horrific things for the screen, but when it comes to real life, I'm a wuss.

"Here," I say, handing her a clean hanky.

I wrap my arms around Amelia and hold her tight, close enough to smell her hair. The familiar scent of shampoo stirs memories of happier times. I can't see a beautiful face, but I've always felt as though I have an instinct for inner beauty. When I think about the night we first met, I can still remember everything about her with such clarity, and how I wanted, *needed*, to know her better. I've always trusted my gut when it comes to people and I'm rarely wrong. I can tell whether someone is good or bad within a couple of minutes of meeting them, and time and life tend to prove me right. Almost always.

"I'll clean that up," I say, stepping away and finding a dustpan and brush in the first cupboard I open.

"How did you know that was in there?" she asks, and I hesitate before answering.

"Lucky guess, I suppose. Are you okay? Do you need your inhaler?"

Amelia has asthma, and sometimes the strangest things can trigger an attack. She once had her eye on a pink coat in a shop window for months. Squirrelled away her money to save up for it. Bought it, wore it one time, and when it was reduced to half price the very next day, she literally had a fit. Amelia has always been someone to count pennies, even though she no longer needs to.

"I really wanted this weekend to be perfect," she says, sounding like she might cry. "It already feels like nothing is going according to plan—"

"Look, this place is a bit creepy, we've had some wine, and we're both tired. Do you think maybe you imagined it?"

I used the tone I reserve for small children, or high-maintenance authors who don't love the screenplays of their books, but I can tell it wasn't the right thing to do even before she erupts.

"No, I didn't bloody imagine it. There. Was. A. Face. In the window outside, looking right at me."

"Okay, I'm sorry!" I say, tipping the broken glass in the bin. "What did they look like?"

"It was a face!"

"A man? A woman?"

"I don't know, it all happened too fast . . . I told you, as soon as I screamed, they ran."

"Maybe it was the mysterious housekeeper?" Amelia stares at me but doesn't answer. "What?"

"Perhaps we should call the housekeeper and tell them that someone is outside?"

"What do you think they're going to do about it?" I say, but she isn't listening, and is already searching for her phone.

"Great," she says, finding it.

"No signal?"

"Not even one bar."

Bob, seemingly bored of our exchange, has wandered out of the kitchen and down the corridor toward the boot room where we came in. We only notice that he's gone when he starts to growl at the old wooden chapel doors, teeth bared, hackles raised. It's the third time our old dog has done something completely out of character since we arrived.

"That's it. I'm going outside to take a look," I say, pulling on my coat.

"Please don't go out there," Amelia whispers, as though someone might be able to hear us.

"Don't be daft," I tell her, attaching the dog's lead to his collar. "I've got Bob for protection. Haven't I, boy?"

Bob stops growling and wags his tail at the sound of his own name.

"Bob is the world's worst guard dog, he's afraid of feathers!" she says.

"Yes, but *they* don't know that. If there *is* someone out there, I'll scare them off and we can open another bottle of wine."

The snow blows inside as soon as I open the doors, and the blast of cold knocks the air from my lungs. Bob goes berserk, growling

and barking and straining on the lead, so much so I struggle to hold on to him. It's pitch-black, and hard to see anything at all at first, but as we blink into the darkness, it soon becomes terrifyingly clear why the dog is so upset. Just outside, no more than a few feet away, there are several pairs of eyes staring at us.

LEATHER

Word of the year:
biblioklept *noun*. A person who steals stories.
A book thief.

28th February 2011—our third anniversary

Dear Adam,

I suspect most couples celebrate anniversaries alone—a table for two at a special restaurant perhaps—but not you and me. Not this year. Tonight, we spent our anniversary with several hundred strangers, and it felt like all eyes were on us.

I have never known anyone who hates parties as much as you do, and yet you seem to go to so many lately. I'm not suggesting that you're antisocial, and I do understand why you dread them so much. Gatherings of more than a handful of people are problematic when you can't recognize a single face. So a fancy film industry party at Tower Bridge, with hundreds of ~~pretentious~~ people who all think you should

know who they are, must be like walking blindfolded into an ego-filled minefield.

"Please go straight in, Mr. Wright," purred the woman on the door, with a wide smile and busy-looking clipboard.

I'd watched while she carefully checked other people's names off her color-coded list, but there was no need with you. Everyone knows who you are now—the new kid on the block who got to stay. Screenwriting is a last laugh business. None of these people gave you a sideways glance when you were down on your luck, but with a blockbuster film under your belt—thanks to Henry Winter's novel—they all want to be your best friend again. For now.

The reason you started inviting me to the big parties, events, and award ceremonies, was so that I could whisper who people are when they approach us, to save you the embarrassment of not recognizing someone that you should. Not that I mind. I quite enjoy it—unlike you—and it's fun dressing up once in a while, getting my hair done, and wearing high heels again. There isn't much call for that sort of thing when you're working with dogs all day.

We have a pretty good routine now. After a few years of listening to you talk about producers, executives, directors, actors, and authors, I had already imagined a cast of their faces. But now I know what they all look like in real life, and we spend evenings like these chatting to people from your world. I rarely have much in common with them, but find it easy enough to talk about books and films and TV dramas— everyone loves a good story.

I was looking forward to seeing inside Tower Bridge for the first time, and the promise of free champagne and posh finger food created by a Michelin-starred chef is still such a treat. But as soon as I spotted Henry Winter's name on the guest list, I dreaded going inside. From that moment, it was obvious that the real reason we were spending our

anniversary with strangers, was because you were hoping to bump into Henry and persuade him to give you another book. You've already asked twice. I told you not to beg, but you ~~always think you know best~~ wouldn't listen. Writing is a hard way to make an easy living.

Tower Bridge was illuminated against the London night sky when we arrived. The party was already in full swing, the dull beat of music and laughter up above us, competing with the gentle lapping of the murky Thames down below. As soon as the lift spat us out onto the top floor, I could tell that it was going to be an interesting evening. The space was smaller than I had imagined, little more than a long corridor crammed full of film types. A waiter squeezed past with a tray of champagne and I was happy to relieve him of two glasses. Having taken a pregnancy test that morning, just in case, I knew there was no reason not to drink. I've stopped telling you the monthly bad news, and you've stopped asking.

"Happy anniversary," you whispered, and we clinked glasses before you took a sip.

I took several myself, so that my champagne flute was already half empty. I find alcohol helps drown my social anxiety, which I still experience every time I attend an event like this. Everyone here knows who you are. The only expectations you still struggle to live up to are your own. But I have never felt as if I fit in with these people, perhaps because I don't. I prefer dogs. I took another sip, then I did what I was there to do and subtly scanned the room, my eyes searching for what yours could not see.

We exchanged anniversary gifts this morning. I gave you a leather satchel with your initials embossed on it in gold lettering. I've watched you carrying your precious manuscripts around in ugly bags for years, so it seemed like an

appropriate present. Your gift to me was a pair of knee-high leather boots I'd had my eye on. I thought I might be too old to wear them—at thirty-two—but you clearly disagreed. I wore them for the first time tonight and I noticed you staring at my legs in the taxi en route to the party. It felt nice to feel wanted.

"Incoming," I whispered into your ear as we made our way down the packed corridor of partygoers.

"Good, bad, or ugly?" you asked.

"Bad. The producer who wanted you to work on that crime novel adaptation last month . . . the one who got snooty when you turned her down. Lisa? Linda? Liz?"

"Lizzy Parks?"

"Yes."

"Shit. Every party has a pooper. Does she look pissed yet?" you asked.

"Very much so."

"Has she seen us?"

"Affirmative."

"Damn. That woman treats writers like factories and their work like tins of baked beans. It wasn't even her book to adapt. She's a walking, talking, biblioklept—"

"Code red."

"Lizzy, darling, how are you? You look wonderful," you said, in that voice you only use when speaking to small children or pretentious people. I hope you never talk to me like that, I'll be upset if you do.

You kissed the air beside each other's cheeks, and I marveled at how you do what you do. It's as though you have a switch, one which I am clearly missing. You become a different version of yourself at parties, the one everyone loves: charming, complimentary, clever, popular, the center of their attention. Nothing like the shy, quiet man I know who

disappears into his new, rather lovely, writing shed every day. It was like watching a performance. I love all the different versions of you, but I prefer my Adam, the real one who only I get to see.

"Incoming," I whispered again, after enjoying a perfectly cooked scallop, topped with a smidgen of pea puree, served on a miniature seashell, and eaten with a tiny silver spoon.

"Who now?" you asked.

I knew this one. "Nathan."

I watched while you shook his hand and listened while you talked shop. The boss of the studio hosting the party is one of those men who is always working the room. Constantly looking over his or your shoulder, to see who else he could or should be chatting up. He was a man who liked to tax joy, always siphoning off a little of someone else's in order to increase his own. You introduced me, and I felt myself shrink a little under his gaze.

"And what do you do?" he asked.

It was a question I hated. Not because of the answer, but because of other people's responses to it.

"I work for Battersea Dogs Home," I said, and made my face smile.

"Oh, gosh. Good for you."

I decided not to explain how or why it wasn't good for me that so many people were cruel or irresponsible when it comes to animals. I also thought it best to ignore his condescending tone. I was taught to always be polite: you can't cross a bridge if you burn it. Luckily the conversation and the company moved on as both always do at these things, and we found ourselves alone at last.

"Any sign of him?" you whispered.

I didn't need to ask who. "Afraid not. We could try the other side?"

We headed down the second corridor, an indoor tunnel

linking one tower to the other above the famous bridge. The view of the Thames and London lit up down below was spectacular.

"Can you see Henry now?" you asked again, and looked so sad when I said that I couldn't. Like a little boy who had been stood up by the girl of his dreams.

There was an invisible queue of people preparing to pounce on you all evening, waiting for their chance to say hello: producers who wanted to work with you, executives who wished they hadn't been unkind to you in the past, and other writers who wished that they were you. My feet were starting to hurt, so I was delighted—as well as surprised—when you suggested leaving early.

You hailed a black cab, and as soon as we were on the backseat, you kissed me. Your hand found the top of my new leather boots, then slid up between my legs and under my dress. As soon as we got home, you started pulling my clothes off in the hallway, until the boots were all I was wearing. Sex on the recently renovated staircase was a new experience. I could still smell the varnish.

Later, we drank whiskey in bed, talked about the party and all the people we met tonight: the good, the bad, and the ugly.

"Do you still love me as much as you did when we got married?" I asked.

"Almost always," you replied with a cheeky grin. It's one of your favorite things to say. You looked so handsome that all I could do was laugh.

I almost always love you too. But I didn't mention that I'd seen Henry Winter several times during the evening, wearing his trademark tweed jacket, bow tie, and a strange expression on his heavily lined face. He looked older than he does in his author photos. With his thick white hair, blue eyes, and extremely pale skin, it was a bit like seeing a ghost.

I didn't tell you that your favorite author had been staring in our direction, constantly following us around the party, desperately trying to get your attention.

Three years and so many secrets.

Are there things that you keep from me too?

All my love,
Your wife

xx

Why did she not tell Adam?

AMELIA

Adam laughs when the sheep outside the chapel door start bleating. Even I find it hard not to smile as he drags Bob—who is still barking like mad—back inside.

When we first saw the multiple sets of eyes staring in our direction, it felt like a scene from a scary movie, but Adam's torch soon revealed that the only nosy neighbors lurking outside the chapel were the small flock of sheep we drove past on the track earlier. They probably followed us here hoping someone might feed them. In the dark, their bodies blended in with the thick blanket of white snow that has covered everything since we arrived, so that all we could see were their eyes.

"We'll laugh about this one day," Adam says, taking off his coat again.

I'm not so sure about that.

I keep my jacket on—I'm freezing—and watch as he locks the front doors with a giant old key. I've never seen it before, but I'm so tired, maybe it was there the whole time and I just didn't notice. I've been planning this trip for so long, I couldn't wait to get away and practically bullied him into coming here, but now I feel strangely homesick.

Adam is a self-confessed hermit. He is happiest in his writing shed with his characters, disappearing so far inside the imaginary world in his head, he sometimes struggles to find his way back. I swear we'd never go anywhere if it weren't for me. He's proud of our home, so am I, but that doesn't mean we should never leave it. The detached, double-fronted Victorian house in Hampstead Village is a long way from the council estate he grew up on, but Adam doesn't tell people about that part of his past. He doesn't just rewrite his own history, he deletes it.

I don't always feel like I belong in such an affluent corner of London, but he fits right in, despite leaving school at sixteen to work in a cinema, with too much ambition and too few academic credits. But everyone loves a trier, and Adam has never learned how to give up. There is a theater director two doors down from our house, a newsreader on our right, and an Oscar-nominated actress lives next door on the left. It can be intimidating: worrying who I might bump into when I walk the dog. I have little in common with our self-made neighbors, unlike my husband. Not that I have anything against social climbers—I've always found the higher you climb in life the better the view. But sometimes his success makes me feel like a failure. Adam is the real deal these days, whereas I'm still more of a first draft; a work in progress.

He kisses me on the forehead then. It's so gentle, like a parent kissing a child good night before turning off the lights. There have been so many times recently when he has made me feel as though I'm not good enough. But maybe I've been projecting my own insecurities. Maybe he *does* still care.

"There's no need to feel embarrassed," he says, and I worry that I might have been thinking out loud.

"About what?"

"Imagining a face in the window and smashing that rather lovely bottle of wine." He smiles at me and I make my face smile back, until he says, "You just need to relax."

Whenever my husband tells me to relax it tends to have the opposite effect. I don't say anything—he wouldn't take me seriously if I did—but I don't think I imagined the face in the window. Unlike him, I live in reality, full-time. I'm sure of what I saw, almost certain, and I can't seem to shake the feeling of being watched.

ROBIN

Robin stepped back from the chapel window as soon as the woman inside saw her, but it was too late. When she started to scream, Robin ran.

It has been a long time since anyone came to visit Blackwater. Over a year since she has seen anyone unexpected here at all, aside from the occasional hiker—lost despite all the gadgets and gizmos they seem to carry nowadays—and there are always plenty of deer and sheep in the valley. But no people. It's too remote and too far off the beaten track for most tourists to visit, and even the locals know to stay away. Blackwater Loch and the chapel beside it have had a reputation for as long as she can remember, and it has never been good.

Luckily, Robin likes her own company and isn't afraid of ghosts. The living have always been more of a concern for her, which is why she's been watching the visitors and their dog ever since they arrived.

Robin had known a storm was coming, so it was a surprise when they drove past her little thatched cottage at the end of the track. She didn't think anyone would be crazy enough to take the coastal

road or risk the mountain lanes in this weather. Robin doesn't own a TV, but there had been several warnings on the radio, and you didn't need to be a meteorologist to look outside the window. It has been cloudy and bitterly cold for days, just like it always is before the snow comes. Robin has spent several years of her life living in the Highlands, so she knows not to trust the Scottish weather, it has a rhythm of its own and no rules. When a storm is on the way, all the locals make time to prepare and take the necessary precautions, because they know from past experience that it could mean being stranded or trapped indoors for days. Nobody in their right mind would come here at this time of year. Unless they *wanted* to get cut off from the rest of the world.

Robin had watched from the window in her cottage, hiding behind her makeshift curtains, transfixed by the sight of the visitors' car as it got closer. It was an old-fashioned, mint green thing, and looked as though it belonged in a museum, not on the road. How they had managed to get all the way to Blackwater was nothing less than a miracle or a mystery. Robin couldn't decide which.

She watched as they carried on down the lane toward the chapel, before parking dangerously close to the edge of the loch. It was pitch-black outside. The wind was picking up and the snow was falling hard, but the visitors seemed oblivious to the danger. The chapel was only a short walk away from her cottage, so she followed them to get a closer look, keeping her distance.

Robin watched them get out of their car, and was pleased to see the big black dog leap from the boot. She has always been fond of animals, but sheep aren't the best when it comes to company. Even from a few meters away she thought the man appeared tired and unhappy, but then long journeys do tend to have that effect on people, and they both looked like they had been on one. Robin stood perfectly still as the couple and their dog walked up to the old chapel, only to find the doors locked and nobody there to greet them. They both seemed so cold and defeated. Someone had to let them in.

The woman had been the one driving the car, and Robin was fascinated by everything about her: the fashionable clothes she wore, the long blond hair, and expertly applied makeup. Robin hasn't had anything new to wear for years, she dresses for warmth and comfort. There is nothing in her wardrobe that isn't made from cotton, wool, or tweed. Most days she wears a uniform of long-sleeved T-shirts beneath her ancient dungarees, along with two pairs of knitted socks to keep her feet warm. Robin's hair is long and gray now, and she cuts it herself when the tangles get too troublesome. Her rosy cheeks are the result of cold winds, not blusher, and even she finds it hard to remember a time before she looked and lived this way.

Robin watched them go inside, then she walked around the chapel, looking in through the stained-glass windows. She wished she could hear what they were saying, but the wind stole their words from her ears. The layers she was wearing had paid off, but she wasn't immune to the cold. Or curiosity. Despite the dust that had settled since the last time someone inhabited the place, the visitors soon seemed to make themselves at home. They lit candles and the fire that had been prepared for them, warmed some food, drank some wine. The dog stretched out on the rug, and the couple almost held hands at one point. From the outside looking in, it was quite a romantic scene. But looks can be deceiving, everyone knows that.

They didn't look *scared* at all.

She wondered if it was because they were together. The world can seem less frightening when you don't have to face it alone. But then life is a game of choices, and some of Robin's have been wrong. She can admit that now, even if only to herself because there is nobody left to tell. Watching the couple start to relax inside the chapel, she knew that they had made poor choices too. And coming here was probably top of the list.

AMELIA

"What's wrong?" Adam says. It's a question my husband frequently asks without really wanting to know the answer.

"Nothing. What now?" I reply as we stand in the boot room staring at each other. I catch sight of my reflection in some of the miniature mirrors on the wall, and look away. This place is a little too *Alice in Wonderland* for my liking. All that's missing is a white rabbit.

"I was looking forward to another glass of wine but you smashed that idea when you dropped the bottle . . ." Adam says.

"Well, you said the crypt was full of them. We could just open another—"

"It was, that's true, and it's your turn to go down there."

"What?"

"Once you see there is nothing to be afraid of, you'll stop being scared."

I'm not sure I agree with his logic, but I do have a feminist backbone, and anything my husband can do I can do just as well. So, although I don't *want* to go down into the crypt, I will. To make a point as well as get some much-needed alcohol.

I notice that Adam closes each door behind us as we head back toward the kitchen, as though trying to keep something *out*. Although I'm sure he must just be trying to keep the heat *in*. When we reach the larder, he heaves open the trapdoor in the floor, and my senses are immediately assaulted by the dank, musty smell.

"What *is* that?" I ask.

He shrugs. "Damp?"

It's far more pungent than any damp smell I've encountered before.

"Pass me the torch," I say.

"The battery is completely dead now, but there is a light switch down there. It's on the right as soon as you reach the bottom."

He holds the trapdoor open as I start down the stone steps. There is no rail to hold on to, so I feel my way down the wall. It isn't just cold, it's wet. Slimy might be a more accurate description. My fingers find the switch, and an ugly fluorescent tube on the ceiling comes to life, creating an eerie green glow. The humming sound it makes is oddly comforting.

Adam was right, there are no ghosts or gargoyles, but the place definitely *feels* spooky. Everything is made of ancient-looking stone—the walls, the ceiling, the floor—and it's so cold down here that I can see my breath. I count three rusted metal rings embedded in the wall, and do my best not to think about what they were used for. I spot the racks of wine in the distance and hurry to take a closer look, keen to get back upstairs. Some of the bottles are coated in so much grime and dust, it's impossible to read the labels, but I spot what looks like a bottle of Malbec.

Then the lights go out.

"Adam?" I call.

The trapdoor up above me slams shut.

"Adam!" I scream, but he doesn't answer, and all I can see is black.

ROBIN

Robin has never been afraid of the dark. Or storms. Or the strange things that sometimes happen at Blackwater Chapel. But, unlike the visitors, Robin is always prepared.

Earlier today, she made the monthly trip to town to get everything she needed. The journey through the valley and the mountains takes just over an hour there and back, and shopping has never been one of Robin's favorite things to do. She's a little rusty when it comes to people skills; living alone for a long time can do that to a person. The solitude of her life is something she has learned to live with, but she still worries about the strange sounds her mouth makes these days, on the rare occasions when she opens it. So she tends to keep it shut.

Being shy and being unfriendly are not the same thing, but sadly most people cannot tell the difference.

Her old Land Rover has seen better days—a bit like its owner—but it is at least easy to drive and dependable, even in the worst kinds of weather. "Town" is really just the nearest village. A sleepy place called Hollowgrove on the wild west Scottish coast. It consists of little more than a handful of houses and a "local store." The

shop—which doubles up as the post office—only stocks essential items at the best of times. Everyone starts to panic buy when they know there's a storm on the way, and a lot of the shelves were already empty. The fresh fruit and veg were all gone, as was the bread, and toilet rolls. Why people needed to stockpile them was beyond her.

Robin snaffled the last pint of milk, some cheese, some matches, candles, and six tins of Heinz spaghetti hoops. She had at least twenty tins of Heinz baked beans at home already, and a cupboard full of nothing but Del Monte tinned mandarins, along with enough cartons of long-life milk to hydrate a primary school. Her dietary choices are nothing to do with the storm. Robin likes tinned food. And she likes to always have enough of it neatly stacked at home, to know that she wouldn't starve anytime soon.

She added the last few jars of baby food on the shelves to her basket. The woman behind the till paused before scanning them—as always—and Robin felt herself shrink a little under the weight of her stare. She had been buying baby food in this shop for as long as anyone could remember, but people knew better than to ask about a baby. They all knew she didn't have one.

The cashier's name badge read: PATTY. Along with the woman's face, it made Robin think of raw burger meat, which made her feel nauseated. Patty was in her fifties but looked older in her frumpy clothes and red apron. She had messy, boyish, blond hair, sallow skin, and dark shadows beneath her beady eyes. Robin noticed that the woman gulped a lot for no reason, which seemed only to accentuate her drooping jowls. Patty was a person who wallowed in bitchy gossip and self-pity. Robin didn't mean to judge the woman who was judging her, she tended to steer clear of rude or unkind human beings, and she had witnessed Patty being both. The woman wore her bitterness like a badge; the kind of person who writes one-star book reviews.

Robin thought about saying hello—knowing that's what

"normal people" do. But if there was a litmus test for kindness, it was clear Patty would fail every time. So even though Robin sometimes longed to strike up a conversation, just to see if she still could, Patty was someone she didn't care to talk to.

By the time Robin got back to the cottage, the power was already out, and the place was dark and cold. It wasn't much—a small stone building with two rooms, a thatched roof, and an outside toilet. But it was hers. And it was as close to a home as she had these days. The cottage had been built by hand more than two hundred years ago, for the priest who looked after the chapel when it was still used for its original purpose. Some of the thick white stone walls have crumbled in places, to reveal dark granite bricks. The fingerprints of the men who made them are still visible, two centuries later, and it always cheers Robin up to think that nobody disappears completely. We all leave some small part of ourselves behind.

Robin's mother sometimes slept in this cottage. Years ago, when Robin was just a child and things were . . . difficult at home. Her mother had a key and would come here whenever she needed to run away, or hide. She was a happy woman trapped inside of a sad one. She loved to sing, and cook, and sew, and had the most wonderful ability to make everything—including herself—look pretty. Even this sad little cottage. Robin would follow her here—she always took her mother's side in any argument—and they would sit together in front of the fire. Comforting each other without words, and waiting for the latest marital storm to blow over. The place became a ramshackle sanctuary for them both. They made it cozy, with homemade curtains and cushions, candles for light, and blankets for warmth. But all of that was long gone when Robin returned years later. Just like Robin's mother. Nothing but the dust of a memory.

The thatch is a little more recent than the cottage's walls, and not without holes, but they can be repaired when the weather gets warmer. Which it will, because it always does. That's the

thing Robin has learned about life now that she is older: the world keeps turning, and the years go by, regardless of how much she wishes she could turn back time. She wonders about that a lot: why people only learn to live in the moment when the moment has passed.

Robin doesn't have much in the way of furniture. Her bed is made from a series of wooden pallets that she found on the side of the road, but it's surprisingly comfy thanks to a thick layer of woolen blankets and homemade cushions. In the room with the fireplace—where she spends most of her time to keep warm—there is a small table with a wonky leg, and an old leather armchair that she rescued from a dumpster in Glencoe. Having belongings that were her own was more important to Robin than how they looked or where they came from. She didn't have much when she arrived here, just a suitcase filled with her favorite things. Robin left everything else behind.

The plates, cutlery, cups, and glasses in the cottage were all borrowed—some might say taken—from cafes and pubs she had visited in the Highlands. Robin never saw it as theft when she slipped the dirty items into her bag, because she always left a tip. She took a guest book from a tea room once, though she wasn't sure why. Maybe all the friendly, handwritten messages inside made her feel less lonely. Robin collected all of the things she *needed* before the money ran out. She didn't have everything she *wanted*, but that was a different story. The cash she had left was kept for emergencies only, and this was definitely one of those.

With no electricity for the foreseeable future, she lights some candles before building a little fire in the grate for warmth. Then she ties a can of baked beans above the flames. Hot meals are important in cold weather, and this isn't the first time Robin has cooked for herself in a storm. When the tin is empty, she'll wash it out, carve two eyes and a smile in the tin, then use it as a candle holder. There are tin-shaped faces all over her little home. Some happy, some sad. Some angry.

Wearing mismatching oven gloves, she removes the can from above the fire and eats the hot beans straight from the tin. It saves on both time and washing up. When she has finished her own dinner, she opens a jar of baby food and spoons the contents into a bowl. She knows he'll eat when he is hungry.

Robin eases into the old leather armchair. She's wearing fingerless mittens indoors, but her hands are still freezing. She throws another log on the fire, then searches inside her cardigan pocket for the wooden pipe, holding on to it like an old friend. It wasn't always hers—something else she borrowed. Sometimes it's enough just to feel it, but not tonight. She takes it out, along with a small, round tin of tobacco. It's a Rattray's pipe, made in Scotland, just like her. A classic Black Swan.

She unscrews the tin, and sprinkles three pinches of tobacco just like *he* taught her when she was a little girl. It feels like feathering a nest before burning it down. A few strands fall onto her lap, where they stay, abandoned by unsteady hands. She notices the dry skin and bitten nails as she strikes a match, so closes her eyes briefly, to hide herself from herself, while she enjoys the smell of the pipe and the nicotine hit she's been craving all day.

Robin stares at the chapel in the distance. From her window she can see that the lights are still on. Unlike her little cottage, the chapel still has power, because the owner suffered too many Scottish storms and installed a generator a few years ago. For all the good it did them. She listens to the radio while she waits; Robin is good at waiting. Patience is the answer to so many of life's questions. She sits and she waits, even when the pipe is empty, and the fire has burned itself out. She listens to the voices on the radio—as familiar as old friends—while they report that the storm has already resulted in several road accidents. Robin wonders if the visitors know what a lucky escape they've had, managing to get here in one piece. When she glances out of the window again, and sees that the chapel is in complete darkness, she thinks that the visitors' good luck might be about to change.

Maybe it has run out altogether, only time will tell.

Robin hears something then, tiny footsteps in the gloom behind her. The bowl of baby food is empty. It's been licked completely clean and that makes her happy. Company is company, in whatever form it takes.

AMELIA

I feel crazy for thinking it, but I don't think I'm alone down in the crypt. I blink into the darkness, and spin around, but I can't see *anything*. In my imagination, the walls are closing in on me, and I think I hear my name being whispered in the shadows.

Amelia. Amelia. Amelia.

My breathing soon starts to get out of control. I feel my chest tighten as though a heavy weight is pressing down on my lungs, and picture invisible hands strangling me as my throat starts to close.

Then the trapdoor opens up above, but I still can't see.

"Are you okay?" Adam's voice calls into the darkness.

"No! What happened?"

"I don't know; power cut, I suspect. I dropped the door when the lights went out, sorry. Try and make your way toward the steps."

"I . . . can't breathe!"

He doesn't just hear my words, he hears the rasping sound of my breaths between them.

"Where is your inhaler?" he shouts.

"Don't . . . know. Handbag."

"Where's that?"

"Can't remember. Kitchen . . . table?"

"Wait there," he says, as if I have a choice.

I've had asthma since I was a little girl—being raised by people who chain-smoked and living in inner-city flats probably didn't help. Not all of my foster parents were child friendly. My asthma isn't as much of a problem these days, but there are still things that can trigger an attack. Being trapped in an underground crypt in the dark seems to be one of them. I edge forward trying to find the steps out of here, but my fingers only find a damp wall, and a cold metal ring. It makes me shudder. If only the torch batteries hadn't died, or I had my phone. I think of all the candles up in the library, wishing that I had one now, but then I remember the matchbox I used to light them. It's still in my pocket.

The first match I strike goes out almost instantly—it's an old box.

I use the second to try and get my bearings, but I still can't see the steps, and I'm struggling to get enough air into my lungs.

The third match I strike briefly illuminates part of the wall, and I notice all the scratch marks on the surface. It looks like someone, or something, once tried to claw their way out of here.

I try to stay calm, remember to breathe, but then the flame burns the tips of my fingers and I drop the final match on the floor.

Everything is black.

And then I hear it again. My name being whispered. Right behind me.

Amelia. Amelia. Amelia.

My breaths are too shallow, but I can't control them and I think I'm going to faint. No matter what direction I look in, all I can see is darkness. Then I hear the sound of scratching.

ADAM

It takes far longer than it should to find Amelia's inhaler.

Her asthma attacks are few and far between, but I always think it is best to be prepared for the worst. Life made me think that way and I'm better off for it. Looking for my wife's handbag is never an easy task—even for her—but trying to guess where she might have left it in an unfamiliar building, in complete darkness, is something that takes time. Time I know she doesn't have. When I finally feel the leather bag, I find the inhaler inside, and rush back to the trapdoor. Bob has started scratching at the wood, and I can hear Amelia crying.

"You need to find the steps," I say.

"What do you think I'm trying . . . to do?"

She can't breathe.

"Okay, I'll come down."

"No! Don't, you'll . . . fall."

"Stop talking and focus on your breathing. I'm coming."

I feel my way slowly, one foot connecting with one step at a time, the sound of Amelia's panicked breathing guiding me in the darkness. I find her against the opposite wall from where she needed

to be, and put the inhaler in her trembling hands. She shakes it and I hear two puffs. Then the power comes back on, the fluorescent tube on the ceiling flickers back to life, and the crypt is bathed in ghostly light.

"There must be a generator," I say, but Amelia doesn't answer. Instead she just clings to me and I wrap my arms around her. We stay like that for a long time and I feel oddly protective of her.

What I *should* feel is guilt, but I don't.

AMELIA

He holds me and I let him, while I wait for my breathing to return to normal. I think about what the marriage counselor asked at our very first session. "Call me Pamela"—as Adam nicknamed her—always sounded as though she knew what she was talking about, but I confess my confidence in her dwindled a little once I discovered she'd been divorced twice herself. *What does marriage mean to you?* I remember how she purred the question and I remember Adam's answer. *Marriage is either a winning lottery ticket or a straitjacket.* He thought it was funny. I didn't.

He kisses me on the forehead, gently, as though scared I might break. But I'm tougher than he realizes. Cleverer too. The kiss feels antiseptic, nothing more than something to soothe.

"How about we take this bottle to bed?" he asks, picking up the Malbec and holding my hand as he leads me out of the crypt. Sometimes it is best to let people think you will follow them, until you are certain that you won't be lost on your own.

There is a circular wooden staircase in the middle of the library lounge, leading up to what must have been a first-floor balcony when this was still a chapel. I'm guessing the woodwork is

all original, it certainly looks it, and every second step creaks in a rather theatrical way. Bob charges ahead, trotting up the stairs, almost like he knows where he is going.

I can't help but stare at the pictures we pass on the whitewashed stone walls. The series of framed black-and-white portraits starts at the bottom of the staircase, and winds all the way to the top, like a photographic family tree. Some of the pictures have almost completely faded, bleached of life by sunlight and time, but the newer ones—closer to the first floor—are in good condition, and even look a little familiar. I don't recognize the faces in them though. And there is no point in asking Adam, who doesn't even recognize his own in the mirror. I notice that three frames are missing; discolored rectangular shapes and rust-colored nails where they used to hang.

A red carpet held in place with metal rods runs up the middle of the stairs—unlike the cold flagstone flooring downstairs—and they open out onto a narrow landing. There are four doors in front of us. All of them are closed and look exactly the same, except for one that has a red DANGER KEEP OUT sign hanging on its handle. There is a tartan dog basket in front of it, along with a typed note like the one we found in the kitchen when we first arrived:

```
No dogs in the bedroom.
Please.
We hope you enjoy your stay.
```

The word "please" seems like an afterthought and a little passive-aggressive on a new line all by itself, but perhaps I'm reading too much into it. Bob sniffs the bed, wags his tail, and sits down contentedly as though it were his own. My dog doesn't suffer from separation anxiety the way I do, and—unlike me—he can sleep anywhere, anytime.

"Well, that's him taken care of. Didn't the note earlier say that one of the bedrooms had been made up for us?" Adam says.

"Yes, but I can't remember which."

"Only one way to find out."

He tries each of the available doors, which are all locked, until the final one opens with a dramatic creak to match the soundtrack of the stairs. Along with the howling wind outside, it's enough to give anyone a dose of the heebie-jeebies.

"This place could really do with some WD-40," Adam says turning on the light, and I follow him inside the room.

I'm shocked by what I see.

The bedroom looks just like ours at home. Not a carbon copy—the furniture is different—but the bed is covered with the same pillows, blankets, and throws. And the walls have been painted in the exact same shade: Mole's Breath by Farrow and Ball. I redecorated as a surprise a couple of years ago, and I'll never forget how much Adam hated it.

We both stand and stare for a moment.

"I don't understand what I'm seeing," I whisper.

"I suppose it does look a bit like ours—"

"A bit?"

"Well, we don't have stained-glass windows in London."

"This is too strange."

"We don't have a grandfather clock either," he says, and that's true. The antique-looking clock in the corner of the room is completely out of place, and the sound of it ticking seems to get louder in my ears.

"Adam, I'm serious. Don't you think this is all a bit weird?"

"Yes and no. They probably just got the idea from the same place as you. Didn't you buy everything in our bedroom from one company because you got a fifty percent discount in the sale? You fell in love with a picture of a bedroom in their brochure, and literally bought it all. I definitely remember the credit card bill. Maybe whoever owns this place did the same?"

What he's saying is true. I *did* fall in love with a picture of a bedroom in a brochure, and I did buy almost everything in it, despite the ridiculous price tags. I suppose it isn't beyond the realm of

possibility that whoever renovated the chapel has similar taste. The place has been beautifully decorated, despite every surface being covered in dust. Which makes me notice that—unlike the rest of the property—the bedroom is spotless. I can even smell furniture polish.

"It's clean," I say.

"Surely that's a good thing?"

"All the other rooms were dusty and—"

"Maybe we should replace our table lamps with these at home?" Adam says, interrupting me and lighting one of the old-fashioned candlestick holders by the bed. He had a box of matches in his pocket, like he knew they would be here. As they start to flicker and cast shadows around the room, I can't help thinking that they look borrowed from the set of *A Christmas Carol*. "They've still got the price stuck to the bottom. They look so old, but they must be new," he says, lifting one.

"It all feels so . . . unauthentic, as if we're in a film of our lives, and someone just dressed the set with cheap replicas of the originals."

"I think they're cool."

"I think they're a fire hazard."

I open another door and find a bathroom that looks nothing like ours at home. Everything is genuinely old, and there are marks on the wall and floor where I'm guessing a claw-foot bath used to be. It was the same in the restroom downstairs—no bath, just an empty space where one clearly once stood. There is mildew on the wall tiles and sink. When I turn on the taps, there is a strange sound but nothing happens.

"I suspect the pipes might be frozen," Adam says from the bedroom.

"Great. I was hoping to take a hot shower," I reply, coming out to join him. The room is now only lit with candlelight, and it does feel cozier. I notice that he's opened the wine and poured two glasses. I want to enjoy it this time, so go to pull the blinds, still a

little creeped out that someone might have been outside watching us earlier. There is an old radiator below the window, but it's freezing cold which explains why I am.

"There are other ways I can think of to keep warm," Adam says, wrapping his arms around my waist and kissing my neck.

It's been a while since I have slept with my husband.

It was different when we first got together—we couldn't keep our hands off each other back then—but I'm sure that's the case for a lot of couples. It sounds daft having been married for so long, but the thought of taking my clothes off fills me with dread. My body doesn't look like it used to.

"I'm just going to freshen up," I say, taking something from the overnight bag before retreating to the bathroom. "Check under the bed for ghosts while you wait."

"Then what?"

"Wait longer."

With the door closed between us, I start to feel calmer again. More in control. I pretend not to know why I am so nervous about being intimate with my own husband, but it's one of those little white lies I tell myself. Just like we all do. I stand barefoot on the cold tiled floor in the unfamiliar bathroom, and stare at the woman in the mirror, then I look away as I remove the rest of my clothes. The new black silk and lace nightdress I bought just for this trip doesn't turn me into someone else, but it might help turn him on. Is it wrong to want to be desired by the man I married?

I open the bathroom door, attempting to look sexy as I step out from behind it, but I needn't have bothered. The bedroom is empty. Adam is gone.

ADAM

Doesn't a KEEP OUT sign make everyone want to see what's behind it? And I've always been rather attracted to danger.

I know Amelia will take forever to "freshen up" in the bathroom and I'm bored waiting. So I take a sip of wine, then step back out onto the landing to see if Bob wants to keep me company. But he's already sound asleep. And snoring.

That's when the DANGER KEEP OUT sign catches my eye and I just can't resist trying the door handle it is hanging on. Surely nothing *that* dangerous could really be lurking behind it. All the other doors up here were locked, but when I turn the knob, this one opens. I don't know what I was expecting, but I suppose I'd hoped for something more exciting than a narrow wooden staircase leading upward. I can see another door at the top of it. Bob has opened one eye and grumbles in my direction. But curiosity killed the cat, not the dog or the man, and now I really want to know what's at the top of the stairs.

There's no light, so I grab one of the candles from the bedroom, then make my way up. One creaky step at a time. I feel something touch my face in the gloom, and imagine tiny fingers, but it's just

cobwebs. I guess nobody has cleaned this part of the house for a long time either. I'm anticipating that the door at the top of the forbidden stairs *will* be locked. But it isn't. As soon as I open it, a huge gust of wind blows out the candle and almost knocks me off my feet.

The bell tower.

The Arctic air outside feels like a slap in the face, but the view from the top of the chapel is spectacular. I feel like I can see the whole world from up here—the valley, the loch, the mountains in the distance, all lit by a fat full moon. The snow has stopped, finally, and the clouds have parted to reveal a black sky decorated with stars. The bell—which is considerably bigger than it looks from the ground—is surrounded by four knee-high white walls. There is no safety rail and barely enough room to sidestep around the main attraction, but it's worth the risk to take in the three-sixty-degree view from every possible angle.

As I look up at the night sky, it seems almost inconceivable to me that something so magical is always there. We're all too busy looking down to remember to look up at the stars. It makes me sad when I think about all the things I might have already missed out on in life, but I plan to change that.

I take my phone out of my pocket to take a picture—the phone my wife thinks is still at home in London. I felt sick when I saw her taking it out of the car glove compartment before we left home, then hiding it in the house. I felt even worse when she lied about where it was, blaming *me* for leaving it behind. She's been behaving strangely for months and now I know I haven't been imagining it.

Amelia went to see a financial advisor recently. She didn't tell me about it until after the event. Said that I spent too much time worrying about the past, and that she wanted to better prepare for the future. I didn't realize at first that she meant *hers*, not *ours*. What other explanation is there for her setting up life insurance in my name and asking me to sign it when she thought I was drunk a couple of weeks ago?

"I just think we're at an age where we need to plan ahead," she said, after eleven on a school night with a pen in her hand.

"I'm only forty."

"And what if something happened to you?" she persisted. "I couldn't afford to pay for a big house in Hampstead Village by myself on my salary. Bob and I would be homeless." The dog—on hearing his name—looked at me then, as if he was in on it.

"You wouldn't be *homeless*. Worst-case scenario, you might have to downsize . . ."

She shook her head and held the pen toward me. I signed the paperwork, because I was too tired to argue and because my wife is one of those women who is difficult to say no to.

Maybe it's because her parents died when she was born, or perhaps it's because of all the sad things she sees at work almost every day, but Amelia thinks about death more than I think is normal. Or healthy. Especially now that she seems so preoccupied with mine.

My wife is planning something, I'm sure of it. I just don't know what.

And I'm not having a midlife crisis.

That's what she keeps accusing me of lately.

I suspect everyone reaches an age where they start to question what they've achieved in life. Whether the choices they've made were the right ones. But I also believe that what I do—telling stories—is important. Stories teach us about our past, enrich our present, and can predict our future. But then I would say that. The words I have written are all that will remain of me when I'm gone.

Actors and directors get all the glory in my business, and most of my career has been spent adapting other people's novels, but those are *my* words that you hear when you watch a TV show or film that I worked on. *Mine.* I didn't even read the book I was asked to adapt last year. I decided that—one way or another—the story that got made was going to belong to me. The producer on the show said she loved my version more than the novel and I was ecstatic. Briefly. Then she asked for changes because that's what these

people do. So I made them and gave in the next draft. Then the director asked for changes, because that's what *they* do. Fast-forward a few months and even one of the actors asked for changes, because of course *they* know the characters better than I do, even though they came from *my* head. So even though I swear my third or fourth draft was much better than their final version, I made the changes because if I hadn't, I would have been fired, and some other shmuck would have replaced me. Because that's how this business works.

My life feels the same as my work, with people always wanting to change me. It started with my mother. When my dad left, she worked double shifts at the hospital to raise me and keep a roof over our heads. We lived on the thirteenth floor of a block of flats on a South London council estate. We didn't have much, but we always had enough. She used to tell me off for watching too much TV when she was working—said my eyes would turn square—but there wasn't much else to do that didn't involve getting into trouble. She preferred to see me reading, so I did, and for my thirteenth birthday she gave me thirteen books. They were all special editions by authors I loved as a boy, and I still have them now, on a little shelf in the shed where I write. She wrote a note in a first edition of my favorite Stephen King novel: *Enjoy the stories of other people's lives, but don't forget to live your own.*

She died three months later.

I left school when I was sixteen because I had to, but I was always determined to make her proud. *Everything* I've done since then was about trying to become someone she wouldn't want to change.

I had a string of girlfriends who tried to change me too, but couldn't, until I met my wife. For the first time in my life, I found someone who loved me for being me, and didn't want to change who that was. I could finally be myself and write my own story, without fear of being abandoned or replaced. Maybe that's why I loved her so much, in the beginning. But marriage changes people whether they like it or not. You can't unbreak an egg when you've already whisked it into an omelette.

I try to shake the negative thoughts from my mind and concentrate on the view. Being this high up reminds me of living on
the thirteenth floor as a kid. At night when I couldn't sleep—the
flat had thin walls—I would open my bedroom window as far as
it would go and stare up at the night sky. The thing I remember
most were the planes—I'd never been on one. I used to count them,
and imagine all those people clever enough, lucky enough, and rich
enough to be flying away somewhere different to me. I felt trapped,
even then. Unlike the view from a block of flats in London, there
are no buildings in any direction here, no sign of life at all, and
everything is covered in snow, bathed in moonlight. We are truly
alone here, which was what Amelia wanted.

People should be more careful what they wish for.

There is a side of my wife that nobody else sees, because she
is so good at hiding it. Just because Amelia works for an animal
charity, it doesn't make her a saint. It doesn't mean she's never done
anything bad, quite the opposite. There are forests less shady than
my wife. She might be able to fool everyone else, but I know who
she really is and what she is capable of. That's why I am emotionally
bankrupt these days—any love I had left for her is spent.

I'm not pretending to be blameless in all this.

I never thought I was the kind of man who would cheat on his
wife.

But I did. And somehow, she found out.

I suppose that makes me sound like the bad guy, but there's also
a bad girl in this story. Two wrongs sometimes make an ugly. And
I wasn't the only one who slept with someone they shouldn't have.
So did Saint Amelia.

AMELIA

"Adam?"

I stand on the landing, holding a candle, and calling his name. But he doesn't answer.

Bob stares up at me, annoyed that I have disturbed his sleep, then he looks at the door with the DANGER KEEP OUT sign and sighs. Sometimes I think our dog is cleverer than we know. But then I remember all the times I have seen him running in circles chasing his own tail, and realize he's just as bemused by life as the rest of us.

I've never been great at sticking to rules, so I ignore the sign and open the door. It reveals a narrow wooden staircase, leading to another door at the top. I take a few steps, then almost drop the candle when I walk into a spider's web. I desperately try to brush it away from my face, but it still feels as though something is crawling across my skin in the dark.

"Adam? Are you up there?"

"Yes, the view is amazing. Bring the wine, and a couple of blankets," he says, and the rush of relief I feel surprises me.

Five minutes later, we are huddled together in the bell tower of

the chapel, and he's right, the view really is quite magical. There isn't a lot of room, and I'm cold—even with the blanket wrapped around my shoulders—but the wine is helping, and when Adam sees me shiver, he puts his arms around me.

"I can't remember the last time I saw a full moon," he whispers.

"Or so many stars," I reply. "The sky is so clear."

"No light pollution. Can you see that brightest star, just to the left of the moon?" he asks, pointing up at the sky. I nod, and watch as he moves his finger as though writing the letter W. "These five stars form the constellation Cassiopeia." Adam is full of random knowledge, sometimes I think it's the reason why there is no room left inside his head to think about us, or me.

"Which one is Cassiopeia again?"

"Cassiopeia was a queen in Greek mythology whose vanity and arrogance led to her downfall." My husband knows more than I do about a great many things. He's well read and a bit of a peacock when it comes to general knowledge. But if there were an IQ test for emotional intelligence, I'd have a higher score every time. There is an edge to his tone as he talks about the stars, and I don't think I am imagining it.

I was having a bit of a clear out recently, sorting through some old things, and I found a pretty box of wedding keepsakes. It was like a marriage time capsule. One that I had carefully curated, then hidden away for my future self to find. There were some cards from friends and colleagues at the Dogs Home, little LEGO cake toppers of a bride and groom, and a lucky sixpence. Adam's superstitions insisted I needed that on our big—rather small—day, and we agreed that his mother's sapphire ring was both my something borrowed and something blue. At the bottom of the box, I found an envelope containing our handwritten vows. All those promise-shaped good intentions made me cry. It reminded me of the us we used to be, and who I thought we'd be forever. But promises lose their value when broken or chipped, like dusty, forgotten antiques. The sad

truth about our present always punctuates my happy memories of our past with full stops.

I wonder if all marriages end the same way eventually. Maybe it is only ever a matter of time before life makes the love unravel. But then I think about those old married couples you see on the news every Valentine's Day, the ones who have been together for sixty years and are still very much in love, grinning false teeth smiles for the cameras like teenage sweethearts. I wonder what their secret is and why nobody ever shared it with us?

My own teeth start to chatter. "Maybe we should head back inside?"

"Whatever you want, my love." Adam only calls me "my love" when he is drunk and I realize that most of the bottle is empty, even though I've only had one glass of wine.

I try to turn back toward the door, but he holds on to me. The view shifts from something spectacular into something sinister; if either of us were to fall from the bell tower, we'd be dead. I don't have a fear of heights, but I do have a fear of dying, so I pull away. As I do, I bump into the bell. Not hard enough to make it ring, just to sway, and as soon as it does, I hear bizarre clicking sounds, followed by a cacophony of high-pitched screeching. It takes my mind a moment to process what it is seeing and hearing.

Bats, lots of them, fly out of the bell and into our faces. Adam staggers backward, dangerously close to the low wall, flinging his arms in front of his face and trying to swat them away. He stumbles and everything seems to switch to slow motion. His mouth is open and his eyes are wide and wild. He's falling backward and reaching for me at the same time, but I seem to be frozen to the spot, paralyzed with fear as the bats continue to fly around our heads. It's as if we are trapped inside our own bespoke horror film. Adam falls hard against the wall, and cries out as part of it crumbles and falls away. I snap out of my trance, grab his arm, and yank him back from the edge. Seconds later there is a loud bang as the ancient bricks crash

down onto the ground below. The sound seems to echo around the valley as the bats fly off in the distance.

I saved him, but he doesn't thank me or display any hint of gratitude. My husband's expression is one I've never seen his face wear before, and it makes me feel afraid.

ADAM

She almost let me fall.

 I know Amelia was scared too, but she *almost let me fall*. That isn't something I can just forget. Or forgive.

We're leaving. I don't care how late it is, or that there's snow on the road. I don't remember us even discussing it. I'm just glad that we are getting out of this place. Even though I don't want to admit it—to myself or anyone else—I am trapped. In this car, in this marriage, in this life. Ten years ago, I thought I could do anything, be anyone. The world seemed full of endless possibilities, but now it's nothing but a series of dead ends. Sometimes I just want to . . . start again.

The road ahead is dark, there are no streetlights, and I know we don't have much petrol left. Amelia isn't talking to me—hasn't spoken for more than an hour—but the silence is a relief. Now that we've given up on the weekend away, the only thing I'm still worried about is the weather. The snow has stopped, but there is heavy rain bouncing off the bonnet, performing an unpleasant percussion. We should slow down, but I think better of saying so—nobody likes

a passenger-seat driver. It's eerie how we haven't seen a single other car or building since we left. I know it's the middle of the night, but even the roads seem strange. The view rarely changes as though we're stuck in a loop. The stars have all disappeared and the sky seems a darker shade of black. I notice that I'm colder than before too.

I turn to look at Amelia and she is an unrecognizable blur, the features on her face swirling like an angry sea. It feels like I am sitting next to a stranger, not my wife. The stench of regret diffuses through the car like a cheap air freshener, and it's impossible not to know how unhappy we both are. When it comes to marriage, you can't always make-do and mend. I try to speak, but the words get stuck in my throat. I'm not even sure what I was going to say.

Then I spot the shape of a woman walking on the road in the distance.

She's dressed in red.

I think it's a coat at first, but as we get nearer, I can see that she is wearing a red kimono.

The rain is falling harder, bouncing off the tarmac, and the woman is soaked to the skin. She shouldn't be outside. She shouldn't be in the road. She's holding something but I can't see what.

"Slow down," I say, but Amelia doesn't hear me, if anything she seems to speed up.

"Slow down!" I say again, louder this time, but she puts her foot on the accelerator.

I look at the speedometer as it rises from seventy miles an hour, to eighty, then ninety, before the dial spins completely out of control. I hold my hands in front of my face, as though trying to protect myself from the scene ahead, and see that my fingers are covered in blood. The pitter-patter of bullet-sized raindrops on the car is deafening, and when I look up, I see that the rain has turned red.

The woman is almost right in front of us now.

She sees our headlights, shields her eyes, but doesn't move out of the way.

I scream as she hits the bonnet. Then watch in horror as her body bounces off the cracked windscreen and soars into the air. Her red silk kimono billows out behind her like a broken cape.

AMELIA

"Wake up!"

I say it three times, gently shaking him, before Adam opens his eyes.

He stares at me. "The woman, she—"

"What woman?"

"The woman in the red—"

This again. I should have known.

"The woman in the red kimono? She isn't real, Adam. Remember? It was just a dream."

He looks at me the way a young child looks at a parent when they are scared. All the color has drained from his face and it's covered in sweat.

"You're okay," I say, taking his clammy hand in mine. "There is no woman in a red kimono. You're here with me. You're safe."

Lies can heal as well as hurt.

He barely spoke to me when we came down from the bell tower earlier. I don't know whether it was the shock of almost falling with the crumbling wall, or the bats, or too much red wine, but he got

undressed, climbed into the unfamiliar bed—that looks just like our own at home—and went straight to sleep without a word.

It's been a while since Adam had one of his nightmares, but they happen often enough and are always the same, except that he sees the accident from a different point of view. Sometimes in the dreams he is in the car, in others he is walking along the street, or there are the dreams where he is watching the scene from the window of a council flat on the thirteenth floor of a tower block, banging his fists on the glass. He never recognizes me straightaway afterward—which is normal for us given his face blindness—but sometimes he thinks I am someone else. It always takes several minutes to calm him down and convince him that I'm not. His dreams have a habit of haunting him, regardless of whether he is asleep or awake. His mind isn't panning for gold; it's searching for something much darker. Tiny nuggets of buried regrets sometimes slip through the gaps, but the heaviest of memories tend to sink rather than rise to the surface.

I wish I knew how to make them stop.

I consider stroking the freckles on his shoulder, or running my fingers through his salt-and-pepper hair like I used to. But I don't. Because I can hear bells.

After playing a creepy tune, the grandfather clock in the corner of the bedroom starts to chime midnight like an apprentice Big Ben. If we weren't fully awake already, we both are now.

"I'm sorry I woke you," he says, his breathing still faster than it should be.

"It's okay. If you hadn't, the clock almost certainly would have," I tell him. Then I do what I always do: take out my pad and a pencil, and write it all down as soon as possible afterward. Because it isn't just a dream—or a nightmare—it's a memory.

He shakes his head. "We don't have to do this tonight—"

I take a silent register of his emotions, ticking off the familiar pattern one by one: fear, regret, sorrow, and guilt. It is the same every time.

"Yes, we do," I say, having already found one of the few blank pages left in the notebook. I always thought I could excavate his unhappy memories and replace them with better ones. Of us. These days I'm not so sure.

Adam sighs, leans back on the bed, and tells me everything that he can remember before the edges of the dream fade too much to see.

The nightmares always begin the same way: with the woman in the red kimono.

Despite the attire, she is not Japanese. Adam finds it hard to describe her face—he struggles with features in dreams the same way he does in real life—but we know that she is a British woman in her early forties, around the same age I am now. She's attractive. He always remembers her red lipstick, in the exact same shade as her kimono. She has long blond hair like me too, but hers is shorter, shoulder length.

He doesn't say her name tonight, but we both know what it is.

The order of what happens in the dream sometimes changes, but the woman in red is always there. So is the car in the rain. It's the reason why Adam doesn't own one and doesn't drive. He never even wanted to learn how.

There is a teenage boy in the nightmares too and he's terrified.

Adam saw it happen: the woman, the car, the accident.

Not just in a dream, in real life.

It was the night his mother died. He was thirteen.

Adam couldn't recognize the person in the car almost thirty years ago, when it mounted the pavement and collided with his mum as he watched. But that doesn't mean he didn't know who they were. It could have been a friend, a teacher, a neighbor—all faces look the same to him. Imagine not knowing if someone you knew was responsible for killing someone you loved. No wonder he struggles to trust people, even me. If my husband didn't suffer from prosopagnosia, his whole life might have unfolded differently, but he wasn't able to describe who he had seen to the police. Not then,

not now. And he still blames himself. His mother was walking his dog when it happened, because he was too lazy to do it.

It makes me feel sad how he idolizes a ghost.

By all accounts, Adam's mother was a nice enough woman—she was a nurse and very popular on the estate where they lived—but she wasn't perfect. And she definitely wasn't a saint. I find it strange how he compares every other woman in his life to her. Including me. The pedestal he put his dead mother on isn't just wonky, it's broken. For example, he seems to have conveniently forgotten *why* she was wearing the red kimono. It's what she always wore—along with the matching lipstick—whenever male "friends" came to visit the little council flat that they lived in. The place had thin walls, thin enough for Adam to hear that his mother had a different "friend" stay in her bed almost every week.

Memories are shape-shifters and dreams are not bound by truth, which is why I write everything he chooses to remember down. I want to fix him. And I want him to love me for it. But not everything that gets broken can be repaired.

One day he might remember the face he saw that night, and the unanswered questions that have haunted him for years might finally get answered. I've tried so hard to make the nightmares stop: herbal remedies, mindfulness podcasts before bed, special tea . . . but nothing seems to help. When everything is written down, I turn off the light so that we are in darkness again, and hope he'll be able to get back to sleep.

It doesn't take long.

Adam is soon gently snoring, but I can't seem to switch off.

I swallow a sleeping pill—they're prescription, and I only take them when nothing else works—but I've been popping more than usual lately. I'm too preoccupied with the growing number of cracks in our relationship, the ones that are too big to fill in or skim over. I know exactly why and when our marriage started to unravel. Life is unpredictable at best, unforgivable at worst.

I must have dozed off at some point—the pill finally kicking

in—because I wake up with an unsettling sense of déjà vu. It takes a few seconds for me to remember where I am—the room is pitch-black—but as I blink into the darkness and my eyes adjust to the light, I remember that we are in Blackwater Chapel. A sliver of moonlight between the window blind and the wall illuminates a tiny corner of the room, and I strain to see the time on the face of the grandfather clock. Its slender metal hands still suggest it is only half past midnight, which means I haven't been asleep for very long. My mind feels fuzzy, but then I remember what woke me because I hear it again.

There is a noise downstairs.

ROBIN

Robin can't sleep either.

She's worried about the visitors. They shouldn't have come here.

When she looks out from behind her curtain and sees that the chapel is in complete darkness, she knows what she needs to do.

It looks farther away than it is. But Robin thinks the distance between places can sometimes be as difficult to perceive as the distance between people. Some couples seem closer than they really are, while others appear further apart. When she watched them eating their frozen dinners on trays on their laps earlier, the visitors didn't look especially happy together. Or in love. But marriage can do that to the best of people as well as the worst. Or perhaps she was just imagining it.

The walk across the fields from her cottage to the chapel would normally take no more than ten minutes. Even less when running, as she discovered earlier. But now that so much snow has fallen, it takes longer than it should to navigate a path for herself without slipping over. It doesn't help that her Wellington boots are several sizes too big. They're secondhand: she doesn't have her own. She would have had to drive all the way to Fort William to buy a pair,

there are no shoe shops selling footwear near Blackwater Loch or even in Hollowgrove. She could have bought some online but that would require a credit card instead of cash, which is all she has nowadays. Robin cut up all her cards a long time ago. She didn't want anyone to have any way of finding her.

She enjoys the sound of snow being compacted beneath her feet, it's the only noise to dent the silence, apart from the distant clicking of bats. She likes to watch them swooping over the loch at night, it's a rather beautiful sight to see. Robin read recently that bats give birth to their babies while hanging upside down. Then they have to catch their children before they fall too far, but that part is the same for all parents. Her path tonight is lit by the light of a full moon, without it the night sky would be a sea of black, as the clouds have hidden all but the brightest stars again now. But that's okay: Robin has never been afraid of the dark.

She isn't bothered by a snowstorm or howling wind, and she doesn't mind being cut off from the rest of the world for a few days—it's not so different from her normal routine if she's honest. And Robin does always try to be truthful, especially with herself. She has gotten used to living here now, even though she only planned to stay for a short while when she arrived. Life makes other plans when people forget to live. Weeks turned into months, and months turned into years, and when what happened, happened, she knew she couldn't leave.

The visitors won't be able to leave when they want to either, not that they know that yet. It's impossible not to feel a tiny bit sorry for them.

Robin reaches their snow-covered car and stops for a moment. She recognized the man as soon as he got out, and the memory of it winds her. She didn't know if she'd ever see him again. Wasn't even sure she wanted to. He's older now, but she rarely forgets a face, and could never forget his. Her mind wanders back in time, and she thinks about what happened when he was a boy. What he saw and what he didn't. The story is as tragic now as it was then, and Robin

wonders if he still has the nightmares about the woman in red. She thinks the time has come for him to be told the truth, but he isn't going to like it. People rarely do.

When Robin reaches the chapel's large wooden doors, she takes one last look around, but there is nobody here to see what she is about to do. The moonlight that was kind enough to light her path reveals the loch and the mountains in the distance, and she can't help but notice how unspoiled and beautiful this place is. People who do ugly things do not belong here she thinks, as she looks at the visitors' Morris Minor covered in snow. It's her favorite kind of weather, because the snow covers the world in a beautiful blanket of white, hiding everything that is dark and ugly underneath.

Life is like a game where pawns can become queens, but not everyone knows how to play. Some people stay pawns their whole lives because they never learned to make the right moves. This is just the beginning. Nobody has played their cards yet because they didn't know they were being dealt.

Robin takes a key from her coat pocket and quietly lets herself inside the chapel.

LINEN

Word of the year:
hornswoggle *verb*. To get the better of
someone by cheating or deception.

29th February 2012—our fourth anniversary

Dear Adam,
I feel as though we have always shared the same dreams—
and nightmares—but it's been a difficult year. You ~~let me down~~ should have been by my side, but you weren't. I sat in the waiting room alone and afraid, despite you promising to be there with me.

After three years of trying, two years of appointments, a whole cast of different doctors and nurses, seemingly endless trips to hospitals and clinics for the last twelve months, and one failed round of IVF, I feel broken. This was not how I wanted to spend our anniversary.

I should have known today would be awful, it didn't start well.

Two young dogs were rescued last night from a flat in South London. They were brought to Battersea and I was one of the first to see them. Despite all my years in this job, even I was shocked. The beagles had been left alone for a long time. The on-call vet guessed at least a week. If they hadn't drunk water from the toilet they would have been dead already. Their emaciated bodies made them look like toys with all the stuffing pulled out. We did everything we could to try and save them, but they died this morning. In the end there was nothing more we could do and it was kinder to put them down. Their owner was on holiday in Spain and I wish we could have given her a lethal injection instead. Sometimes I despise human beings, so maybe it is just as well we've never been able to make one.

We were supposed to meet at London Bridge at one o'clock this afternoon. I've been having problems sleeping recently, I'm exhausted, but I was still there and on time. Because the appointment at the fertility clinic was important to me. I thought it was important to us, but you've been more ~~selfish~~ distracted than ever lately. I was worried you might forget, so I texted to remind you.

Five times.

You didn't reply.

On this occasion I really do think you should have put your wife before your writing.

London Bridge was busy and loud, and not just with commuters. Men in hard hats seemed to be everywhere when I stepped outside the station, and there was an impressive collection of cranes blocking my view of the sky. The Shard is very much under construction and, according to the passersby that I eavesdropped on, it is going to be the

tallest building in Europe. I'm sure it will be for a while. Until someone builds something taller. I'm willing to bet it won't take long, because humans are always trying to outdo one another.

Even when they pretend to care.

I called you when I reached the entrance of the clinic. Your phone rang twice before being diverted to voicemail. I know who you were with. A producer who has shown an interest in your first-ever screenplay: *Rock Paper Scissors*. It's the manuscript I found in a drawer that inspired me to write secret letters of my own, to you. A flicker of attention from someone in the business about a story you have written, opposed to an adaptation of someone else's, and you're like a dog in heat. I wonder if all writers are egomaniacs with low self-esteem? Or is it just you? You said the lunch meeting with her wouldn't take long, but I guess getting your firstborn into production was more important than us making a real child of our own.

Our GP referred us to the clinic in London Bridge. Eventually. Everything to do with us trying for a child has been a battle from day one. I just never thought it would result in us fighting with each other. I've become familiar with the sterile, soulless place over the last few months. If I were to add up all the hours that I sat in that waiting room—often alone—I suspect I must have spent several days of my life there. Waiting for something I always knew might never happen.

It took months to get an appointment, followed by several more months of being prodded, poked, and interviewed by counselors who intruded into our most private sorrow. Looking back now, I sometimes wonder how we managed to survive this long. Whenever I felt most alone, I told myself that you loved me and that I loved you. It became a silent mantra inside my head, there to steady me whenever it felt

like I might fall. But our marriage isn't as solid or stable as I thought.

I know you found the appointments difficult. I'm sure stepping into a private room, being able to lock the door, choose some porn to look at, and jerk off into a sample pot must be very stressful. Sorry. I don't wish to belittle your experience, but I think most right-minded people would agree that your contribution to this process was less dramatic, albeit still psychologically invasive.

I've had to spread my legs, sometimes for a room full of doctors and nurses, and let them put metal instruments in my body. The same strangers have seen me naked, scanned me, felt me, touched me, some of them even put their hands inside me. I've been tested, repeatedly stuck with needles, pumped full of drugs, put to sleep, and operated on. I've had my eggs harvested, pissed blood for days afterward, and couldn't stand, let alone walk due to crippling pain after a bungled operation. But we got through it, together. You said everything would be okay. You promised, and I believed you.

After all, other people have children.

People we know, people we don't. They make it look so easy. Some of them even get pregnant by accident, they don't even have to try. Some of them kill the children growing inside them, because they didn't want them in the first place. Some people we know didn't want to have children, but had them anyway. Because they could. Because everyone else does. Everyone except us. That's how it feels: as though we are the only couple in history that this has happened to. Sometimes it's even worse than that: it feels as if I am alone in the world, and that you are the one who abandoned me.

I wanted a baby so badly that it physically hurt. Then today, at our first appointment after our second—and possibly final—round of IVF, you weren't there.

You weren't there when the receptionist called us and I

had to go into that room alone. Or when the man we nick-named Doctor Doom sat down behind his desk, and gestured to the two empty chairs opposite him. Or while we waited for you in awkward silence, and he checked his folder to re-mind himself of our names. The clinic never really treated us like human beings, more like lonely walking checkbooks.

Worst of all, you weren't there to hear the news we had been waiting for.

After everything we have been through, the doctor finally said that I was pregnant.

I didn't believe him at first.

I made him repeat it. Then made him check the file, con-vinced he was reading the results from someone else's notes. But it was true.

Doctor Doom even got me to lie on the bed and scanned my tummy. He pointed out a tiny speck on the screen and said it was our embryo. The contents of your sample pot and my egg, grown together in a lab, had been successfully implanted in my womb, and it was there on the screen. Alive and growing inside me.

You missed it.

You arrived in the reception of the clinic just as I was leav-ing, and when you started trying to explain, I told you not to bother. I'm sick of hearing you talk about your work as if it's the only thing that matters. You make shit up for a living and your agent sells it. I think it's about time you all got over yourselves. The producers, directors, actors, and authors you tell me stories about sound like a class of spoiled children, and I don't understand why you indulge them, or their tem-per tantrums. You've been truly hornswoggled by at least one of them, even if you are too blind to see it.

I'm sorry. I hope you never find this letter and in the un-likely event that you do, I didn't mean what I said. I'm just hurting too much right now; and that hurt needs somewhere

to go. It breaks my heart sometimes, the way you give these people all of your time and save none of yourself for me. I'm your wife. My stories are real. Does that make them not worth listening to?

I wanted to get the tube, but you insisted we take a cab. I refused to speak to you for the first half of the journey. I'm sorry for that now too, but I've never been one to wash my dirty linen in public. I do wish I'd told you sooner, though. We could have been happier for longer than we were.

I didn't tell you until we got home. I'd already laid the kitchen table with a linen cloth—an anniversary should always be celebrated—but my face gave the news away when I took a bottle of champagne from the new Smeg fridge. Renovating the house has helped keep me busy and take my mind off other things. The ground floor is finally finished, and I'm proud that I did most of the work myself: sanding floors, plastering walls, making roman blinds—it's amazing what you can learn just by watching a few videos on YouTube.

You cried when I told you I was pregnant. I cried when I showed you the scan. Having dreamed of that moment for so long, that black-and-white image was the only thing that made any of it feel real. Because you weren't there to hear it, I kept worrying that I might have imagined what the doctor said.

"I hope it's a girl," I whispered.

"Why? I hope it's a boy. Let's rock paper scissors for it."

I laughed. "You want to play rock paper scissors to determine the sex of our unborn child?"

"Is there a more scientific way?" you replied, with a serious face.

My scissors cut your paper, just like always.

"You let me win!" I said.

"Yes, because I don't really mind whether it's a boy or a girl. I'll love them either way, but I'll always love you more."

You opened the champagne—I only had a small glass—and we ordered a pizza.

"I didn't forget our anniversary, by the way," you said, gorging on your third slice of Pepperoni Passion an hour later.

"Is that so?" I asked, sipping lemonade from a champagne flute.

"I struggled with the linen theme, and this morning I was worried I'd bought the wrong thing—"

"So give it to me now. Then you'll know."

You reached inside the leather satchel I had given you the year before, and handed me a square parcel. It was soft. I'm normally so careful when I unwrap things, but I was aware the pizza was getting cold so tore at the paper. There was a linen cushion inside. It had my name stitched on it along with the following words beneath:

SHE BELIEVED SHE COULD, SO SHE DID.

I tried not to, but I cried again. Happy tears. It felt as if you'd already known I was pregnant. You believed in me, even when I wasn't able to believe in myself.

I was about to thank you, when I looked up and noticed the strange expression on your face. You were staring down at my legs and when I followed your gaze I could see why. A thick trickle of bright red blood had made its way right down to my slippers. When I stood up in panic, there was more.

According to the first doctor we saw in the emergency room, I wasn't pregnant long enough to call it a miscarriage. The gynecologist who examined me next was a little more sympathetic, but not much. Looking back now, I wish I'd never told you at all—you wouldn't be able to grieve for something you never knew you had. And I'm sorry and broken enough for both of us.

I went straight to our bedroom when we got home, even

let Bob stretch out on the end of the bed. I tried crying my-self to sleep, but it didn't work, nothing does. I might talk to the GP about getting some sleeping pills. I noticed that my watch had stopped at three minutes past eight, and I won-dered if that was the exact time our baby died. I took the watch off my wrist and I don't want to see it, or wear it, ever again. I'll always remember what you said when you came upstairs and held me:

"I love you. Always have, always will."

"Not almost always?" I asked, trying to make you smile, even though I was broken. But you didn't. Smile. Instead, you looked more serious than I have ever seen you.

"Always always. I'm so sorry that we can't seem to have children, because I know how much it means to you, and what a wonderful mother you would be. But it doesn't change a thing for me. I'm with you for life, no matter what, because this is our family: you, me, and Bob. We don't need anyone or anything else. Nothing will ever change that."

But words can't fix everything, no matter how fond you are of them.

Hours later, when you were sleeping but I still couldn't, I thought I may as well get up and come downstairs. Bob followed me, as if he knew something was very wrong. I put the cold, uneaten pizza—which was still where we had left it when I started to bleed—in the bin, along with the linen cushion you had given me. The words stitched on it are too painful to ever read again. You believed that I could, then briefly I did. Now I'm not sure of anything. I don't know who I'm supposed to be if I can't be the me I dreamed I would be. And I don't know what that means for us.

I have grown fond of writing letters I will never let you read. I find it cathartic. They make me feel better, even though I know it would destroy you if you found them.

That's why I hide them away. I'll keep the scan from the hospital with this one. A reminder of what we almost had. I've already tucked it inside the envelope the clinic gave me with my name on:

Mrs. A Wright.

I'm holding it now. Can't quite let go. The receptionist used swirly handwriting on my initial, as though it were something pretty. I remember when we got married, and I first took your surname, I practiced signing my new signature for weeks with swirly letters of my own. I was so happy to be your wife, but none of the wishes I've made since have come true. I think that might be my fault, not yours. I hope that if you ever find out the truth, you'll be able to forgive me and love me no matter what. Always always. Like you promised.

Your wife

xx

AMELIA

I hear another noise downstairs in the chapel and I know I'm not imagining it.

I reach blindly for the light switch by the bed, but it doesn't work. Either there has been another power cut—which seems odd if there is a generator—or someone has cut the power. I try not to allow my overactive imagination to make this experience even scarier than it is. I tell myself that there must be a rational explanation. But then I hear the unmistakable sound of a footstep at the bottom of the creaking stairs.

I hold my breath, determined to hear nothing but silence.

But there is another groan from elderly floorboards, followed by another creak, and the sound of someone climbing the staircase is getting louder. And closer. I have to cover my mouth with my hand to stop myself from screaming when the footsteps stop right outside the bedroom door.

I want to reach for Adam but I am frozen with fear.

When I hear the sound of the door handle start to turn, I practically fall out of the bed in my hurry to get away from whoever is out there, and wish that I was wearing more than just a flimsy

nightdress. I grip the unfamiliar furniture, feeling my way in the shadows, walking as quickly and quietly as I can toward the bathroom. I'm fairly sure its door had a lock. As soon as I find what I'm looking for, I close the door behind me and barricade myself inside. The light switch doesn't work in here either, but maybe that's a good thing.

I hear the bedroom door slowly open and more creeping footsteps. I blink into the darkness, willing my eyes to adjust to the low light, then hold my breath and step back as far as I can while the sound of creaking floorboards gets closer. I realize I've been twisting my engagement ring around my finger—something I only do when I'm most anxious. The ring—which once belonged to Adam's mother—doesn't come off anymore, and has started to feel too tight. My chest feels the same way, and my heart is thumping so loudly, I'm scared that whoever is out there can hear it when they stop right outside the bathroom door.

The handle turns very slowly. When they discover that the door is locked, they try again. More aggressively this time. I feel like I'm in *The Shining*, but the only window in this bathroom is made of stained glass—even if it *did* open, I'd never fit through it, and the fall from this height down onto the ground below would probably kill me. I search for a weapon, anything to defend myself with, but find little comfort in my Gillette Venus razor. I hold it out in front of me regardless, then press myself up against the wall, unable to get any farther away. The tiles on my bare back are icy cold.

Everything is quiet for a few seconds. Then the silence is smashed by the sound of a fist banging on the door. I'm so scared I start to cry, tears streaming down my cheeks.

"Amelia, are you in there? Is everything all right?"

My husband's voice confuses and calms me at the same time.

"Adam? Is that you?"

"Who else would it be?"

I open the door and see him standing there in his pajama

bottoms, stifling a yawn, with his bed hair sticking out in all directions. The light from the old-fashioned candlestick holder he is carrying casts ghostly shadows around the bedroom, so that now I feel like I'm in a Charles Dickens novel.

"Why are you crying? Are you okay?" he asks.

My words trip over themselves in my hurry to say them. "No, I'm not. Something woke me, I heard a noise downstairs, the lights wouldn't work, then I heard someone coming up the stairs and—"

"It was just me, silly. I was thirsty and I went to get a glass of water. But I guess *all* of the pipes must be frozen because none of the taps work."

"There's no water?"

"Or power. The storm must have out taken out the generator. I tried to find a fuse box while I was down there—just in case I could fix something—but no joy. Good job we have these creepy candlesticks!"

He holds the flickering flame below his chin and pulls a series of silly faces, like children do with torches at Halloween. I start to feel better. A little bit. At least there is a rational explanation. Then I feel foolish . . .

"I thought I heard a noise downstairs. The sound of someone creeping around. I was so scared—"

"Me too, that's what woke me," Adam interrupts.

After a brief absence, my terror returns. "What?"

"That was the other reason I went downstairs, to check everything was okay. But the main doors are still locked, there is no other way in or out, this place is like Fort Knox. I had a good look around, no burglars—or sheep—have managed to break in and everything is fine. Just as we left it. Besides, Bob would have barked if a stranger had let themselves in."

That is true: Bob does growl if a stranger comes to the front door at home, but only until we open it. Then he wags his tail at double speed and rolls over to show the visitors his tummy—Labradors are too friendly to be good guard dogs.

We climb back into bed and I ask a question he never wants to answer.

"Do you ever wish that we'd had children?"

"No."

"Why?"

I expect Adam to change the subject—that's what normally happens next—but he doesn't. "Sometimes I'm glad we don't have kids, because I'm scared that we might have fucked them up somehow, the way our parents fucked us up. I think maybe our line came to an end for a reason."

I think I preferred it when he didn't answer. I don't like him describing us like that, but part of me does wonder whether he might be right. I've always felt abandoned by people I was foolish enough to care about, including my parents. Yes, they died in a car crash before I was born, but the result—me growing up alone—is the same as if they deserted me deliberately. If you don't have anyone to love or be loved by as a child, then how do you learn?

But then, isn't love like breathing? Isn't it instinct? Something we're born knowing how to do? Or is love like speaking French? If nobody teaches you, you'll never be fluent, and if you don't practice you forget how . . .

I wonder if my husband really still loves me.

"I don't like it here," I confess.

"No, me neither. Maybe we should leave in the morning? Find a nice hotel somewhere a bit less remote?"

"That sounds good."

"Okay. Let's try to get some sleep until it is light outside, then pack up and go. Maybe take another sleeping pill, it might help?"

I do as he says—despite the warnings on the prescription—because I'm exhausted, and if I'm going to have to drive for hours again tomorrow, I need to get some rest. But before I close my eyes, I notice that the grandfather clock in the corner of the room has stopped. I'm glad, at least *that* won't wake us up again in the night. I squint at the time and see that it stopped at three minutes past eight,

which seems strange—I thought we heard the bells at midnight—but my mind is too tired to even try to understand. Adam slips his arm around my waist and pulls me to him. I can't remember the last time he did that in bed, or made me feel safe like this. If nothing else, the trip has already brought us closer together. As usual, he is asleep within minutes.

ADAM

I pretend to be asleep, and wonder how long I'll have to hold her before I can get back to what I was doing downstairs.

Amelia has always struggled to sleep, but the pills help, and her breathing changes when they work. So all I have to do is wait. And listen. The same way I did a little earlier. The second pill should do the trick—it normally does, even when I secretly crush them and put them in her tea. She's a very anxious individual. It's for her own good. As soon as she is asleep again, I slide out from beneath the sheets, take the candlestick from beside the bed, and leave the room as quietly as possible. I don't really need it to light my way—I know where I'm going—but make a mental note to avoid the noisiest floorboards: I know which ones creak.

Bob follows me down the wooden spiral staircase, and I love that about having a dog: they are so loving and loyal. Dogs aren't unforgiving or suspicious. They don't get jealous and start fights all the time so that you dread being with them. Dogs don't *lie*. He might be a bit deaf these days, but Bob is always happy to see me, whereas Amelia only sees things from her point of view.

I'm tired. Of all of it.

I used to believe in love, but then, I used to believe in Father Christmas and the Tooth Fairy. I've heard people describe marriage as two missing pieces of a puzzle coming together, and discovering that they are a perfect fit. But that's just wrong. People are *different* and that's a good thing. Two pieces of different puzzles cannot and will not fit together, unless one has been forced to bend or break or change to fit around the other. I can see now that my wife has spent a lot of time trying to change me, to make *me* feel smaller, so that we would be a better fit.

Nobody should promise to love somebody else forever, the most any sane individual should do is promise to try. What if the person you married becomes unrecognizable ten years later? People change and promises—even the ones we try to keep—sometimes get broken.

I started running again a few months ago. Writing is a solitary profession and it's also not terribly active. I spend a scary amount of time sitting on my arse in the shed, and the only part of my body that gets a decent workout are my fingers, tapping away on the keyboard. Bob takes me for walks once a day but—like me—he's getting on in years. The running was just about getting fit and trying to take better care of myself. But *of course*, my wife presumed it meant I was planning to have an affair. A couple of weeks ago, she put my running shoes out with the trash the night before the bins got collected. I *saw* her do it. That is not normal behavior.

I just bought new running shoes, but they're not the only thing in my life that needs replacing. I might not be good at recognizing faces, but I can tell I'm looking older. I certainly feel it. Perhaps because everyone else in my industry seems to be getting younger these days: the executives, the producers, the agents. Almost everyone in the last writer's room I was involved in looked like they should have been in school instead. That used to be me. I was the new kid on the block once. It's strange when you still *feel* young, but everyone starts to treat you as though you are old. I'm only in my forties, not ready for retirement quite yet.

Am I attracted to other people? Sure, I'm human, we are designed to be. Never because of a pretty face—I can't see those anyway. People are a bit like books for me in that way, and I tend to be genuinely turned on by what's on the inside rather than just a flashy cover. I admit I've been thinking about someone else a lot lately, imagining what it would be like if I was with them instead. But doesn't everyone have little fantasies occasionally? That's all they are and it doesn't mean I'm actually going to *do* something about it. The last time I slept with someone I shouldn't have it did not end well for me. I've learned that lesson. I think. Besides, I'm always working, I don't have time to have an affair these days. I do my best to placate my wife's constant jealousy, but no matter what I say she just doesn't seem capable of trusting me.

In some ways, she's right not to.

I have never been completely honest with my wife, but that's for her own good.

There are so many things I can't tell her; a bit like the sleeping pills I sometimes pop into her hot drinks before bedtime. Things she doesn't need to know. It was me who turned the power off when she was down in the crypt earlier. She doesn't understand fuse boxes—all I had to do was flick a switch and drop the trapdoor. I forgot about the generator outside, but I've turned that off now too, and we won't be getting power back any time soon.

WOOD

Word of the year:
mensch *noun*. A good person. Someone who is
kind and acts with integrity and honor.

28th February 2013—our fifth anniversary

Dear Adam,

I'm sorry I've been acting so jealous lately, I'm hoping we can put these past few months behind us. It would seem strange not to mention the baby stuff at all. I can't pretend it didn't happen, or that I didn't want to be a mother. It was never about having your children (sorry), I just wanted my own. I've given up on giving up so many things in life, but I knew I couldn't keep trying for a baby. Not after the last round of IVF didn't work. The heartbreak was killing me, and my unhappiness was killing our marriage.

I still secretly hoped it might happen for a while. I've read all those stories about couples who get pregnant as soon as

they stop trying, but that isn't what life had planned for us. For the first few months I still cried every time my period arrived, not that ~~you asked~~ I told you that. But I think I've moved on now, or at least moved far enough away to breathe again. Life can start to feel full of holes when the love has nowhere to go.

Bob isn't a baby—I know that—but I suppose I do treat him like a surrogate child. And I've thrown myself back into my work at the dogs home these last few months. The unexpected promotion I've been given doesn't pay much more than before, but it's nice to feel recognized. And I've realized I'm a good person. Not being able to get pregnant wasn't a punishment, it just wasn't the plan. When I was a child I was repeatedly told that I was bad, and sometimes I still believed it. But they were wrong about me. All of them.

We had a row last week, our first in ages, do you remember? I still feel guilty about that. To be fair, I think a lot of wives might have reacted the same way. You came home drunk, and considerably later than you said you would. It might not have bothered me so much if I hadn't made the effort to cook. But instead of picking up on my silent anger when I made a scene of scraping your cold, uneaten dinner into the bin, you told me all about October O'Brien. The young, award-winning Irish actress had fallen in love with your screenplay: *Rock Paper Scissors*. She'd gotten in touch via your agent, and an afternoon meeting for three turned into drinks and a meal for two. Just you and her. I hadn't been worried at all until I Googled the girl and saw how beautiful she was.

"You'll have to meet her yourself," you babbled with a ridiculous grin on your face. Your lips were a little stained with red wine, at least I hoped that's what it was. "Her thoughts about how to improve the script are just . . . genius!" I helped you with that script years ago. I might not be a Hollywood actress, but I read. A lot. And I thought Team Us did a pretty

good job. "You're going to love her . . ." you gushed, but I
very much doubted that. "She's simply delightful . . . so utterly charming, and clever, and—"

"I didn't realize she was old enough to drink," I interrupted. I'd had some wine myself while I stayed up waiting.

"Don't be like that," you said, with a look that made me
want to punch you.

"Like what? It isn't as though we haven't been here before.
An actor or actress says they love your story, they won't rest
until it gets made in Hollywood—"

"This is different."

"Is it? The girl is barely out of school—"

"She's in her twenties and she's already won a Bafta—"

"You won a Bafta in your twenties, but it still didn't get
you what you wanted. Surely it's a producer you need to
back the project . . . or a studio."

"I've got a much better chance with an actress like October attached. If she knocks on doors in LA they will open
for her. Whereas with me, unless I get another big book to
adapt soon, all the doors seem to be closing." I felt bad then.
It's been tough for you this year. You're still getting work,
but not the kind you really want. I was about to change the
subject, try to be a little kinder, but then you lashed out in
self-defense. "It's a shame you aren't still as passionate about
your career, then maybe you would understand."

"That's not fair," I said, even though it was.

"Isn't it? You haven't had a decent pay rise from Battersea
for years, but you still stay."

"Because I love working there."

"No, because you're too scared to even consider working
somewhere else."

"We don't all want to rule the world, some of us just want
to make it a better place."

The thought of you not being proud of me ~~was utterly~~

~~devastating~~ hurt. A lot. I know you think I could be doing more with my life, but it isn't all my fault. When the person you love has too many bright ideas, they can completely eclipse yours. And I still do. Love you. I spent my ambition on your dreams instead of my own.

You slept in the spare room that night, but we've made up since. Just in time for this year's anniversary.

You were awake before me this morning, which is practically unheard of, and unexpected given how late you were up rewriting a ten-year-old screenplay again last night. When you carried a tray of breakfast into our bedroom, I thought I must be dreaming. In all the years we have been together, you've never done that before. So I should have known something was wrong.

We ate dippy eggs, as I like to call them—soft-boiled is your preferred grown-up term—with toast. I was looking forward to spending the day together, so I couldn't understand why you were up so early, or why you seemed to be so keen to take the dirty cups and plates back downstairs.

"We don't need to rush, do we?" I asked.

Your face confessed before you did. "I'm so sorry, I need to go and see my agent. It really won't take long—"

"But we agreed to spend the whole day together this year. I took annual leave."

"And we will, it's just for a couple of hours. I really think *Rock Paper Scissors* might actually get made this time. I just want to talk to him, in person—you know it's the only way I can tell what he really thinks about anything—while the project has momentum again. See if he agrees about the next steps and . . ."

I know you couldn't see whatever face I pulled, but you must have read my body language.

"I know it's our anniversary but I promise I'll make it up to you tonight."

"We'll still have dinner?" I said.

"It will be drinks o'clock by five P.M. at the latest. I'll call you as soon as I'm done, and I got you this."

It was a ticket for a matinee performance of a show I have wanted to see for months. It's been sold out since it opened. The ticket was for today, so at least I'd have something fun to do while you were working. But it also meant that you *knew* I would need something to do. Alone. There was only one ticket. I gave you your anniversary present then. Five years is meant to be a wooden gift so I got you a ruler with an inscription:

FIVE YEARS MARRIED, WHO WOOD BELIEVE IT?

You smiled, held up two ties and asked me to choose one. I loathe them both to be honest, but pointed at the one with the birds. It seemed strange even at the time, given that you never normally dress up to see your agent.

"It's not for me, it's for you," you said, reading my mind.

You wrapped the silk tie around my face to cover my eyes. Then you took me by the hand and led me downstairs.

"I can't go outside in my nightie!" I whispered, when I heard you open the front door.

"Sure you can, you still look just as beautiful as the day we got married, and besides, it's the only way to show you your real anniversary present."

"I thought it was the theater ticket," I said.

"Give me some credit."

"Can't, sorry. You're already in too much debt."

"This year's gift is meant to be made of wood, right?"

I took a few more uncertain steps, the cold path biting my bare feet, until they reached the grass. We stopped and you removed my makeshift blindfold.

There was a leafless and ugly little tree in the middle of what used to be my perfect lawn.

"It's a tree," you said.

"I can see that."

"I know you've always wanted a magnolia so—"

"Is that what it is?" You looked hurt. "I'm sorry, it's really sweet of you. I love it. I mean, not right now maybe, but when the flowers come out, I bet it will look amazing." You looked happy again. "Thank you, it's the perfect gift. Now go and get your screenplay made into a Hollywood blockbuster, so Bob and I can walk down a red carpet in Leicester Square."

As soon as you had my permission you were out the door, and I was alone on our anniversary. Again.

Looking back now—hindsight is such a bitch—I think everything would have been fine had a smoke alarm not gone off at the theater that afternoon. Everyone in the audience was evacuated not long after the curtain went up, the fire brigade was called, and the matinee performance I was meant to see got canceled.

That's why I came back to the house earlier than planned.

I found myself staring at a couple on the tube ride home. They were our age, but holding hands and grinning at each other like two smitten teenagers. I bet that they always spent anniversaries together, and I started to wonder where we sat on the scale of normal. The jury in my head was still out when I arrived back at Hampstead station. The heavens opened as I started walking and I was drenched by the time I reached our garden gate. I felt inexplicable rage at the sight of the ~~ugly~~ magnolia tree you had planted, and by the time I reached the front door my hands were shaking with crankiness and cold.

As I struggled to slot the key in the lock, I heard a woman laughing inside our home. When I opened the door and stepped into the hall, I felt like I must be dreaming. There was a Hollywood actress drinking wine in my kitchen. With you. On our anniversary.

"What are you doing home so early?" you asked, looking as upset as I felt.

"The play was canceled," I said, staring at her the whole time—I couldn't help it. October O'Brien was even more beautiful in real life than she was in all the pictures I'd Googled online. Her extremely pale, porcelain-like skin was flawless, and her copper, pixie-cut hair shone beneath our kitchen lights. If I had mine styled that way I would look like a boy, but she looked like a happy elf princess, with her big green eyes and wide white smile. Even in my twenties I never looked that good.

Then you introduced us, as though coming home to find your husband drinking wine in the afternoon with another woman—who you have only ever seen on TV and in films— was normal. I was about to make a complete tit of myself, but then October's perfect red lips smiled and she explained what you should have.

"It's so lovely to meet you," she purred, holding out a perfectly manicured hand. For a moment I wasn't sure whether to shake it, kiss it, or slap it away. I had an odd urge to curtsy. "Your husband confessed last night that he has never cooked you an anniversary meal. I said I didn't want anything to do with his screenplay until that situation was rectified, and when he said he couldn't cook, I offered to help. It was supposed to be a surprise . . . but maybe it was a bad one?"

I felt my face get hot for several reasons all at once.

Firstly, I wished I had cleaned our fridge more recently, then I panicked about the condition of our old pots and pans—worried what she must think about me and us and the state of our kitchen. Then I wished I'd worn a little more makeup, because next to this beautiful creature, I felt like a bedraggled old bat.

I needn't have worried. I don't think I've ever met a more kind or generous woman—no wonder you wanted to work with her. Even Bob fell in love with our houseguest, but he loves everyone. I insisted that October stay and eat the meal

she had prepared with us—you didn't argue—and once I had changed into some dry clothes and opened another bottle, we had the most wonderful evening. All three courses were delicious—especially the chocolate pudding. I thought I'd be intimidated by someone like October O'Brien. She's so stunning, successful, and smart . . . but she was utterly charming, modest, and sweet. It made me realize that regardless of who everyone thinks celebrities are, at the end of the day they're just people. Like you and me. Even the disturbingly beautiful ones.

"I knew you'd love her too if you met her," you said when October left.

"You were right, but I love you more."

"Almost always?" you asked and smiled. "So you don't mind me working with her now? And you won't get jealous?"

"Who says I was jealous?" I replied, and you raised an eyebrow.

"You've no need to be. She's lovely, but she's still an actress."

"Do you think I'm lovely?"

"You're my MIP," you said.

"MIP?"

"Most Important Person."

Thank you for a very memorable anniversary this year, one I certainly won't forget. Five years. Where did it go? So many memories, mostly happy ones, and I'm looking forward to making more with you in the future. I suspect everyone has a Most Important Person. I am yours and you are mine. Now and forever.

Your wife

xx

ROBIN

Robin sits perfectly still, hiding in a cold, dark corner of the chapel, until the visitors are all back upstairs again. The man came down *twice*, and she almost got caught. She wonders if he would recognize her at all now. Regardless of his face blindness, she fears she must have changed beyond all recognition since they last met.

When Robin let herself inside more than an hour ago, she thought they'd gone to bed for the night, and had to hide when she heard him coming down the old, wooden spiral staircase. He somehow managed to avoid all the creakiest steps. Luckily, the lounge—which she always thought was more of a library with sofas—had plenty of dark spaces, and the bookcases provided ample cover until she could see who it was. After that she let herself into the secret room. Secrets are only secrets for the people who don't know them yet. They can morph into lies when shared, and like caterpillars turning into butterflies, beautiful lies can fly far, far away. There is nothing Robin doesn't know about this old chapel: she used to live here.

She could still live here now if she wanted, but chooses not to. Robin doesn't like being inside the place any longer than

necessary these days. She always has to summon a colossal amount of courage to step inside those old chapel doors, and on the rare occasions when doing so can't be avoided, she does what she needs to do as quickly as possible before getting out again. The visitors would want to get out too if they knew the truth about where they were staying, but people see what they want to see.

The secret room is tucked behind the library and Robin hates this part of the chapel the most. It's easy enough to find behind the bookcase—if you know where to look—but you have to use your eyes. Most people go through life with their eyes shut. And books are good at hiding all kinds of things, especially closed books, just like closed people.

Some memories are claustrophobic, and the variety this room invokes always smother her, making it hard to breathe. Robin stays as still as possible, studying the parquet floor in the secret room as if it were a puzzle she might be able to solve, trying not to look at anything that will remind her of a past she would rather forget. But memories don't take orders; they come and go as they please.

The moon is full and bright tonight. It shines through the stained-glass windows casting a series of patterns that seem strange and unfamiliar. The sight of her own shadow on the wall catches her eye, and it makes her feel small. Even her shadow looks sad. Robin doesn't mean to make a fist, but when she sees her silhouette do the same, she holds her hand higher, changing the shape of her fingers. First a rock. Then flat, like paper. Then she makes a cutting motion, like scissors, and smiles.

When she is sure it is safe to do so, Robin stands to leave. She freezes when she thinks she sees someone, but it is only her own reflection in the mirror above the mantelpiece. The sight shocks her: she almost didn't recognize herself. There are no mirrors back in her little cottage. The woman in the mirror here, staring back at her in the secret room looks so old, and her pale skin is so white she could be mistaken for a ghost.

Robin reaches inside her pocket for the key to lock the secret room behind her, but her fingers find something else instead, providing her with a small wave of much needed comfort: her favorite red lipstick. It's worn down to a flattened stump. She remembers the first time she used it: it rained that night and she got badly hurt. But it reinforced the importance of not trusting anyone except herself.

The best lessons are often the ones we don't realize we're being taught.

Robin applies a tiny bit of lipstick—wanting to save what is left for as long as possible—then admires her new reflection in the mirror. She smiles again but it doesn't take, her mouth soon turning down at the edges. Still, it's an improvement, and it gives her the courage to do what she came here to do.

The visitors didn't *look* happy when they arrived, or when she watched them through the window. As she lurked downstairs, running her fingers along the spines of the books in the lounge that is more like a library, she noted that the visitors didn't *sound* happy either. She listened to them as they talked in the bedroom upstairs. Their voices carried, and their words seemed to bounce from the double-height vaulted ceiling up above straight down into her ears.

It seems strange to her that the visitors really thought they could stay here for free. Only fools believe in something for nothing. She had to suppress a laugh when she heard them agreeing to leave in the morning. But her amusement soon turned into anger. That's the biggest problem with people nowadays: they don't appreciate what they *have*, they always want more. They don't want to *work* for it. They don't want to *earn* it. And they bitch and moan like spoiled brats when they don't get their own way. Too many people think the world owes them something, and blame others for their own poor life choices. And everyone thinks they can just run away if things don't go according to their plans.

That won't be happening here.

The visitors can *say* what they like, they can even choose to believe it if that helps them sleep when they lay their heads back down on her pillows. The storm *outside* might have stopped—for now—but nobody is leaving here tomorrow morning. After what she has already seen and heard, Robin is fairly sure that at least one of them will never leave this place again.

AMELIA

It's still dark outside, but I shake Adam awake.

"Bob's gone. I can't find him!"

I watch impatiently as my husband rubs the sleep from his eyes, blinks into the darkness, and peers around the bedroom. It *smells* as though we are in a chapel now. That musty scent of old Bibles and blind faith. The only source of light is the flame from the candlestick I'm holding, and it takes Adam a while to remember where we are. It's as cold in here as I suspect it is outside now thanks to the complete loss of power overnight, and he instinctively pulls the bedcovers around himself.

I pull them back off. "Did you hear me? Bob is missing!"

"He was sleeping out on the landing," Adam says, suppressing a yawn.

"Well, he isn't there now."

"Maybe he went downstairs—"

"He isn't there either! I searched the whole place, he's not here!"

Now Adam looks worried.

He is finally hearing what I am saying. The unfamiliar concern on his face makes me feel worse—*I'm* the one who worries, not

him. When I am most anxious, he always remains calm. We balance each other's emotions, that's how our marriage works. Or used to.

"Well, the front doors were definitely locked and Bob doesn't have a key, so he *must* be here somewhere. I'll help you look," he says, lighting the other candle and pulling on a sweater over his pajamas—a feeble attempt to combat the cold. "I'm sure if we put some food in his bowl he'll come running—he normally does."

Adam is still half asleep, but drags himself out of bed and hurries onto the landing. He pauses to stare at the empty dog bed—as though I might be making it up that Bob is missing—then hurries ahead of me down the stairs. I notice that he deliberately misses some of the steps, which creak loudly when I walk on them.

"How did you know which steps not to walk on?" I ask, following him a little more closely.

"What?"

"You skipped some of the steps. The ones that creak."

"Oh . . . well it annoys me. Like squeaky cupboards or doors."

"But we only arrived last night. How did you know which—"

"I might not be able to remember faces, but facts and figures, or the things most people overlook—like which steps creak—tend to stick in my mind. You know that about me."

Adam does often remember peculiar details. A photographic memory of sorts, for unimportant things. I decide to drop it—we have bigger issues to worry about right now—and together we search every corner of every room for the missing dog.

"I don't understand it, the doors are still locked, he can't have got out," Adam says.

"Well, he didn't vanish into thin air," I reply, pouring some kibble into Bob's food bowl and calling his name.

The invitation is met with a silence that sounds even more ominous than before. I don't know what to do. I pick up my phone, but of course there is no signal, and who would I call even if there were?

"We should search outside," Adam says, and we hurry to the boot room.

He unlocks the old chapel doors, and heaves them open.

The scene they reveal stops us both in our tracks.

The sun is starting to rise behind a mountain in the distance, and there is just enough light outside for us to see a wall of snow higher than my knees. Everything is covered in a thick blanket of white, and I can barely make out the shape of our car on the driveway. If Bob really is out there somewhere, in snow this deep, he won't last long.

Adam reads my mind and does his best to calm the panicked thoughts swirling inside it.

"You saw me open the doors, they were definitely locked. The snow is taller than Bob—even if he could have got out, he wouldn't have—that dog doesn't even like the rain. He *must* be inside—did you look in the crypt?"

"After last night? With just a candle? Of course not."

"I'll use the torch on my phone," he says.

I'm about to correct him—he's forgotten that his mobile is still back in London—but then I watch as he hurries to find the old leather satchel he uses for his work. It's so tatty, I should get him something new. He reaches inside and pulls out his phone.

The one he pretended he couldn't find in the car when he had it with him all along.

The reason why a person lies is almost always more interesting than the lie itself. My husband shouldn't tell them; he isn't very good at it.

ADAM

I grab my mobile, turn on the torch, and hurry to the trapdoor. It's closed, so I don't see how Bob could have got down there, but it's also the only place we haven't looked. I open it and rush down the stone steps as fast as I dare. All I find are the same dusty wine racks, and a dirty, homemade-looking pamphlet on the floor: "The History of Blackwater Chapel."

I'm sure that wasn't there before.

"Bob isn't down there," I say, coming up the steps, distracted by the piece of paper in my hands.

Amelia doesn't reply, just stares. If I could see the expression on her face, I know it would be a bad one—her arms are folded and she's standing in that stance that means trouble. For me.

"What?" I ask.

"I thought you couldn't find your phone?"

Busted.

The guilt I feel is soon replaced with anger.

"Well, luckily I noticed you removing my phone from the car before we left. You lied to me about that and you've been acting

strange for weeks. Is there anything else you've been lying to me about? Is Bob really missing?"

"Don't do that. You know I love Bob."

"I thought you loved me."

The idea that Amelia had something to do with Bob's disappearance is unthinkable, but after her crazy behavior recently, I don't know what to think.

"All I wanted was a nice weekend away. Just the two of us, for once. Not me, you, and your bloody work. The writing, the books, the screenplays . . . that's *all* you ever seem to care about these days. That's why I took your phone out of the car, because you spend so many hours looking at it all the time you make *me* feel invisible."

She starts to cry then—always her Get Out of Jail Free card—and I can't stay angry with her. It isn't as though *I've* been honest about everything.

"Do you have a signal on your phone, maybe we could call someone?" she asks. I'm on a different network from her, so it's a sensible question.

"No. I already checked."

Her body language suggests she's relieved, but that doesn't make sense. I must be reading her wrong. I hate who we've become, but I'm not to blame for all of it. Trust can't be borrowed; if you take it away, you can't give it back.

"There's something I need to tell you."

I say the words so quietly I'm surprised she hears them.

Amelia steps away from me. "What?"

"Last night . . . I didn't come downstairs to get a glass of water. I saw . . . something down here, before we went to bed. I didn't want to scare you, so I waited until you were asleep, then came back downstairs to try and make sense of it. You were already so upset after the crypt incident; I didn't want to make matters worse—"

"Can you please get to the point."

"I would if you'd let me."

"What did you find?"

"This," I say, opening one of the kitchen drawers. It is crammed full of old newspaper articles about October O'Brien. "She's the actress who—"

"I know who she is, Adam. It's not something I'm likely to forget," Amelia snaps, pulling the neatly cut press clippings out one by one, and laying them on the kitchen table. "I don't understand. Why would *these* be *here*—"

"And I found this down in the crypt just now. I thought about hiding that from you too—I know how much this weekend meant to you—but I also know you don't like secrets."

I show her the pamphlet.

"What is it?"

"I think you should just read it for yourself. I don't think we're really welcome here."

"But then why offer a free weekend as a raffle prize? *They* invited us."

"*Who* did?"

Amelia doesn't answer because she doesn't know.

She picks up the flimsy piece of white paper covered in typed words, then lingers on the front page as if scared to open it. I watch in silence while she reads.

The History of Blackwater Chapel

A chapel has stood on this site, next to Blackwater Loch, since at least the mid-ninth century. When the current owner purchased the property and surrounding land, it had already been abandoned for several years. With a great deal of love and hard work, they decided to transform this derelict building into a beautiful home.

The original features include several carved stones, which are dated between 820–840, and it is one of the oldest Scottish chapels on record. We know that the chapel has not been used for its original purpose since the last priest, Father Douglas Dalton, left in 1948. There are no surviving accounts of his time here, only local (unsubstantiated) rumors that he fell to his death from the bell tower.

According to other records, the chapel's congregation dwindled down to almost nothing as the local population aged, and that was why it was left abandoned. Not much was known about the chapel's true history, until building work began to convert what was by then a crumbling wreck into a livable space.

Excavations in the crypt, to make a stronger foundation, revealed that the chapel had been used as a witch's prison in the 1500s. Iron rings were found in the crypt's walls, where women and children convicted of witchcraft were chained before being burned at the stake. The bones of more than one hundred suspected witches were found buried in the floor, along with

their offspring. Tests revealed that one skeleton was that of a five-year-old girl.

A collection of local anecdotes and urban legends all share similar stories about Blackwater Chapel. Most include tales of ghostly figures that can be seen floating over the loch at night. There are several accounts of women dressed as witches, with burned faces and singed clothes. Rumor has it they walk around the chapel after sundown, peering in through the stained-glass windows, searching for their murdered children. There have been several reports of such sightings in the local press over the years, before people got so scared that they stayed away.

Almost all of the builders involved in the renovation of the property said they felt inexplicably cold in the crypt, and some claim they heard their own names being whispered when they were down there. But it's important to note that not everybody who visits Blackwater Chapel witnesses paranormal activity or ghostly apparitions.

We hope you enjoy your stay.

AMELIA

"We need to find Bob, and get out of here," I say, as soon as I've finished reading.

Adam puts the pamphlet and newspaper clippings about October O'Brien in a kitchen drawer, then closes it firmly, as if making them disappear might help. I'm not sure what the link is yet between October and this place, but he can't seem to look me in the eye.

"I didn't want to scare you—"

"I'm not *scared*. I'm angry," I interrupt. "I don't believe in ghosts. Someone is trying to frighten us. I don't know who yet or why—"

"I don't think we should jump to conclusions."

"I agree. We should find Bob, pack up, and jump in the car instead."

We're dressed less than five minutes later. After searching the whole chapel again for the dog, there's nowhere left to look except outside.

Now that the snow has stopped falling, it feels like stepping into a painting. The sky has turned from black to gray to pale blue since I woke up, and I can see so much more than when we arrived in the

dark last night. There are snow-covered mountains and dense forests in the distance. A handful of white clouds are reflected on the
still, glassy surface of the vast loch, and the old white chapel seems
to shine in the early morning sun. Then I notice the bell tower and
remember last night. The part of the wall that collapsed is impossible to miss. No wonder the sign on the door read DANGER.

"Adam . . ."

"What?"

"The fallen wall."

"What about it?"

"What if Bob somehow got up to the bell tower, and the dam-
aged wall . . . and fell?"

"Then he'd be lying broken in the snow."

I don't like the way he answered the question, but I know Adam
is right. We start searching outside in silence. This is undoubtedly
one of the most beautiful and unspoiled corners of the world, but
I can't wait to leave.

I didn't bring the best clothes or shoes for this weather. The
snow is so high we have no choice but to wade through it in our
trainers. My socks and feet are wet within seconds, and the bottom
half of my jeans are soaking and heavy with freezing cold water.
I'm so worried about the dog, I barely notice. Seeing the place in
daylight, we can now truly appreciate the isolation and scale of
the vast valley we're in. We don't find what we are looking for,
but we soon discover what happened to all the missing bathtubs in
the property. Three claw-foot roll top baths are hidden around the
back, and have been filled with plants—heather by the looks of it,
in various shades of pink and purple.

They aren't the only unexpected discoveries.

We stumble across a small graveyard—as I suppose might be
expected behind an ancient church—with a collection of elderly
looking headstones almost completely hidden by the snow. There
are also a series of dark wooden sculptures dotted around outside the chapel, at least two or three in every direction that I look.

Hand-carved rabbits that appear to be leaping out of the frozen ground, an enormous tortoise, and giant wooden owls, perched on the tree stumps they have been fashioned from. They all have huge, hand-chiseled eyes, which seem to stare in our direction, as though they are as cold and scared as we are. Even the trees have faces carved into them, so it's impossible not to feel watched.

I call Bob's name over and over, but after twenty minutes of walking in circles, I don't know what to do. A non–dog person wouldn't understand, but it's just as distressing as losing a child.

"Do you think someone has taken him?" I ask, when we seem to have run out of all other ideas.

"Why would anyone do that?" Adam says.

"Why does anyone do anything?"

"Who then? We're in the middle of nowhere."

"What about that little thatched cottage we passed on the track in?"

"It looked empty."

"Shouldn't we check?"

He shakes his head. "We can't just accuse someone of—"

"No, but we could ask for their help? They're a lot closer to the main road than we are, so might still have power . . . or at least a phone we can use. It's not that far to walk. It's worth trying, isn't it? If Bob did get out somehow, they might have seen him?"

Adam never really wanted to get a puppy. The childhood memories that still haunt his dreams put him off—understandably—but that changed when he met Bob. My husband hides it well sometimes, but I know he loves that dog just as much as I do.

"Okay, let's go," Adam says. He takes my hand and I let him.

Some parts of the loch are frozen, and again my thoughts turn to Bob. He hates rain, or sleet, or snow, or anything falling from the sky, but he loves the water—always jumping in rivers or running into the sea. But surely our silly old dog would have known to keep away from a frozen loch. I try not to think about it as we trudge toward the cottage in the distance. Except for the sound of

our footsteps compacting the fresh snow, the cold air is hushed and muted. Silence can be eerie when you're not used to it, and living in London and working at Battersea, I'm definitely not. Sometimes I hear dogs barking in my sleep. But here, it's *so* quiet. Unnaturally so. There aren't even any birds singing. Now I think about it, I don't remember seeing any.

It didn't look that far when we set out, but it takes us more than fifteen minutes to reach the cottage. It's a tiny thing, with white-washed walls just like the chapel, and a thatched roof. Almost like a Hobbit house. It's so small and remote that I can't imagine why anyone would want to live in it, but there is a car parked outside—almost completely hidden from view—which gives me hope that someone does. It's a big vehicle, an old Land Rover perhaps. It's hard to tell with it being half buried by snow. Whatever it is, I'm sure it will cope better than my car in this weather.

I clear my throat before knocking on the bright red door. I'm nervous for some reason, and not even sure what I'm going to say if someone opens it.

I needn't have worried; nobody does.

It's strange because I could have sworn I heard voices when we walked up the path—a radio perhaps, or someone talking to a child in a hushed tone. I look at Adam, who shrugs, then I knock again. A little harder this time. There's still no answer, no sign or sound of life at all.

"Look at that," Adam says, staring at the roof.

I presume he means the thatch, but when I look up, I see the smoking chimney. Somebody *must* be inside.

"Maybe they can't hear us," he says. "You stay here and I'll take a quick look around the back."

He disappears before I can answer, and is gone so long I start to worry.

"Anything?" I ask, when he finally returns. It might just be the cold, or my imagination, but he looks paler than he did.

"Yes and no," he says.

"What does that mean? We just need to find Bob."

"It's a mess around back, completely overgrown and there's even an outside toilet. No outside bath this time at least, but I think whoever lives here must be old. There's no other door, just a couple of dirty windows. I saw a woman inside, sitting next to a fire."

"Great—"

"Possibly not," he says, interrupting my positive thoughts with more of his negative ones. "I knocked on the window to get her attention and I think I scared her."

"Well, that's understandable—I doubt she gets many visitors all the way out here. We can just apologize. I'm sure she'll want to help once we explain."

"I don't think so. There were candles everywhere—"

"Well, there has been a power cut and it is probably rather dark in there."

"No, I mean *everywhere*. Hundreds of them. She looked like a witch casting a spell."

"Don't be daft. That stupid pamphlet has put silly ideas in your head—"

"That wasn't all. She had an animal on her lap."

I picture poor Bob and feel sick. "What kind of animal?"

"A white rabbit, I think . . ." Relief floods my fear. For a moment I was terrified of what Adam might say. "I didn't have very long to take it all in before she saw me."

"And what happened when she did?"

"She stared at me for a long time, then just walked right up to the window, as close as I am to you now. Still carrying the fat white rabbit, *if* that's what it was. Then she pulled the curtains shut."

ROBIN

Robin didn't just pull one set of curtains; she closed them all.

She blows out every candle too—there were only a handful, not hundreds, but men are predisposed to exaggeration—then she sits in the dark, waiting for her heart to stop beating so fast. It never occurred to her that someone would be rude enough to trespass on her property or walk around the back uninvited—peering in through the glass as if she were an animal in a zoo. The curtains aren't really curtains at all—they are secondhand bedsheets nailed above the windows. She notices the yellow tinge of pipe smoke on the threadbare fabric. It used to be white. But it doesn't matter what something *used* to be, so long as it does the job. And things don't need to be beautiful to serve a purpose. Robin might not be pretty anymore, but she has every right to be here.

Not like them.

Robin used to sit in the dark, just like this, when she was scared as a child. It was an all too regular occurrence. She does what she did then to try to calm herself down: crossing her legs, closing her eyes, then focusing on her breathing. Slow, deep, breaths. In and

out. In . . . and . . . out. At least it was only *him* who saw her, that's something to be glad about.

It seems obvious now that she thinks about it—of course the visitors would come here looking for help—she's just annoyed that they managed to catch her off guard.

Robin wonders what they must be thinking now.

This is hardly a normal situation for any of them, far from it, and she expects that the stress and fear must be starting to take its toll. Married couples always think they know their partners better than anyone else—especially when they have a couple of years under their belts—but that doesn't mean it is true. Robin knows things about both of them that she is certain they do not know about each other.

She saw *him* looking at the rabbit on her lap, with a mixture of horror and disgust on his face. But Oscar the rabbit is her only companion these days. Like her, he is a creature of habit, and always tends to jump up on the armchair after his breakfast of grass, fresh vegetables, or—when the snow comes—tinned jars of baby food. At least he's real, unlike the characters *Adam Wright* makes up inside his head and spends all *his* time with. Mr. *Wright* is sometimes wrong. Robin will not be judged by these people.

She crawls toward the front of the cottage on all fours avoiding the windows. She needs to know whether the visitors have gone yet—there is so much to do and so little time. But they haven't. Gone. So she slides down to sit with her ear against the sealed-up letter box, still holding the rabbit, stroking its fur. It is surreal to hear *them* talking about her on the other side of the door. They might not know who she is, but Robin knows who *they* are. She invited them here after all, even if they don't realize it yet.

They will soon enough.

AMELIA

"We should try knocking again," I say.

"I don't think that's a good idea," Adam replies. "She looked like a nutter."

"Shh! She can probably hear you; this place isn't double glazed. How do you know it was a woman?"

He shrugs. "Long hair?"

Sometimes Adam's inability to recognize features on faces is more annoying than others.

"If it *is* a woman," I say, "then maybe *I* should try talking to her. I don't see any other buildings nearby, she might be the only one who can help us."

"What if she doesn't *want* to help us?" Adam whispers.

I'm already freezing, but I feel colder than I did before when he says that. I think about the October O'Brien newspaper clippings he found stuffed inside one of the kitchen drawers at the chapel and I feel sick. It's such a long time ago now, but Adam worked with the actress before what happened, happened, and I sometimes still wonder—

"Do you think she might be who you saw outside the window last night?" he whispers.

I shrug and it turns into a shiver. Relieved a little that at least he believes me about that now. "I don't know. Do you?"

"How would I know? I didn't see what you saw, and we both know I wouldn't be able to recognize them again even if I did."

"Well, was the person you saw just now fat or thin? Old or young?"

"Medium build I guess, and she had long gray hair."

"So, old then?"

"Maybe."

"I wonder if she is the housekeeper?"

"If she is, she's a bad one."

"Someone wrote those notes for us to find," I remind him.

"Don't housekeepers clean things? From what I saw through the window, she doesn't look like she knows how to use a feather duster. She may have a broom . . . for flying around at night—"

"This isn't the time for making jokes."

"Who says I'm joking? You didn't see what I saw with all the candles and the white rabbit on her lap like she was casting a spell. We've got enough problems right now without upsetting the local witch."

Sometimes having an overactive imagination is a curse. I take out my mobile and hold it up to see that I still don't have any signal. Adam watches, then does the same with his.

"Anything?" I ask, looking over his shoulder. But he shakes his head, and puts his phone back in his pocket before I see the screen.

"Not even one bar. Why don't we climb to the top of that hill, I think I can see a footpath," he says, pointing at what looks like a small mountain to me. "One of us might get a signal up there, and if not, at least we'll have a view of the whole valley. If there are any other houses, or people, or even a busy road where we could flag someone down, we'll be able to see it."

It's not a completely crazy idea.

"Okay. That sounds like a good plan. I'm still going to write a quick note though, just in case."

I reach inside my handbag for a pen, and find an old envelope to scribble on.

Sorry to disturb you, we didn't mean to intrude. We are staying at Blackwater Chapel. There is no phone at the property, and no power due to the storm, no water thanks to frozen pipes, and no mobile signal. If you have a phone we could borrow, we'd really appreciate it and promise to reimburse you for the call. We've lost our dog. If you see him, his name is Bob and we're offering a generous reward for his safe return.

Many thanks,
Amelia

I show the note to Adam.

"Why did you add that bit about the reward?"

"Just in case she *is* a witch and wants to turn Bob into a rabbit too," I whisper, before trying to push the note through the letter box. It seems to be sealed up, so I slide the envelope beneath the door instead. I hear a noise then, and take a quick step back. "Come on, let's go."

"What's the hurry?" Adam asks.

I watch as he salutes a blackbird, just in case it's a magpie. It's one of his many superstitious habits that often make me love and loathe him at the same time. The idea that failing to salute a magpie will result in bad luck waiting for you around the next corner, is a myth my logical mind has never believed in. But he does. Because his mother did. Given our current circumstances, maybe I should start saluting too.

"I heard something," I whisper, when we are a little farther away. "I think she was on the other side of the door the whole time we were standing there talking. Which means she heard every word."

ROBIN

Robin did hear every word.

She reads the note that the woman pushed under the door, then screws it up into a ball before throwing it on the fire.

Robin isn't a witch—not that she cares what they think—but has frankly been called far worse. So what if she doesn't keep the cottage spotlessly clean? It's *her* home and how she chooses to live is *her* business. *Some people* think money is the answer to all of life's problems, but they're wrong, sometimes money is the cause of them. *Some people* think money can buy love, or happiness, or even other people. But Robin won't be bought. Everything she has now is *hers*. She earned it, or found it, or made it all by herself. She doesn't need or want anyone else's *money* or *things* or *opinions*. Robin can take care of Robin. Besides, this cottage might not look like much, but it was somewhere she used to run away to as a child. Just like her mother before her. Sometimes home is more of a memory than a place.

The comments about her personal appearance hurt a bit, more than they should have. But name-calling stings no more than nettles these days, and the initial irritation soon fades to nothing. Besides, being dismissed as an elderly woman amuses her in some ways. Just

because her hair has turned gray, it doesn't mean that Robin is *old*. She tells herself that *he* doesn't know what he's talking about—the man can't even recognize his own reflection. But although vanity has never been one of her qualities, it doesn't mean she is immune to insults.

She tidies herself and the place up a little—because she *wants* to, not because of what *he* said—then carefully pulls back the corner of one bedsheet curtain, to check that the visitors aren't still lurking outside. She is pleased to see that they are halfway up the hill already. Out of the way and earshot.

Now that she is sure they cannot see or hear anything else that they shouldn't, Robin sits down in the old leather chair and lights her pipe. She just needs a little something to steady herself and her nerves, and this is the last chance she'll get to smoke it. The only visitors she is used to these days are Patrick the postman—who knows better than to knock or say hello—and Ewan, the local farmer who grazes his sheep on the land around Blackwater Loch. He sometimes drops by with milk or eggs to say thank you—she lets the animals feed for free, and understands that farming has become a tough business. He also tells her snippets of gossip about various characters in town—not that Robin wants to know—but *most* people stay away.

Because *all* the locals know the stories about Blackwater Chapel.

Robin looks out of the window to check on the visitors one last time. They're near the top of the hill now, so it's safe to go out. She puts on her coat and Oscar stares up at her. A few years ago, Robin would have thought that a house rabbit was a ridiculous idea, but as it turns out, they make surprisingly good companions. Robin slips a red leather collar inside her pocket, then heads off toward the chapel alone. She knows what happened to the visitors' dog because she took him. But Robin doesn't feel guilty about that at all, even though she used to own a dog herself, and knows how upset they must be.

Bad people deserve the bad things that happen to them.

IRON

Word of the year:
chuffed *adjective.* Feeling happy or very pleased.

28th February 2014—our sixth anniversary

Dear Adam,
This has been a good year for us both, hasn't it? You were
happy, which made me happy, as though it were contagious.
Henry Winter asked you to adapt another of his novels for
film—a murder mystery with a hint of horror this time,
called *The Black House*—and things seem to be moving in the
right direction with your own screenplays too, with *Rock Paper Scissors* now in preproduction!

We have October O'Brien to thank for that. Having an
A-list actress on board didn't just help open doors for your
own projects in Hollywood, it attracted the attention of a
great producer, someone you trust. The three of you have
spent ~~an insane amount~~ lots of time together this year, with

you disappearing to LA with them more than once, not that I mind. Besides, thanks to October, we've just had one of our best anniversaries ever.

I told her that we've never been away for our anniversary because you're always too busy working—it's true—and that's when she suggested we celebrate our sixth in style at her French villa. It was very kind, especially when she's had such a horrible time lately. The press found out about a speeding ticket, one of many as it turns out. October's pretty face—and very expensive car—was in the newspapers for all the wrong reasons. October loves driving fast cars, but now she has to go to court and because of all the previous offenses, it sounds like she might lose her license.

The Eurotunnel crossing was much faster than I imagined it would be. We parked on the train, and just over thirty minutes later we were in Calais, as if by magic. Bob used his pet passport for the first time, and it was so easy to travel with a dog. I saw one woman crossing the channel with a rabbit in the passenger seat of her car. It wore a tiny red harness and walked on a lead, I'd never seen anything like it!

We drove through Paris—I wanted to see Notre Dame—and after lunch in a little café on the bank of the River Seine, we strolled through the "Bouquinistes of Paris," and the booksellers of Paris did not disappoint. Each had their own display of secondhand books—hundreds of them—beneath a sea of green-roofed huts lining the path along the river. Just as their predecessors had been doing for hundreds of years.

You were in your element.

"Do you know these bookstalls were declared a UNESCO World Heritage Site in 1991?" you said, stopping to literally smell the books. It's something you always do, and although I once found it a little peculiar, I now find it endearing. I love the way you pick up a book in your hands, carefully turning

the pages as if the paper were made of gold, then smell them, as if you might be able to breathe in the story.

"I did not know that," I replied, having heard you tell this tale several times before.

That's a funny thing about marriage that nobody ever mentions. People think that when a couple run out of stories to tell each other, their time is up. I could listen to your stories all day, even the ones I've already heard, because every time you tell a story it's a little different. Nobody knows everything about another person, no matter how long they've been together, but if you ever feel like you know too much then something is wrong.

"It is said that the River Seine is the only river in the world that runs between two bookshelves," you said, and you held my hand.

"I like that," I replied, because I did. I still do.

"I like you," you replied, then you kissed me.

We haven't kissed in public like that for years. At first, I felt self-conscious—I wasn't sure I could remember how—but then I gave in to the idea of us being us again. The people we used to be. We time traveled to the moment when I was the girl you wanted to marry, and you were the man I hoped might ask.

October has loaned us her French home in Champagne while she is filming another movie in America. She has four different homes dotted around the world. Maybe that's why she's so good at changing her accent and look. Her French house is a twenty-minute walk from Moët & Chandon on Avenue de Champagne—which I'm quite convinced is the best address I've ever heard—and I can see why she likes living here more than London or Dublin. I feel like we are in Disneyland for wine lovers. The main avenue is a cobblestoned wonderland for anyone who enjoys a glass of fizz. Elegant châteaus line the street on either side, each owned

by the world's oldest and best-known winemakers. The town itself is filled with award-winning restaurants and cute little bars, all serving champagne as if it were lemonade.

Your favorite actress's French hideaway is in the perfect location: close enough to walk to the center of town, but far away enough to feel like we are in the countryside, with sweeping views of vineyards and the valley below. The building was once a small, derelict, former independent winery. Now it is a luxury house, all wooden beams and big glass windows. Modern, but with enough original features to make it feel like a home. Not too shabby at all for a woman under thirty. She seems to have caught the renovation bug, and already has her eye on another abandoned property she wants to transform, according to you. Somewhere a little more remote.

We arrived late, so after a supper of cooked Camembert, jam, and fresh French bread, washed down with a bottle of champagne—*bien sûr*—it was straight to bed.

"Happy anniversary," you said the next morning, kissing me awake.

I wasn't sure where I was at first, but then relaxed when I saw the stunning view from the guest bedroom: nothing but blue sky, sunshine, and vineyards. You smiled when you gave me my gift and looked rather pleased with yourself. I'm so sorry if I looked a little disappointed when I opened it; I was still half asleep and wasn't expecting you to give me a bookmark. Don't get me wrong, as bookmarks go it's a very nice one: made of iron to represent our sixth year and engraved:

IRON SO GLAD I MARRIED YOU.

You seemed to think that was hilarious.

"I'm just chuffed that you love reading as much as I do these days," you said. "It's nice when we spend an evening with a couple of books and a bottle of something good in front of the fire, isn't it?"

"Nobody under seventy uses the word 'chuffed' anymore," I replied.

It is true—I do read as much as you these days. What choice do I have? It's either read together or be alone.

I gave you your gift: a very elaborate-looking vintage iron key. You seemed as unimpressed as I probably did a few minutes earlier, and I decided we might need to work on our gift buying choices.

"What does it open?" you asked.

"A secret," I said, and reached beneath the white sheets.

I think you'll remember what we did then, twice, in October O'Brien's bedroom. It was the best sex we've had in a long time. There were several photos of our lovely host hanging on the walls: October winning a Bafta, or posing with members of the royal family for the charity work she does, or smiling with other young, beautiful, Hollywood A-listers that I should probably know the names of, but don't. I had to turn away at one point, worried she was watching us.

I hate myself for thinking it, but I hope it was me you were picturing in her bed.

I had a little nose about the place while you were taking a shower. Who wouldn't? There were inspirational mottos dotted around, including a framed print that read: YOU GET WHAT YOU WORK FOR, NOT WHAT YOU WISH FOR and—my personal favorite—BE THE PERSON YOUR DOG THINKS YOU ARE. I didn't know she had one. There was also some unopened mail on the doormat, and two of the envelopes I picked up were addressed to an R. O'Brien.

"I didn't know October was married," I said, putting the post on the dressing table, and having a quick peek inside her drawers.

"She isn't," you replied from the bathroom.

"Then who is R. O'Brien?"

"What?" you asked, shouting over the sound of the shower.

"These letters are all addressed to someone called R. O'Brien."

"October is just her stage name. It helps keep her private life private," you said. "Good thing too the way the press sometimes goes after her. That business about the speeding ticket and all the headlines it generated, you'd have thought she killed someone." Then you immediately changed the subject, and I was glad, because I wanted this time away to be all about us. Only us.

I gave you that iron key because I want to tell you the truth about everything. All of it. We're so happy at the moment, and I don't want there to be secrets between us anymore. But when you unwrapped it, and held the key to everything in your hand, something felt wrong. Why ruin our present or jeopardize our future with my past? Better to let us live this happy version of us a little while longer.

All my love,
Your wife
xx

ADAM

I take better care of myself than my wife, she spends too long taking care of others. By the time we reach the top of the hill, she is red in the face and more than a little out of breath. I could have made it easier, gone a little slower perhaps, but I wanted to get us both as far away from that cottage as soon as possible.

"I can't see anything," she says.

"That's because there is nothing to see."

Strictly speaking, neither of these things are true.

There is a full three-sixty-degree view of the valley from up here—just as I predicted there would be—with only snowy mountains and wilderness as far as the eye can see. It's stunning, but a view of another house, or a petrol station, or a phone box, might have been preferable, given the circumstances. A beautiful but barren landscape is exactly what I feared: nowhere to run. Or hide. We are completely cut off.

I did see something though.

Back at the cottage.

It's been bothering me ever since.

I didn't recognize the woman—I never recognize anyone—but I

did get a strange sense of déjà vu. I try to tuck it away in one of the darker corners of my mind—out of sight—and look at my wife instead. She has her back to me, busy taking in the view of the valley. I can tell she is trying to catch her breath and gather her thoughts, both seem to have escaped her. I wish I could see my wife the way other people do. I recognize the shape of Amelia's body, the length and style of her hair. I know the smell of her shampoo, her moisturizing cream, and the perfume I give her for birthdays or Christmas. I know her voice, her quirks, and mannerisms.

But when I stare at her face, I could be looking at anyone.

I read a thriller about a woman with prosopagnosia last year. I was genuinely excited at first—not much has been written about face blindness. I thought it might be a good premise and make a good TV drama, as well as help raise awareness of the condition, but sadly not. The writing was as disappointing and mediocre as the plot, and I turned the job down. I spend so much time rewriting other people's stories, I wish I was better at rewriting my own.

Sometimes I think that I should have been an author. An author's words are treated like gold, they're untouchable and get to live happily ever after inside their books—even the bad ones. A screenwriter's words are jelly beans in comparison; if an executive doesn't like them, they chew them up and spit them out. Along with whoever wrote them. My own real-life experience would have made a better thriller than that novel. Imagine not being able to recognize your wife, or your best friend, or the person responsible for killing your mother right in front of you as a kid.

My mother was the person who taught me to read and fall in love with stories. We would devour novels from the library together in the council flat I grew up in, and she said that books would take me anywhere if I let them. Kind lies are the cousins of white ones. She also said that my eyes would turn square from all the TV I insisted on watching, but when our battered old set broke, my mother sold all of her jewelry—except for her beloved sapphire ring—at the pawn shop to get me another one. She knew that the characters I

loved in books, films, and TV shows, filled the gaps left by absent family and nonexistent friends when I was a child.

Watching her die will always be the worst thing that ever happened to me.

"What shall we do now?" Amelia asks, interrupting my thoughts.

It was a long and steep climb to the top of this hill, both of us are unsuitably dressed for the hike *and* the weather, and it seems it was all for nothing. Neither of us has a signal on our phones, even up here. There's no sign of Bob or any way of calling for help. I can see the chapel in the distance down below, and it looks so much smaller than before. Less threatening. The sky, on the other hand, has darkened since we left. The clouds seem determined to block out the sun, and Amelia is shivering. It was okay when we were on the move, but I feel the cold too since we stopped, and I know we shouldn't stand still for long.

When you reach the top of a hill, you can often look back and see the whole path you took to make the journey. But while you're on the path, it's sometimes impossible to see where you are going or where you have been. It feels like a metaphor for life, and I'd be tempted to write the thought down if I wasn't so damn cold. I take one final look around, but other than the chapel and the cottage, there really is nothing to see except a snow-covered landscape for miles in all directions.

"I guess we really are in the middle of nowhere," I say.

"I'm freezing," she replies through chattering teeth. "Poor Bob."

I take off my jacket and wrap it around her. "Come on, let's go. We'll light the fire when we get back, get warm, and come up with another plan. It will be easier going down."

I'm wrong about that.

The ground seems even more slippery now than it did on the way up, and a combination of snow and ice makes our progress slow. The muddy sky turns a darker shade of gray, and although we both do a good job of pretending not to notice the first few drops of sleet, seconds later it is impossible to ignore. Our clothes are

not designed to withstand extreme winter weather, and neither are we. The wind blows the sleet at us from all directions, and within minutes we are both soaked to the skin. Even I'm shivering now.

Just when I think things can't get any worse—weatherwise—the sleet turns to hail, raining down from the sky like bullets. I predict we will both be covered in bruises when we get back. *If* we get back. Whenever I dare to look up, risking a face full of tiny ice pellets, I notice that we don't seem to be getting any farther down the hill. The chapel still looks tiny and very far away.

The pelting from above eases off, and the hail turns into snow.

"Let's try and make a bit more progress while we can," I say, reaching out to help Amelia down from one part of the rocky path to another. But she doesn't take my hand.

"I can see someone," she says, staring into the distance.

I shield my eyes, scan the valley below, but see nothing. "Where?"

"Going into the chapel," Amelia whispers, as though they might hear her from what must still be over a mile away.

Sure enough, I spot the shape of a person walking up the chapel steps.

I feel for the giant key I locked the old wooden doors with before we left, and start to relax when I find it in my pocket. But my brief sense of comfort evaporates as I watch the shadowy figure open the doors and disappear inside. I'm sure I must have imagined it—though it's hard to be certain of anything from this distance—but it looked like they might have been wearing a red kimono. Just like the one my mother used to wear when she invited . . . friends to stay. I try to Control-Alt-Delete the thought, as always, but the keys in my mind get stuck. I might have imagined what they were wearing, but someone *did* just go into the chapel. Even if I ran down the hill, and managed not to slip on the ice or fall in the snow, I guess it would take at least twenty minutes to get back down there and confront whoever just let themselves in.

"Tell me how we ended up staying at this place again," I say, in a shaky voice that sounds like a poor imitation of my own.

"I already told you. I won the weekend away in the staff Christmas raffle."

"And you found out when you received an email?"

"Yes."

"And the email was from . . . ?"

"The housekeeper. I told you already."

"Did anyone else you know at work win something similar?"

"Nina got a box of Quality Street chocolates, but she bought twenty raffle tickets so was bound to win something."

"How many raffle tickets did you buy?" I ask, already dreading the answer.

"Only one."

ROBIN

It doesn't take Robin long to walk from the cottage to the chapel.

Oscar looked very sorry for himself when she left him behind, his big white floppy ears seemed to droop even more than normal. Robin was in desperate need of some comfort and company when she first arrived in Blackwater, and Oscar seemed like a good name for the companion she found. Robin had always been rather fond of those solid bronze statues the film industry gave out once a year. *Her* only Oscar might be a rabbit, but she loves him.

She spotted the visitors at the viewpoint on top of the hill in the distance, and knew she had at least half an hour to do everything she needed to do. They couldn't get back in time to stop her even if they tried. Unlike them, she has proper winter weather gear. Even if her borrowed boots are too big, they're still better than trendy trainers for trekking across snow-covered hills and fields.

She stops outside the chapel briefly before going in, taking a moment to stare up at the stained-glass windows and the small, white bell tower perched on top of the building. With the loch and mountains in the background, it's like looking at a painting. She realizes that she has been here too long in more ways than one; a person can

become immune to beauty when exposed to it too often. As Robin lets herself inside, so does the wind, blowing a cloud of dust motes masquerading as snow into the air. It amuses her that the visitors think she is the housekeeper. That isn't why she has a key.

Robin removes her boots in the boot room—the place might be filthy, but there is no need to make things worse—then she walks through to the kitchen. Her socks have more holes than a pair of fishnets, but waste not, want not. The chapel is even colder than usual, and already smells different from how it did before they arrived. Traces of the dog, along with the woman's overpowering perfume now permeate the stale air.

She hurries to the lounge that looks more like a library, then pulls the glove off her right hand, and runs her fingers along the spines of the novels that line the shelves. She does this every time she comes here, the same way some people can't resist touching tips of wheat in a field. She notices the faint smell of smoke, and sees that the visitors burned all the logs she left for them last night. Not that it matters now. At least, not to her. It might matter to them later.

When she grips the banister of the spiral staircase, a million unwanted memories flood her mind, drowning her courage and clouding her concentration.

Your focus determines your future.

Robin is rather fond of inspirational mottos like these. She repeats the words to herself until her thoughts feel steady again, then makes her way up the creaky stairs, ignoring the missing faces among the framed photos on the wall.

The bed where the visitors slept last night has not been made. It still feels strange to have let *them* sleep here. But it doesn't take long for Robin to tuck in the sheets, straighten the duvet, and puff up the pillows. It's the least she can do: if the visitors are still here tonight—and they will be—they will need their rest. Then she looks inside their bags, and studies their things, because she can and because she wants to.

She starts in the bathroom. Robin finds the woman's shampoo, then smells it before tipping the contents down the sink. Seeing their pink and blue toothbrushes side by side provokes another wave of irritation, so she grabs them both and uses them to clean the toilet bowl. She scrubs so hard that the bristles look flattened. Then she puts everything back how she found it.

The pots of face cream left on the windowsill look expensive, so Robin applies some to her own cheeks. It has been a while since her skin care routine consisted of anything more than a wet flannel once a day, and the moisturizer feels so good she decides to keep it, slipping the jar into her pocket. She returns to the bedroom then, and takes one last look around, noticing that the drawer to one of the bedside tables is slightly open. She takes a closer look, hoping something might have been left inside.

The way some people blindly trust others has always baffled Robin. At least one of the visitors believed they were coming here for a weekend away, and that Blackwater Chapel was some kind of holiday rental. It's not and never will be. At least not while she's alive.

When Robin thinks about the properties people pay vast amounts of money to stay in: hotels, Airbnbs, overpriced cottages by the sea, she can't help thinking about all the other hundreds of strangers who have slept in the same bedsheets, drunk from the same cups, or shat in the same toilet before. All those people, using the same access codes every changeover day—different hands slipping the same keys into different pockets once a week. Locks are rarely changed, even when the keys to rental properties get lost, so who knows how many people might really have a copy. Anyone who has ever stayed there could come back at any time and let themselves in.

She finds a wallet in the drawer. It seems odd that the man would have left it behind, but animal owners do act strangely when worried about their pets. Robin can understand that. She slides the credit cards out of his wallet one by one, rubbing her thumb across

the embossed name. Then she finds a crumpled paper shape between the leather folds. She holds it up to the light and sees that it is an origami crane. It's a little burned around the edges, but Robin knows that cranes are supposed to bring good luck, and the fact that *he* carries it around in his wallet makes her hate him a little less. She puts everything else back as she found it.

There is an inhaler in the drawer on the other side of the bed. Robin puts it in her mouth and takes a puff, but it isn't nearly as satisfying as her pipe. She expels the rest of its contents into the air, then takes the empty inhaler with her, along with the prescription sleeping pills she has found. After a quick trip to the tower to ring the chapel bell, Robin heads back inside to finish what they started.

AMELIA

Adam starts to run down the hill toward the chapel, but I can't keep up.

He's been somewhat preoccupied with his own health and fitness recently, and started taking vitamins and supplements, which is new. His obsession with jogging at least twice a week is finally paying off, and I tell him not to wait; the sooner one of us gets back the better. I keep having to stop to catch my breath. I forgot to bring my inhaler—foolishly leaving it next to the bed in my panic to find Bob—but I know I'll be okay, so long as I take my time and try to stay calm.

It sounds easier in my head than it is in reality.

If we hadn't both seen someone letting themselves into the chapel, I might have thought I imagined it. But it was real. Maybe it *is* the mysterious housekeeper? Come to check we are okay after the storm? I tell myself that whoever it is will be able to help us. And want to. Because none of the other possibilities auditioning inside my mind are good. When I reach the snow-covered track at the bottom of the hill, I'm relieved to be on a flat surface again. Adam's lead has increased. He isn't far from the chapel now, so I hurry on as fast as I can, trying to catch up.

I stop when the bell in the tower starts to ring.

The snow pummels my face. I didn't see Adam go inside but he must have, because when I look up—shielding my eyes from the relentless blizzard—he's vanished. Did *he* ring the bell? I remember earlier, when Adam said that the main doors were the only way in, and out, of the chapel. I haven't seen anyone leave, which means whoever we saw go inside is still there. Anything could be happening. The latest snowstorm seems to have turned the world black and white. I can barely see my own hand when I hold it in front of my face. I try to run faster but I keep slipping and my chest starts to hurt. My heart is beating too quickly, and my breaths are too shallow. My anxiety is made worse knowing that even in a medical emergency, we have no way of calling for help.

When I finally reach the huge chapel doors, I don't need to worry about knocking—they are wide open and the floor of the boot room is covered in snow. I spot a pair of large, unfamiliar Wellington boots next to the old church bench, and notice that someone has drawn several smiley faces in the dust on its wooden surface now. I wonder if it means something and lift the lid, but it's empty. When I look up, I catch sight of my reflection in the wall of tiny mirrors. I look wrecked.

"Adam?" I call, but am met with an eerie silence.

The kitchen is empty, as is the lounge full of books. I hurry up the wooden spiral staircase to the first floor, wheezing, and gripping the banister like a cane. I ignore the DANGER KEEP OUT sign on the farthest door, and climb the steps to the bell tower. But there's nobody there, and the bedroom is empty too. It doesn't make sense. The pain in my chest isn't getting any better, so I pull open the drawer beside the bed. My inhaler has gone. I'm *sure* that's where I left it, and now panic starts to ripple through me.

I need to find Adam. Back out on the landing I try the other doors, but they're all still locked. He isn't here, I've already searched every room. Then I remember the crypt.

"Adam!" I yell again.

Silence.

I run so fast that I almost fall down the creaking stairs.

"I'm in here!" he calls when I reach the lounge, but I can't *see* him.

"Where are you?" I shout back.

"Behind the bookcase on the back wall."

I hear his words but fail to make sense of them.

I follow the sound of his voice, staring at the shelves lined with books from floor to ceiling. I don't understand until I see the sliver of light revealing a secret door, covered in the spines of old books. I hesitate before pushing it open, once again feeling as though I might have fallen down the rabbit hole, or become trapped in one of the dark and disturbing novels my husband loves to adapt.

The thin door squeaks open to reveal another room. It's a study, but unlike any I have seen before. The long, narrow, dark space only has one stained-glass window for light. There is an antique desk at one end, and my husband is sitting at it.

"Whoever was here has gone," Adam says without looking up. "I searched the whole place. The only thing that I noticed was different was that the door to this room was open."

"I don't understand—"

"I think I'm starting to. I recognize this room."

He doesn't seem to notice that I can barely breathe. There are no supplements for people who suffer from a sympathy deficit, and my husband has always been easily distracted by his own thoughts and feelings. "You do?"

"Yes, I've seen it before. I couldn't think where at first and then I noticed this," he says, tapping the shiny wooden desktop. "I've seen a picture of this study in a magazine, albeit a few years ago. And I remember who the article was about. You say that you won a weekend away by chance, in a raffle, but that can't be true. It's all too much of a coincidence. I know who this property belongs to now."

COPPER

Word of the year:
discombobulated *adjective.* Feeling confused
and disconcerted.

28th February 2015—our seventh anniversary

Dear Adam,

It's been a difficult year.

October O'Brien was found dead in a London hotel a few
months ago, and you were one of the last people to see her
alive. Suspected suicide according to the newspapers. There
was no note, but empty bottles of alcohol and pills were
found by her bed. It was obviously devastating. And surprising; the woman always seemed so happy and positive, at least
on the outside. Barely thirty years old and everything to live
for. The two of you had become quite close—I was rather
fond of her myself—but it also means that the filming of

Rock Paper Scissors has been canceled. You can't make a TV series without the star of the show.

The funeral was awful. You could tell that so many people there were merely acting out what they thought grief should be. ~~Two-faced shysters~~. It seems that genuine friends are even harder to come by when you're famous. I was surprised to discover that October's real name was Rainbow O'Brien. Her parents were hippies, and nobody at the service wore black.

"Thank goodness she used a stage name," you whispered.

I nodded, but wasn't sure whether I agreed. She was a bit like a rainbow: beautiful, captivating, colorful, and gone from our lives almost as soon as she appeared in them. I used to think a name was just a name. Now I'm not so sure. I had become quite friendly with October myself—occasional drinks, dog walks, and visits to art galleries—and I miss her too. It does feel like something, not just someone, is missing from both of our lives now that she is no longer in them.

A trip to New York sounded like a great way to spend our seventh anniversary and take our minds off it all, until I realized that it coincided with the premiere of Henry Winter's latest film, *The Black House*. You were ~~so eager to please~~ flattered when he told his agent and the studio that he would only attend if you did. You thought it was because he was pleased with the adaptation, and wanted you to get the credit you deserved for writing the screenplay. But that wasn't why he wanted you there. Or why he suggested you invite your wife.

You've been ~~moody as hell~~ a little distant recently, and I didn't want to start another fight, but playing gooseberry to a pair of writers while they basked in the temporary warmth of Hollywood's fickle sun didn't appeal much. Neither did walking down the red carpet at the old movie theater in Manhattan where the premiere was held. The Ziegfeld was

my kind of place—an old-school cinema decorated in red and gold, with a sea of plush red velvet seats. But being photographed on the way in made me feel like a fraud. I hate having my picture taken at the best of times, and compared with all the beautiful creatures in attendance—with their tiny waists and big hair—I worried that I must be a disappointment to you. It's hard to shine when surrounded by stars. The idea of just being normal seems to make you so unhappy, but it's all I ever wanted us to be.

The deal was that we would spend time alone together after the premiere, but then Henry wanted you to accompany him to a few more events the next day. I understand why you couldn't say no; I just wish that you hadn't wanted to say yes. I get that you've always been a huge fan of his, and I understand how grateful you are that he let you adapt his work. I know what it's meant for your career, but haven't I already paid the price for that? Wandering around a city on my own while you hold an author's hand instead of mine, is not my idea of a happy anniversary.

You haven't been yourself for a while. I know that you are grieving for October, I understand that she was more than just a colleague, and the dream of seeing your own work on screen stalling, again, must also be upsetting. But it still feels as if there is something else going on. Something you're not telling me. There are residents in our lives, the ones who stay for years, and then there are the tourists just passing through. Sometimes it can be hard to tell the difference. We can't, and don't, and shouldn't try to hold on to everyone that we meet, and I've met a lot of tourists in my life, people I should have kept at a safe distance. If you don't let anyone get too close, they can't hurt you.

I spent today alone, visiting the parts of New York I'd never seen before, while you followed Henry Winter around the city. The elderly author might seem charming to you, on

the rare occasions when you have been in his company, but in real life the man lives like a hermit, drinks like a fish, and is impossible to please. I can't tell you that, because I shouldn't know. I've read all of his novels, too, just like you. His most recent was mediocre at best, but you still act as though the man is Shakespeare reincarnated.

I tried not to think about it when I visited the Statue of Liberty. The ferry to the island was jam-packed, but I still felt alone. Inside the monument, I joined a group of strangers for a tour. There were families, couples, friends, and as we climbed the staircase, I realized that everyone seemed to have someone to share the experience with. Except me. A friend from work texted to ask how the trip was going. I haven't known them very long, and it seemed a little overfamiliar, so I didn't reply.

There are three hundred and fifty-four steps to the Statue of Liberty's crown. I silently counted the reasons why we were still together as I climbed them. There are still plenty of good things about our marriage, but a growing number of bad ones make me feel like we are starting to unravel. This distance between us, the empty spaces in our hearts and words; it scares me. A lot of married couples we know are muddling along, but most of those have the glue of a young family to keep them stuck together. We only have us. I did something I never do at the top . . . I took a selfie.

I headed to Coney Island after that. I guess it must be busier in summer, but I quite liked wandering around the closed arcades. I even found a last-minute gift for you—the copper theme this year posed a bit of a challenge. We've had so many highs and lows over the course of our relationship, but I suppose year seven is supposed to be difficult. I've heard about the seven-year itch and I'm sure you must have too. Whatever happens, I know I won't be the first to scratch it.

When my feet ached from all the walking, I headed back to

the aptly named Library Hotel. It's a small but perfectly formed boutique hideaway, full of books and personality. Every room has a subject and ours was math. Horror might have been more appropriate; given the way this evening has turned out.

I'd booked us a table for dinner—I knew you would forget to remember—at a nearby steak house called Benjamin that the concierge recommended. The decor and atmosphere made me think of *The Shining* meets *The Godfather*—which again seems rather fitting in hindsight—but the service and steaks were perfection. As was the wine. We drank two bottles of red while I listened to you tell me about your day with Henry. You didn't ask about mine, or notice the new dress I'd bought in Bloomingdale's. Paying me a compliment is something you only do by accident these days.

I forgot to wave tonight when you walked in to the restaurant, but somehow you still knew it was me. Given that all faces look the same to you, and I was wearing something you had never seen, your confidence as you sat down at our table was out of character and surprising. I was equally baffled by how much attention you paid the waitress, wondering how you recognized the beauty of her twentysomething features if you couldn't see her face.

I think I knew we were going to argue even before you said what you said. Sometimes fights are like storms, and you can see them coming.

"I'm sorry to do this, but Henry wants me to go with him to LA. Given all the buzz around this film, the studio wants to adapt another of his books, and he says he'll only entertain the idea if I go along to meet them and agree to write the screenplay."

"What about *Rock Paper Scissors*? You're not going to give up on that, are you? It's terrible about October, but there are other actresses. Working on Henry's novels was only supposed to be a stepping-stone to—"

"I hardly think writing a blockbuster film script of a best-selling novel, written by one of the most successful authors of all time, is a stepping-stone."

"But the whole point of this was to help you to make TV shows and films of your own—not his—to do what you really wanted."

"This is what I want. I'm sorry if my career choices aren't good enough for you."

We both knew that wasn't what I meant, and I could see you weren't really sorry at all.

"What about what I want? It was your idea to spend a few days in New York together and so far I've barely seen you—"

"Because I couldn't leave you behind. I never would have heard the end of it."

For once, it feels like I'm the one who can't recognize my spouse. "What?"

"You don't seem to have any friends or even a life of your own these days."

"I have friends," I say, struggling to think of the names of any to help back up my claim.

It's hard when everyone my age that I used to know seems to have children now. They all disappeared inside their shiny new happy families, and the invites dried up. It reminded me of school a little . . . being shunned by the cool kids because I didn't own the latest must-have accessory. I changed schools more than once growing up. I was always the new girl and everyone else had already known each other for years. I didn't fit—I never do—but teenage girls can be cruel. I tried to make friends, and I succeeded for a while, but I was always on the outer solar system of those childhood relationships. Like a smaller, quieter planet, distantly orbiting the brighter, more beautiful, and popular ones.

I still tried to stay in touch—attending the occasional birthday party, or obligatory bachelorette party or wedding

for someone I hadn't spoken to for years—but as we all grew up, and grew apart, I guess I grew more distant. My child-hood relationships set the tone for the ones I formed as an adult. It was self-preservation more than anything else on my part. I'll never forget the woman who pretended to breast-feed her children until they were four years old. Always mak-ing excuses to avoid seeing me—as if my infertility might be catching. I care more about liking myself than being liked by others these days, and I don't waste my time on fake friends anymore.

You reached for my hand, but I pulled it away, so you reached for your wine instead.

"I'm sorry," you said, but I knew that you weren't, not really. "I didn't mean that," you added, but it was just another lie. You did. "Henry is a sensitive writer. He really cares about his work and who he will trust with it. He's had a difficult year—"

"I've had several. What about me? You're acting like he's your best friend all of a sudden. You hardly know the man."

"I know him very well; we talk all the time."

It's been a while since I felt so discombobulated. I almost choked on my steak. "What?"

"Henry and I talk quite regularly. On the phone."

"Since when? You've never mentioned it."

"I didn't know I had to tell you about everyone I speak to, or get your permission."

We stared at each other for a moment.

"Happy anniversary," I said, putting a tiny paper parcel on the table.

You pulled a face that made me think you had forgotten to get me a gift, but then surprised me by taking something out of your pocket.

You insisted I open yours first, so I did. It was a small cop-per and glass hanging frame. Inside were seven one penny

copper coins. They all had different dates on them, one from each of the seven years we have been married. It must have taken a lot of thought and time to find them all.

You cleared your throat, looked a little sheepish. "Happy anniversary."

I said thank you, and wanted to be grateful, but something still seemed broken between us. It felt like I had spent the evening with someone who looked and sounded like my husband, but wasn't. You opened my hastily bought gift, and I blushed with embarrassment after all the effort you had made.

"Where did you get this?" you asked, holding the American penny up to the candlelight. It had a smiley face carved into it, next to the word "liberty."

"Coney Island this afternoon," I replied. "I stumbled across this arcade machine that said Lucky Pennies. The paper crane I gave you is looking a little worn out, so I thought I'd give you something new for good luck to keep in your wallet."

"I'll treasure them both," you replied, tucking the penny away with your crane.

You were soon back to talking about Henry Winter again. Your favorite subject. As I half listened, I couldn't stop thinking about October O'Brien's untimely death, or how you seem to care more about Henry's writing these days than you do about your own. There are plenty of horror stories in Hollywood, and I don't mean the ones that get made into films. I've heard them all. Maybe I should just be grateful that you're a screenwriter who is still getting work; it's not always the case, and the competition is fierce. Some writers are like apples, and soon turn rotten if they don't get picked.

You poured the rest of the wine into your glass and drank it.

"You wouldn't worry about my career so much if you

cared more about your own," you said with slurred words, and not for the first time. I wanted to smash the bottle over your head. I love my job at Battersea Dogs Home. It makes me feel better about myself. Maybe because—like the animals I spend my time caring for—I too have often felt abandoned by the world. It's rarely their fault that they are unloved and unwanted, just like it was never mine.

"I'm sure I could write something just as good as you, or Henry Winter for that matter—"

"Yes, everyone thinks they can write until they sit down and try to do it," you interrupted with your most patronizing smile.

"I care more about the real world than indulging fantasies," I said.

"Indulging my fantasies paid for our house."

You reached for your glass again before realizing it was empty.

"Tell me about your dad," I said, without really thinking it through. You put the glass down with a little too much force, I'm surprised it didn't break.

"Why are you bringing that up?" you asked without making eye contact. "You know he left when I was a toddler. I don't think Henry Winter is secretly my long-lost father if that's where you were going—"

"Don't you?"

Your cheeks turned red. You leaned forward before replying and lowered your voice, as if you were worried who might hear.

"The guy is my hero. He's an incredible writer and I'm very grateful for everything he has done for me, and therefore us. That's not the same thing as imagining him as some kind of surrogate father."

"Isn't it?"

"I don't know what you're trying to say—"

"I'm not trying to say anything, I'm telling you that I think you've developed some kind of emotional attachment to the man . . . it's like an obsession. You've abandoned all your own projects to work night and day on his. Henry Winter kick-started your career when you were down on your luck, so yes you owe him some gratitude, but the way you now constantly seek his approval whenever you write something new is . . . at best needy, at worst narcissistic."

"Wow," you said, leaning back as if I had tried to physically hit you.

"You should believe in yourself enough by now to know your work is good without needing him to say so."

"I don't know what you're talking about. Henry has never said he likes my work—"

"Exactly! But it's so obvious—to him and everyone else—how desperate you are for him to endorse you in some way. You need to stop secretly hoping that he will. He rarely says anything kind about another writer's work—he rarely has a kind word to say about anything or anyone at all—just accept the relationship for what it is. He's an author, you're a screenwriter who adapted a couple of his novels. The end."

"I think I'm old enough to make my own choices and choose my own friends, thank you."

"Henry Winter is not your friend."

When we left, I didn't break the uncomfortable silence to let you know that I'd spotted Henry sitting a few tables away from us in the restaurant. He was hard to miss, wearing one of his trademark tweed jackets and a silk bow tie. His white hair was thinning, and he looked like a harmless little old man, but the piercing blue eyes were still the same as always. He'd been watching us the entire time we were there.

You continued to talk about him all the way to the Library Hotel, my words on the matter forgotten almost as soon

as I'd said them. From the gleeful look on your face, any-one would have thought you had spent the day with Father Christmas, rather than a book-shaped Ebenezer Scrooge.

When we got back to our math-themed room, things weren't adding up for me. I ate both the chocolates on our pillows while you were in the shower—even though I hate dark chocolate—I guess I wanted to hurt you back some-how, childish as that sounds. My phone buzzed and for a mo-ment I thought it might be you, texting me from the hotel bathroom—nobody else sends me messages late at night. Or in the day. But it wasn't you, it was my new friend at work saying that they missed me. The idea of anyone missing me made my eyes fill with tears. I sent them the selfie of me at the top of the Statue of Liberty and they replied straightaway with a thumbs-up. And a kiss.

You're asleep now, but I'm awake as usual, writing you a letter I'll never let you read. This time on hotel letterhead. A seven-year rash of resentment might be more accurate than an itch. I can't be honest with you, but I need to be honest with myself.

I ~~hate~~ don't like you right now, but I still love you.

Your wife

XX

ROBIN

Robin stays where she is until both visitors are in the secret study. Then she unlocks the door of the room she's been hiding in, creeps down the staircase—avoiding the steps she knows will creak—and leaves the chapel. She meets her silent companion exactly where she left him. He does not look impressed about being abandoned out in the cold. Robin does what she needs to do outside as quickly and quietly as she can, then waits.

She's good at waiting. Practice can make a person good at anything, and at least she isn't alone this time. The snow has stopped falling but it is still cold. Robin would rather get back to the cottage, but there is no point rushing something this important. She has been careful to step in the visitors' earlier footprints, but trying to go unnoticed isn't always easy. That's the problem with following in someone else's footsteps; if you leave a bigger mark than they did they tend to get upset. Robin learned the hard way that it's always best to take her time, and late is better than never. Sometimes the early bird eats too many worms and dies.

Stained-glass windows are beautiful, but they let the cold in and the sound out, which is why she is listening outside the one in the

study. She unlocked the secret door and left it open deliberately, so that the visitors could find it for themselves. Once the penny drops things shouldn't take too much longer.

Listening to *them* in the place where *she* used to live, and laugh, and dream, is such a strange and surreal experience. A bit like food poisoning. She feels sick and feverish, but already knows she'll feel better again once she gets whatever was rotten out of her system. She wants the visitors out of the chapel, but not yet. There is still too much to say and do before this unpleasant chapter in her life can come to an end.

"Everything will be okay, you'll see," she says to her companion, but he doesn't reply. He just stares back at her, looking as sad and cold as she is starting to feel.

Whenever her life has taken a wrong turn in the past, Robin has tried to pinpoint the exact moment she got lost. There always is one. If you are prepared to open your eyes, and look far enough back, you can normally see the instant you made a poor choice, said something you shouldn't, or did something you lived to regret. One bad decision often leads to another and then, before you know it, there is no way back to where you were.

But everyone makes mistakes.

Sometimes, the most innocent-seeming people turn out to be guilty of horrific things. Sometimes, the people who do bad things, are just bad people. But there is *always* a reason why a person behaves the way that they do. The woman at the local store was a good example of someone with a much darker past than you'd expect. Patty, the unfriendly shopkeeper, with her red face, beady eyes, bad breath, and a habit of shortchanging strangers, had a list of convictions longer than the Bible she kept behind the counter. From aggravated assault to driving when over the limit. Everyone in town knew, but they had to get their supplies from somewhere. Few people are genuinely capable of forgiveness, and nobody ever really forgets. Sometimes you just know a person is bad news as soon as you meet them, because they're rotten, inside and out, and instinct tells you to stay away.

Lives carry on regardless of whether the people they belong to do. Robin wanted to move on, she tried so hard to put her own mistakes behind her, and not be consumed by regrets. But our secrets have a habit of finding us, and everything she tried to run away from caught up with her eventually. Covering her present with the dust of her past.

Her companion starts to fidget.

"Shh," she whispers. "Just wait a little longer."

He still looks unimpressed but does what she says, just like always.

AMELIA

Time freezes when Adam says he knows who the chapel belongs to.

I look around the secret study, thinking it might reveal the answer before he does, but all I can see are more dusty books, an old desk, and my husband. His handsome features have twisted into a disappointed frown and ugly scowl. He looks more angry than afraid. As if this is all somehow *my* fault.

I think when you feel abandoned by your own parents, it's impossible not to spend the rest of your life suspecting people of plotting to leave you. It's something I always feel anxious about with everyone, even Adam, despite how long we've been together. Whenever I get close to someone—partners, friends, colleagues—there inevitably comes a point when I have to back away. I rebuild barriers, higher than before, to make myself feel safe. A constant fear of abandonment makes it impossible to trust anyone, even my husband.

I'd managed to calm my breathing when I found him in here, but this new anxiety is pressing on my chest.

"Writers are a peculiar breed of human being," Adam says, still staring at the antique desk as though he is talking to it, not me. It's

so cold in this room that I can see his breath. "There are people I've worked with over the years—people I *trusted*—who turned out to be nothing more than . . ."

The light from the stained-glass windows casts shattered fragments of color on the parquet floor, and he seems too distracted by them to finish his thought. I try to think of anyone he has fallen out with since I've known him, but there aren't many. He's had the same agent since the beginning. Everyone loves Adam, even the people who don't.

"Do you remember the film *Gremlins*?" he asks. I'm glad he doesn't wait for a reply because I don't know what to say or see how this is relevant. "There were three rules: don't get them wet, don't expose them to bright lights, and don't feed them after midnight. Otherwise bad shit happens. Authors are like Gremlins. They all start off like Gizmo—these individual and interesting creatures that are fun to have around—but if you break the rules: if they don't like the adaptation of their book, or they think you changed too much of the original story, authors turn into bigger monsters than the ones they write about."

"What are you talking about, Adam? Who owns this property?"

"Henry Winter."

I freeze. I've always been afraid of Henry, and not just because of the dark and twisted books he writes. The thing that scared me the most the first time I saw him, were his eyes. They're too blue, and too piercing, almost as though he could look inside a person, not just at them. See things he shouldn't be able to see. Know things he shouldn't know. My breathing starts to get a little out of control again.

"Are you all right? Where's your inhaler?" Adam asks.

"I'm fine," I insist, grabbing the back of the chair.

"The *Daily Mail* wanted to do a feature on where Henry wrote his novels when the last film came out. He wouldn't let them send a journalist or, heaven forbid, a photographer—he always hated those. I'd known him for years by then, but he wouldn't even tell

me where he lived when not in London—always obsessively worried about privacy for reasons I could never fully understand. I only ever saw one picture of him in his study—which the newspaper said was 'supplied by the author.' This is it. The room where he writes. I remember the picture of him sitting at this desk," Adam says, touching the dark wooden table. It's a peculiar old thing on wheels, with lots of little drawers. "It once belonged to Agatha Christie, and Henry paid a small fortune for it at some charity auction years ago. He became quite superstitious about it; once told me that he didn't think he could write another novel anywhere else."

"Are you sure?"

"Yes. Look at the shelves in this room."

I turn and do as he says, but the bookcases that line the back wall of the study look exactly the same as the ones in the lounge. Then I notice the spines of the books, and I see that they are all written by Henry Winter. There must be hundreds of them, including translations and special editions. It's a giant vanity wall and exactly what I would expect from a man like him.

"So, what is this? A prank? A bad joke?" I ask. "Why would Henry send an email from a fake account, telling me that I've won a weekend at his secret Scottish hideaway? Why is everything covered in dust? Where is he? And where is Bob?"

"Are you sure you're all right?" Adam asks. "Your breathing sounds—"

"I'm fine."

He looks unconvinced but carries on anyway. "I think he might be upset with me. Ever since I said I didn't want to adapt his books anymore—"

I stare at him, taken aback. "You did what? I don't understand."

"I just decided that maybe it *was* time to focus on my own work."

"You didn't tell me—"

"I couldn't bear the inevitable I told you so's. He didn't take the news well at all. It was like a spoiled child throwing a tantrum. I'd had Henry Winter on too high a pedestal my whole life. I looked

up to him even when he looked down on me. But then I saw him for who he was for the first time: a selfish, spiteful, and lonely old man."

I take in his words, processing what they mean for him, and for us.

"When was this?"

"A while back. I tried to keep things friendly, but then he ignored my calls, and I haven't spoken to him for . . . a long time. His books were all he had. But if there's one thing I have learned from life as well as fiction, it's that nobody is ever *just* a hero or *just* a villain. We all have it in us to be both."

Adam glares at me when he says that last sentence. I'm about to ask why when I spot my inhaler on the desk behind him.

"Why do you have that?" I ask.

"Your inhaler?" he says. "I didn't even notice it was there."

I stare at him for a long time. I can normally tell when he's lying and I don't think he is.

I grab the inhaler and slip it in my pocket. "I think we're both exhausted, and now that we know who this place belongs to, I just want to find Bob and get out of here."

As soon as I say his name, I hear a dog barking outside.

ADAM

We run out into the snow.

I don't know what to expect. Henry Winter standing outside the chapel? Holding Bob's lead, and laughing manically like a comedy villain? Maybe he *has* finally lost his remaining marbles? The man writes dark and twisted fiction, but I still struggle to believe he would be capable of something like this in real life.

The sound of a dog barking stops as soon as we step outside.

"Bob!" Amelia calls.

It's pointless—the poor old thing is practically deaf at the best of times—but I start shouting his name too.

The valley is now eerily silent.

"Maybe it wasn't Bob?" I say.

"It *was* him, I know it," she insists. "There were a pair of men's Wellington boots by the door when I got back, now they're gone. Whoever was here before left and they've got Bob with them."

She runs farther out into the snow and I have no choice but to follow her.

The sheep are back. They stare in our direction, but aren't as scary as they were in the dark last night. We both stop in our tracks

when we see the back of a person wearing a tweed jacket, dark trousers, and what looks like a panama hat . . . in the middle of winter . . . in freezing cold snow up to their knees. Amelia looks in my direction. I can't read the expression on her face, but if it's anything like what I'm feeling, I expect it is one of terror.

I remind myself that I used to know this man—as well as you can know someone you work with and have only met a handful of times. I clear my throat and take a step closer.

"Henry?" I say gently.

For some reason, I remember the antlers on the wall of the boot room. It occurs to me that authors of murder mysteries and thrillers probably know a lot of ways to kill a person without getting caught, and I don't especially want to have my remains mounted on a wall. He doesn't move. I tell myself he's probably just a bit deaf, like the dog, and carry on until we are face-to-face.

Except he doesn't have a face.

What I appear to be looking at is some kind of scarecrow, but with the head of a snowman. He has wine corks for eyes, a carrot for a nose, a pipe sticking out of the space where his mouth should be, and one of Henry Winter's silk blue bow ties tied around his neck. It's a shade darker than it should be, saturated with melting snow. Henry's walking stick, the one with the silver rabbit's head handle is leaning against it, as though for support.

Amelia comes to stand by my side. "What the—"

"I don't know anymore."

"This wasn't here before, was it?"

"No. I think we would have noticed. I really don't understand what is happening."

We stand side by side in silence, staring at the scarecrow snowman as his head slowly melts. One of his cork eyes has already slipped halfway down his face. Apart from the odd dead-looking tree and creepy-looking wooden sculptures, we are in the middle of a vast open area. Whoever did this must be close by. And if Bob is near enough to be heard barking, we should be able to spot him,

but all I can see is empty white space. Thanks to the sheep, the snow has been disturbed almost everywhere outside the chapel. If there were any footprints to follow, there aren't now.

"We have to find Bob. He's out here somewhere, we both heard him, and we just have to keep looking," Amelia says, and I follow her.

There is a small cemetery at the back of the chapel. The old gravestones are barely visible thanks to the snow, but one stands out as I get nearer. The reason it catches my eye is because someone has wiped it clean, so that the dark gray granite stands out against everything else covered in white. And, unlike all the other headstones, this one looks relatively new.

That isn't all.

There is a red leather collar sitting on top of it.

Amelia picks it up and I see Bob's name on the tag, as though there had been any doubt in my mind that it belonged to him.

"I don't understand. Why remove the dog's collar and leave it here?" she says.

But I don't reply. I'm too busy staring at the headstone.

HENRY WINTER
FATHER OF ONE, AUTHOR OF MANY.

1937–2018

AMELIA

"I don't understand. If Henry died two years ago, wouldn't we have known about it?" I ask.

Adam doesn't answer. We stand side by side in silence, staring at the granite headstone, as if doing so might make the words engraved on it disappear. No matter how many times I rearrange the pieces of this puzzle inside my head, they just don't fit. I can see the confusion and fear and grief on my husband's face. I know he thought everything we have was a result of Henry Winter giving him his big break, and trusting him with his novels. A silly falling-out didn't change that. The man dying when they weren't even on speaking terms is going to hit him hard. But Adam must realize we have bigger problems right now: if Henry didn't trick us into coming here, then who did?

"We should get back inside," Adam says.

He's still looking at the headstone, like he can't believe what he's seeing.

"What about Bob?" I ask.

"Bob didn't take off his own collar and leave it here for us to find.

Someone else did that. I don't know what's going on, but we're not safe."

His words sound so melodramatic, but I agree.

As soon as we are back inside the chapel, Adam locks the doors, and pushes the large wooden church bench in front of them.

"Whoever we saw letting themselves in earlier must have had a key. This will stop them getting back in without us hearing," he says, heading toward the kitchen. "Can you show me the email you were sent about winning a weekend in this place again?"

I feel for my phone inside my pocket, but find my inhaler instead. Now that my breathing has returned to normal, I don't need it, but I feel better knowing it's close at hand.

I find the email on my mobile and hand it to Adam.

"info@blackwaterchapel.com, that's the email address they used?" he asks.

"Yes. It sounded like a genuine holiday rental."

"Henry had a thing about the number three and the color black. A lot of his novels were set in Blackdown or Blacksand . . . I think there may have been a Blackwater too . . ."

"You never mentioned that before."

"I didn't realize there was a connection until now. But Henry can't have sent this email—he doesn't *do* emails, or the internet, doesn't even have a mobile phone. He thinks they cause cancer. *Thought.*"

For a moment, I think Adam might cry.

I put my hand on his shoulder, "I'm sorry, I know how much you—"

"I'm fine. He hadn't even been in touch since . . ."

Adam trails off and stares into space.

"What is it?" I ask.

"I hadn't heard anything from or about him since last September, when his latest agent sent me a copy of his latest book. Luckily, this agent approves of screen adaptations, not like Henry's first one. He's a nice guy, we even joked about how Henry wasn't speaking to

him either, but the author had still sent his manuscript, three days before his deadline, wrapped in brown paper and tied with string just like usual."

"So?"

"The headstone outside says he died two years ago. Dead people can't write novels or send them to their agents."

It takes me a few seconds to process this latest piece of information. "Are you saying that you think he *isn't* really dead?"

"I don't know what to think anymore."

"Did he have any family? Surely someone would have known if he passed away. One of my old foster parents died last year, do you remember? Charlie, the guy who worked at the supermarket all his life, and always brought home free food that was about to go off. I hadn't spoken to him for over a decade, but I still knew when he died. Henry Winter is a world-famous author; we would have read about his death in the newspapers or—"

Adam shakes his head. "There was nobody. He was a self-confessed hermit, and liked living his life that way . . . most of the time. Whenever he drank too much whiskey, Henry would get all teary-eyed about not having any children—nobody to look after his books when he was gone. That's all he really cared about: the books. The man was stoic as a tree at all other times."

"Well, someone must have been helping him. Henry was no spring chicken if he was born in 1937," I say.

Adam's eyes narrow. "That's an odd detail to remember."

"Not really. It was written on the headstone and Amelia Earhart went missing in 1937. I was named after her. Don't you remember why you were called what you were? I think names are important."

Adam stares at me as though my IQ has dropped to a dangerously low level. "Henry Winter didn't have any children; he didn't have any family at all. I think the only person he had left in his life other than his agent was me, and we weren't even on speaking terms when he died . . ."

His voice wobbles and he looks away.

"The headstone outside said 'Father of one.' Someone had that made, and someone buried him. He couldn't have done *that* by himself."

The way Adam looks at me scares me a little. It's hard not to say the wrong thing when nothing feels right. I sometimes think that his inability to recognize other people's faces might make it harder for him to control the expressions on his own. The well-worn frown has gone, and it's almost like he is . . . smiling. It vanishes as quickly as it appeared.

"We should get out of here while it's still light," he says, adopting a serious face once more to match his tone.

"What about Bob?"

"We'll find a police station, explain the situation, and ask them to help."

"The car is snowed in. The roads look dangerous—"

"I'm sure we can dig it out. I'd feel safer out there than I would do staying here for another night, wouldn't you?"

He opens the door to the walk-in larder where we saw the wall of tools when we arrived. The industrial-sized chest freezer hums an eerie soundtrack, and I avoid looking at the trapdoor to the crypt. I'd rather forget what happened down there.

"Are you going to chop our way out?" I ask when Adam takes an axe off the wall.

"No, I just think having something for self-defense might not be a bad idea," he replies, taking a shovel down off a rusty hook with his other hand.

The Morris Minor is covered in so much snow, it blends in with the scenery. I feel like a spare part as Adam begins to dig it away from the car's wheels. It's freezing cold, but he's still sweating from the effort. Until he stops and stares at the front wheel as though it has offended him. He drops the shovel and bends down behind the front left-hand side of the car, so that I can no longer see what he is doing.

"I don't believe it," he says, sounding breathless.

"What?"

"We appear to have a flat tire."

I hurry over. "It's okay, on these roads in this car it's to be expected. I have a repair kit in the boot, so long as we can find the hole and it's small enough I can—"

I stop talking when I see it for myself. It won't be a problem to find the hole because it's the size of a fist. There is a smile-shaped gash in the rubber: the tire has clearly been slashed. I was already so cold that I could barely feel my hands or feet, but the chill I feel now spreads through my entire body.

"Maybe we drove over some glass?" he says.

I don't answer. Adam's knowledge of cars is very limited as a result of never owning one. I used to find it endearing, now not so much. He starts digging out the back wheel, then abruptly stops. Again.

"Have you ever had two flat tires at the same time?" he asks.

It looks like the back wheel has been slashed as well. It's the same with the other two.

Someone really doesn't want us to leave.

ROBIN

Robin lets herself back inside the cottage and locks the door. She takes a small red towel from a hook on the wall, then wipes the snow from the dog's feet, legs, and belly, before taking care of herself. He wags his tail while she dries him, then licks her face. Robin smiles, she likes all animals, especially dogs like this one. Even Oscar the rabbit has warmed to their new houseguest.

By now, the visitors will know that the chapel belonged to Henry and that he is dead. Robin wishes that she could have seen their faces when they found the headstone, but she and Bob were long gone by then. He's a very friendly and affectionate dog—even if he does bark at the wind occasionally—the kind who trusts everyone.

It's cold, even *inside* the cottage. Robin lights the fire and sits down on the rug next to it, trying to warm her bones. She misses her pipe but that's gone now, so she opens a packet of Jammie Dodgers. The dog lies down by her side resting his chin on her legs, staring up at her while she eats, hoping she might drop something. Robin likes to nibble each biscuit, biting off tiny pieces of the

outer edges until only the jam center is left—making the pleasure it brings her last as long as possible.

Despite sitting so close to the open flames, she can still hardly feel her hands. Her fingers were a rainbow of red and then blue after using them to wipe all that snow off Henry's headstone. But the visitors never would have found it if she hadn't, and she needs things to stay on track. There is a reason why she invited them here this weekend, and not any other.

Robin remembers when Henry died.

"I need you to come."

That's what he said when he called. Not "hello" or "how are you?" Just five little words. *I need you to come.* He didn't need to say *where*, even though they hadn't spoken for such a long time. He didn't need to say *why* either, but he did.

"I'm ill," were the two extra little words offered when she didn't reply. That turned out to be rather an understatement.

She knew Henry had sold his London flat by then and was living in his Scottish hideaway full-time. He'd always been a hermit who preferred his own company. What she didn't expect, was that she would be the one he would call in his hour of need. But then having nobody else was one of the few things they had in common. Writers are capable of creating the most elaborate and popular worlds, sometimes leaving rather small ones for themselves. Some horses need blinders to do what they do best and win the race. They need to feel alone and with no distractions. Some authors are the same; it's a solitary profession.

Silence cannot be misquoted. It was one of Robin's mottos. But when she still didn't speak, the phone line crackled, and Henry spoke once more before hanging up.

"I'm dying. Come or don't come. Just don't tell anyone."

She can still hear the dial tone now if she closes her eyes.

He explained later that he had run out of change for the hospital pay phone. Insisted that he had not been deliberately dramatic or

rude. Robin didn't believe him. She never did. But she got in the car anyway, because life can be as unpredictable as death.

She didn't recognize the man perched on the edge of the hospital bed. His last official author photo had been taken at least ten years earlier, and Henry had not aged well. The trademark tweed jacket looked too big, like it belonged to someone else, there was no silk bow tie, and all that was left of the shock of white hair were a few thin strands, combed over his pink balding head. It seemed odd that his face was not more familiar to her, but then people lose touch all the time. Distance wasn't a deciding factor in such matters. Even neighbors living side by side don't always know each other's names.

There was no greeting. No hug. No thanks.

"I want to go home," was all he said.

Robin watched as Henry signed the release forms using a fountain pen from his inside jacket pocket. His shaky fingers gripped the barrel so hard that the bones in his hand looked like they might burst through his paper-thin skin. She waited without a word while he initialed various statements to acknowledge that he was leaving the hospital against medical advice.

The hospital was more than an hour away from Blackwater, and they sat in silence for the entire journey along winding Highland roads. Once back inside the chapel he had turned into a home, Henry hobbled through to the lounge that he had turned into a library, beckoning for her to follow. Then he opened the secret door in the back wall of books. Robin wasn't impressed—she had *seen* it before—but it was the first time he had ever invited her *inside* his study.

She stared at the white rabbits that seemed to cover every surface. The wallpaper was covered in a shimmery pattern of them, the roman blinds were stitched with a leaping variety, there were matching big ears and bobtails sewn onto the window seat cushions, there was even a rabbit in one of the stained-glass windows.

Then she noticed the cage in the corner of the room. Big enough

to hold a small child. *That* was something she'd never seen before, and it wasn't empty.

"You have a rabbit for a pet?" Robin asked, staring at the creature.

"More of a companion really. I'm rather fond of white rabbits."

"I noticed," she replied, taking in the room again. "Does it have a name?"

He smiled. "*She* does. I called her Robin."

Robin didn't know what to make of that. "Why?"

His smile faded. "She reminded me of you."

Henry shuffled over to the chair at his desk and sat down.

"I don't know how much time we have, so best not to waste it. I'd like to show you where my will is kept. Everything is arranged, I just need someone to push the button so to speak, when the time comes. There are plans written down for what I would like to happen to me. I want to be cremated, but everything you need to know is in the folder. I'm halfway through my latest novel, I won't be able to finish it now. My agent will look after almost everything book-shaped when the time comes. But there might be some decisions about my literary estate that I would prefer . . ." He looked at her, his big blue eyes pleading as though waiting for Robin to say something. When she didn't, he seemed to give in, gently picking up his weary thoughts almost from where he had left them. "You must do whatever you think is right. That's all any of us can do in the end. I promise I tried to. There are a couple of other email addresses you should probably have—people who need to know that I'm dead before they read it in the newspapers—why don't I scribble them down now while I remember."

Robin watched as he took a laptop from the desk drawer. Henry's face stretched into something resembling a smile when he saw the expression on hers, the plentiful lines and creases on his skin doubling in number.

"I know, I know. Everyone thinks I don't understand how to use modern technology, but I'm old, not senile. I quite like that they think

I'm so ancient that I write the novels with a feather quill and a pot of ink, but this little laptop saves me a lot of time. It's much easier to edit for starters. I use the typewriter for the final version to send to my agent—to maintain the illusion of the person they think that I am—but I use a computer for all other drafts. I draw the line at mobile phones though—those things cause cancer, you mark my words."

He typed the password into the laptop using just his index finger, and very slowly, so she saw what it was without really meaning to: Robin. The knowledge that he used her name for his passwords as well as his pet made her feel an overwhelming sense of bewilderment and guilt. She didn't know what to say so—once again—said nothing. He opened up his email account using the same password, and it made her want to cry. She knew him well enough to know that he wanted to live—and write—forever. But all the money in the world cannot buy more time.

"Probably stuff and nonsense, it normally is," Henry said, turning his attention to some unopened post on the desk. He took a silver letter opener, which looked heavy in his frail hand, and sliced between the folds of the top envelope. His fingers shook a little as he removed what was inside: a letter from his agent. Robin read it over his shoulder, and saw how the old man beamed when he learned that his latest novel was a *New York Times* bestseller.

"Isn't that something?" he said, looking much more like his old self, the one she remembered. "I didn't know when I was writing it, but that was the last book I'll ever publish. It means the world to me that my readers liked it."

"Well, their opinions always mattered most," Robin said, and his face crumpled. "I mean, congratulations," she added, because what else could she say to a dying man? She looked at the laptop again. "Your agent still writes you letters and sends them in the post?"

"Yes."

"He doesn't know that you have email?"

Henry smiled. "There are a lot of things my agent doesn't know about me."

An unspoken conversation took place between them, a rare moment of understanding. Then they reset themselves and it was gone.

"There is some champagne in the crypt," he said. "Go and get us a bottle, will you? Have one drink with me to celebrate my last bestseller? Then I promise I'll tell you everything else you need to know. I locked the trapdoor—even I get the heebie-jeebies sometimes."

"But all those stories about bodies being found in the crypt, and witches, and ghosts . . . *you* made all that up to keep people away from here."

He grinned. "Yes, all just a figment of my dark and twisted imagination. But it worked, didn't it! The only thing the builders found down in the crypt when we restored the place, was damp. I like peace and quiet and privacy. I don't want people bothering me, but sometimes I scare myself. I spent so many years inside those stories, that the world I made up felt more real to me than the one I lived in." His blue eyes watered, and Robin could tell that his mind had wandered somewhere far away. But then he blinked and was back. "The key for the padlock on the trapdoor is in one of the kitchen drawers . . . I forget which."

Robin hesitated, but then did as he asked. The first thing she saw when she walked into the larder was the giant freezer, then she noticed all the tools lined up on the wall, including all the woodwork chisels and stone masonry tools neatly arranged according to size. The axe frightened her just as much then as it always had. For years, Henry had enjoyed carving things out of wood and stone, he said it was a bit like carving fiction from real life. It just required patience, imagination, and a steady hand. Every summer, he would chop down an old tree that was blocking his view of the loch with that axe, then carefully carve an animal sculpture into the remaining stump. Owls and rabbits were his favorites. All with spooky, oversized eyes, a bit like his own.

The trapdoor really was locked, and it took her forever to find the key. The smell of damp as she walked down the stone steps

reminded her of so many things that she would rather have forgotten. But there were no ghosts in the crypt—at least not that variety and not that day—only alcohol. By the time she returned to the study holding a dusty champagne bottle, she was surprised to find Henry still staring at the fragile clipping of the *New York Times* bestseller list. His agent had circled his book in red. It was number one.

Robin poured two glasses and held one out for the old man to take, but he didn't. When she looked a bit closer, she could see that he wasn't moving and his blue eyes hadn't blinked for some time. She felt for a pulse but there wasn't one. On the desk, she noticed some items that hadn't been there before: an empty bottle of pills, a list of instructions, and a will. She drank the glass of champagne that was in her hand. Not in celebration, but because she required alcohol. At least he died happy.

Robin buried Henry that night, scared that someone might see if she waited for the sun to come up. She wrapped his body in an old bedsheet along with some of his favorite books, then dragged him out of the chapel. In his will, he had asked to be cremated, but having a cemetery right outside, and a shovel, had proved to be very convenient. Albeit hard work. There were other instructions Robin chose to ignore, too. Like telling anyone at all that Henry had died. The following morning, she ordered a very nice-looking headstone online using Henry's bank account details, and when it arrived, she engraved it herself using Henry's tools. He had a staggering amount of money—more than she'd imagined—but Robin never spent a penny of it on herself. Despite it being clear in his will that the author had left her a considerable sum. The only time she ever used his bank card again, was to buy props for the visitors, because that was for *them*, not her. Two days after Henry died, she sacked his cleaner, knowing that nobody else ever came to visit the recluse. Even the Blackwater Inn had closed down years earlier, thanks to Henry. He would be as alone in death as he chose to be in life.

When Robin found Henry's work in progress on his laptop, she read it out of curiosity more than anything else. It was another

typically dark and twisty Henry Winter novel. She hadn't realized that she was holding her breath during a particularly frightening scene, until the rabbit made an unexpected sound in its cage and made her jump. Robin didn't like her namesake being locked up. She carried the enormous white rabbit outside the chapel, and when it didn't run away, she closed the doors behind it, hoping that she would never see it again. But it didn't budge. When she carried it farther away, closer to the long grass and the loch, it just came back, sitting outside those huge gothic doors as though waiting to be let in. She didn't understand back then, but not everyone wants to be set free.

BRONZE

Word of the year:
atelophobia *noun*. The fear of not doing
something right or the fear of not being good
enough. An extreme anxiety of failure to
achieve perfection.

29th February 2016—our eighth anniversary

Dear Adam,
We didn't celebrate our anniversary this year.

I've been spending a lot of time with a friend from work
and you've been, well, spending time with your work. You
struggled with the latest adaptation of Henry Winter's
books. Personally, I think because you were trying too hard
to please the author instead of being true to yourself. But as
you said when I offered to try and help a couple of weeks
ago, what do I know?

I do know that the lies we tell ourselves are always the most dangerous. And I know that sometimes the thoughts we hide in the margins of our minds are the most honest, because they are ours alone, and we think nobody else will see them. While you've been thinking about Henry Winter and his books, I have been thinking about leaving you.

My friend at work is kind, and caring, and genuinely interested in me. They never make me feel stupid, or insignificant, or taken for granted. Face blindness isn't the only way that you make me feel invisible. You make me feel as though I'm not good enough every single day. It's a terrible thing to confess, but sometimes I wonder if the only reason I stay is for Bob. And this house.

I love this big old beautiful Victorian relic, hidden away in a corner of London that time forgot. My blood, sweat, and tears literally went into every inch of the place while I restored it. With little and mostly no help from you. When we were younger, I didn't dare to imagine we might share a home like this one day. You probably did; your dreams have always been bigger than mine. But then so are your nightmares. You and I had the kind of childhoods that are better forgotten, but seeds of ambition grow best in shallow soil.

How dare you invite *him* here without even asking me first.

I'd had such a difficult day at work—and, no offense, but my job is a real one, I don't just sit around ~~making shit up~~ writing all day—all I wanted was to come home, shower, and open a bottle of wine. I could hear voices inside the house before I had even put my key in the door. Yours and one other. And it smelled like something was burning. I found you in the lounge, drinking whiskey with Henry Winter, while he smoked a pipe in our non-smoking home. I thought

I was imagining it at first, but the tweed jacket and silk bow tie looked authentic enough to be real.

"Hello, darling. We have a visitor," you said, as if I couldn't see that for myself.

Anyone else would have recognized the look of horror on my face, he did, but you didn't because you can't. Still, I would have thought you could have picked up on my extreme discomfort in another way. Sometimes you display the emotional intelligence of a brain-damaged frog.

Both of you stared at me, waiting for me to speak, but what could I say? One of you was completely clueless about the situation, while the other seemed only too happy about it.

"Look, this is Henry's new book," you said, holding up a bright red hardback and looking pleased as punch, as though you had written it yourself and wanted a gold star.

Henry gave a shrug of false modesty. "It's probably not your cup of tea."

"Not really, no. I see enough horror in the real world," I replied. You might not be able to read the expressions on my face, but I'm fluent in yours, and if looks could kill I would have been in the morgue. We could have cut the tension with a teaspoon, so it wasn't surprising that Henry picked up on it.

"I'm so sorry to intrude. I sold my London flat last year and retreated to my Scottish hideaway full-time—you and Adam must come to visit—I've got a meeting with my publisher in town tomorrow, but there was some last-minute problem with my hotel reservation, and your husband insisted I stay here"—I didn't say a word—"but I don't want to intrude. I could always—"

"You're more than welcome here. Isn't he, darling?" you interrupted, looking at me.

"Of course," I said. "I'm actually just getting changed and

popping out to see a friend. I hope you have a lovely evening."

I felt like an unwanted guest in my own home.

I practically ran up the stairs and packed a bag. I spent the entire weekend with my friend from work. We went to an art gallery one day, and the theater the next. I felt alive, and happy, and free. I enjoy her company more than yours these days. She tends to like animals more than people too, that's why she started volunteering at Battersea Dogs Home. She listens to me, laughs at my jokes, and doesn't make me feel second-best all the time. She's a bit too fond of microwave meals and tinned food for lunch—I've never seen her eat a salad or anything green—but nobody is perfect and there are plenty of worse things in life to be addicted to.

When I came home at the end of the weekend, I was relieved that Henry was gone. It made me sad that you didn't seem to really care where I had been or who I was with. You knew it was a friend from work, but you didn't even ask what their name was. Instead, you just stared at me with a peculiar look on your face.

"What's wrong?" I asked, fussing over Bob who clearly missed me more than you did.

"Nothing is wrong," you said in that sulky man-boy tone that meant something was. "You've changed your hair."

"Just a trim."

You recognize my hair more than you recognize my face, and it always seems to bother you a little when I change it. It's honestly only an inch shorter, and with a few more highlights than before, but it's nice to feel noticed. I felt like pampering myself a little, as though I deserved a treat, but I could tell from your face that something else was on your mind.

"Do you want to tell me what's bothering you now or after dinner?" I asked.

"Nothing is bothering me." You pouted like a spoiled child. "I finished my screenplay today . . . and I wondered if you might like a drink at the pub to celebrate?" I was about to politely protest that I was tired, but you preempted my refusal with more words of your own. "Also, I wondered if you might read it, before I send it to my agent?"

And there it was, not just in your voice, but in your eyes. You still needed me.

Despite all the writer-shaped colleagues and friends in your life, in London and LA, you still cared what I thought of your work. Just like when we first met.

"I didn't think I was still your first reader?" I said, my turn to sound petulant.

"Of course. Your opinion has always mattered most. Who do you think I'm secretly writing all these stories for?"

I tried very hard not to cry. "Me?"

"Almost always."

That made me smile. "I'll think about it."

"Maybe a game of rock paper scissors would help make the decision?"

"Maybe we should play for something else?" I said, forcing myself to look you in the eye.

"Like what?"

"Like . . . whether or not we should still be together?"

That got your attention—even more than the hair—and neither of us was smiling then. I don't know what I expected you to say, but it wasn't . . .

"Okay. Let's do it. A game of rock paper scissors shall decide the future of our marriage. If I lose, it's over."

I was no longer sure who was calling whose bluff or if that was what it was. You have always let me win whenever we played the game. My scissors would cut your paper. Every. Single. Time. I don't know what made me want things

to be different, but my hand formed a new shape. To my surprise, yours did too.

On the first go, we both formed a rock, and it was a tie.

But if I hadn't changed my choice . . . you would have won.

On the second go, we both chose paper.

With the stakes considerably higher than normal, the third round of this child's game felt ridiculously tense.

We played again. I chose to twist, but you decided to stick. Your paper-shaped fingers wrapped around my rock-shaped fist, and you won.

"I guess that means we stay together," I said.

You held on to both of my hands then, and pulled me closer.

"It means sometimes life changes people, even us. We are both different versions of ourselves compared with who we were when we first met. Almost unrecognizable in some ways. But I love all the versions of you. And no matter how much we change, how I feel about you never will," you said, and I wanted to believe you. We've come so far, you and I, and we did it together. That's why I can't let us fall apart.

We didn't go to the pub, and we didn't do very much to celebrate our anniversary this year, I stayed up late to read your work instead. It was good. Maybe your best. Feeling needed isn't the same as feeling loved, but it's close enough to remind me of who we used to be. I want to find that version of us again, and warn them not to let life change who they are too much.

I left my notes about the manuscript, along with my anniversary gift to you on the kitchen table, before leaving for work early the next day. It was a small bronze statue of a rabbit leaping into the air. You thought it was something to do with *Alice's Adventures in Wonderland*—knowing that was one of my favorite books as a child—but you were wrong. I

bought it because it reminded me of a Russian proverb that an old man once taught me. I'm still rather fond of it:

If you chase two rabbits, you will not catch either one.

You gave me a bronze compass a few days later, with the following inscription:

SO YOU CAN ALWAYS FIND YOUR WAY BACK TO ME.

I hadn't realized that you thought I was lost.

Your wife

xx

AMELIA

Adam abandons the car with its flat tires, and storms back inside the chapel. I follow him through the boot room, the kitchen, then the lounge, until we are both standing in the middle of Henry Winter's secret study. Adam stares around the room. I'm not sure what he's looking for or hoping to find. I preferred it when I thought we were leaving.

White rabbits are definitely a theme in here . . . they leap all over the wallpaper, the blinds, the cushions. The interior design choices are unexpected for a man in his eighties who liked writing dark and disturbing books. But then as Adam always says, the best writers tend to have nothing and everything in common with their characters.

Adam stares at me with a strange look on his face.

"If you know anything about what is really going on here, then now would be a good time to tell me," he says, in a tone he usually reserves for cold callers.

"Don't start trying to blame me. This place belongs to the author whose novels you've spent the last ten years of your life adapting. I *never* liked him. Or his books. And everything I've seen this weekend suggests that *you're* the reason we're trapped here."

Adam looks at the antique desk again, the one that used to belong to Agatha Christie. It's made of a dark wood, and quite small, but there are ten tiny little drawers built into it, which I only really notice when he starts pulling them out. Each looks like a miniature wooden box, and when he tips the first onto the palm of his hand, a small bronze statue of a rabbit falls out.

"I've seen this before," he mutters, already moving to the next drawer.

Inside that, he finds an origami paper bird, just like the one he always carries around in his wallet. I watch in silence as the color seems to drain from his face.

I do not enjoy seeing my husband like this. Other people all see a different version to the man I know. They have no knowledge of his moods, or his insecurities, or his regular nightmares about a woman in a red kimono being hit by a car. He doesn't just wake up breathless and covered in sweat when he dreams about her, sometimes he screams. Adam has spent a lifetime running away from the things that scared him the most, and although the boy now looks like a man, he hasn't changed so much.

Not in my eyes.

He opens another drawer and holds up an antique-looking iron key.

The next is filled with copper pennies. There must be over a hundred of them, each one with holes for eyes and a carved smiley face.

POTTERY

Word of the year:
monachopsis *noun*. The subtle but persistent
feeling of being out of place. Unable to
recognize your intended habitat, never feeling
as though you are at home.

28th February 2017—our ninth anniversary

Dear Adam,
Our house doesn't feel like our home anymore, but at least
you didn't forget our anniversary this year. That's something,
I suppose. You've been busy writing again, and I have made
myself busy doing other things with other people.

We opted for a quiet evening in—just like we do most
nights—but with a bottle of champagne and a takeaway to
~~celebrate~~ mark our nine years of marriage. We both agreed
that eating in the lounge while watching a movie was the
best way to go—sitting in silence only highlights our struggle

to have a conversation these days. You gave me a printed voucher ~~purchased from a last-minute website~~ for a pottery class. I gave you a mug that said GO AWAY I'M WRITING. I've considered suggesting that we see a marriage counselor, but so far, the time has never felt quite right. We're both treading so carefully we've come to a standstill.

I felt a mix of relief and excitement when the doorbell rang and saved us from ourselves. You jumped up to answer it, and spent so long out in the hallway I presumed it was someone you knew. But it was my friend from work. She was crying. I had a slight wobble when I saw the two of you together. I try not to talk about us with her, but she always asks, so it's hard not to without sounding rude. I guess I just wanted to keep her to myself, a friend of my own who had nothing to do with you, silly as that might sound.

"What's wrong?" I asked, taking in the sight of you both standing there in the doorway, you in your slippers, her in high heels with tears streaming down her face.

She started as a volunteer at Battersea Dogs Home last year. If we actually had to pay everyone who works for the charity, we'd soon be bankrupt. Volunteers help staff with just about everything: caring for the animals, washing them, walking them, feeding them. They clean out kennels, they help raise awareness and funds at events, and some even help me in the office. That's how we met. In return, I helped her get a full-time, paid job earlier this year, so now we see each other almost every day.

My colleagues didn't warm to her the way I did. They made jokes that we could be twins were it not for my hair being blond and straight, and hers a mop of mousy brown curls. But I think most of the bitchy comments were green-eyed. Gossip is almost always jealousy's love child. She's shy and socially awkward, in that way that makes people suspicious. She's also a tad too quiet, and always speaks as though

doubting everything that comes out of her own mouth, trying the words on for size as if worried they might not fit. But
not tonight.

"I'm so sorry to turn up like this, uninvited," she said,
wiping her tearstained face with the back of her hand. She
was wearing an enormous puffy coat with a hood, which
didn't match the heels at all.

"What's happened? Are you all right?" I asked and she
started to sob. "Come in—"

"No, I really can't. Adam says it's your anniversary . . ."

Your name on her lips sounded foreign to my ears.

"Oh, don't worry about that. We've been married for almost a decade; we don't even have sex anymore."

The look you gave me then was priceless.

I wonder what my own face did when she accepted the
invitation, stepped inside, and lowered her hood to reveal a
head of blond hair. The mousy curls were gone, instead it
was styled straight just like mine, and dyed exactly the same
shade.

"Oh . . ." she said, clocking my reaction as she removed
her coat. "I got my hair done."

"So I see," I said, taking in the rest of the makeover.
Her work uniform of a Battersea sweatshirt, old jeans, and
trainers—which was pretty much all I had ever seen her
wear—had been replaced with a tight-fitting red dress. She
looked different yet familiar: she looked like me. She even
sounded a bit like me. The East End twang I'd gotten used
to was gone, but then a lot of people sound different when
they are nervous. And she seemed super-nervous around
you.

"I wanted to look nice because I had a date . . . but it was
a bad one. He said he wanted to pick me up and I thought he
was being old-fashioned and kind, but now he knows where I
live. He threatened me and got very aggressive when I didn't

invite him in and . . . I'm so sorry, I don't know anyone else in London except you and—"

"It's okay, you're safe now. Would a glass of champagne help?" you suggested, and she smiled with teeth that seemed whiter than before.

You're always a better husband when we have an audience.

I felt so sorry for her as the three of us sat in the lounge, drinking our anniversary champagne, and listening to her seemingly endless horror stories about single life. I couldn't imagine being on my own at our age. The world has changed so much—online dating, speed dating, dating apps—it all sounds awful. I had never seen it before—perhaps because she did such a good job of hiding it beneath the baggy T-shirts and old jeans she normally wore—but my friend is quite beautiful when she makes an effort. If single life is so hard for her, imagine what it would be like for us mere mortals. I felt far too old for that sort of malarkey. I watched you, watching her and being so kind and considerate. She beamed constantly as you made polite conversation, as though there were a smile quota she had to fulfill before the end of the night. I was glad that the two of you seemed to get on. As we opened another bottle, and sat and listened to her talk about dreadful dates with terrible men, I realized just how lucky I was to have one of the good ones.

"Well, it was nice to finally meet your work wife," you whispered, as we climbed into bed. She was asleep in our spare room, and given the amount of alcohol she consumed there was probably no need to lower your voice.

"I don't know why I've never invited her over before. Now I think of it, I'm not sure how she knew where to find me—I don't think I've ever given her our address—but I'm glad that she did."

"She isn't quite what I pictured from the way you described her. She seems . . . nice."

"You said that like it was an insult. Did you find her attractive?"

You laughed. "No."

"Really? Even with the hair and heels and makeup—"

"Really, no. Besides I can't see all that, remember? I only see what's inside."

"And what did you see? Inside?"

"An actress. I've met enough of them to know."

I laughed. "That's bonkers . . . she's a quiet little mouse most of the time."

"Not all actresses are on the stage. Some walk among us, masquerading as normal people." We both laughed and you held me closer. There is something quite magical about being in a warm bed when it's cold outside. Sharing body heat with someone you love. Or used to. But just because we still share a bed, it doesn't mean that we still share the same opinions.

"What do you see inside me?" I asked.

"Same as always, my beautiful wife."

You stared at me then and I felt seen.

"What happened to us?" I asked, expecting you to look away, or change the subject, but you didn't.

"I'm not who I was ten years ago, and neither are you, and that's okay. The only question we need to ask ourselves, is do we love who we are now? Listening to your friend tonight made me feel lonely and lucky at the same time. The success of a relationship can't be measured by longevity alone. I love that we celebrate these milestones every anniversary, and even I smile at those news items about couples who have been together for seventy years, but I also think it's possible to have a one-night stand that might be more profound than some marriages. It's not about how long a relationship lasts, it's about what it teaches you about each other and yourself."

"What are you saying?"

You smiled. "Rock paper scissors."

"What?"

"You heard me, rock paper scissors. If you win, we stay together forever."

It must be a year since we last played that game. But you let me win just like you always used to, my scissors cutting your paper. It sounds silly, but I felt as if it was a sign that maybe we were more like who we used to be too.

"What would have happened if I'd lost?" I asked.

"We would stay together forever anyway, because I love you, Mrs. Wright," you replied, slipping your arm around my waist. If it was the alcohol talking, I didn't care. You spend all day working with words, but those were the only three I needed to hear.

"I love you more," I said, and we made love for the first time in a long time.

I'm an eggs-in-one-basket girl when it comes to relationships, and it's a dangerous way to be. One bad fall, or an unfortunate slipup, and everything I care about could get broken and smashed. I found my person when I found you, and I've never really needed or wanted anyone else since. Rightly or wrongly, I poured every emotional part of myself into us. I adopted your hopes and dreams and loved them as though they were my own. I cared about you so much, I had nothing left to give anyone else, even myself. I was content with a social circle big enough for two. You were always enough for me, but I never felt as though I was quite enough for you. Maybe that can change. Maybe if I try to love you a little less, the scales might tip in my favor, and you might love me a little more?

I care about my friend at work very much, but I don't want to end up like her. Seeing her here in our home—so lonely, and sad, and broken—was a bit of a wake-up call. Funny how another person's misfortune can make you realize what you have. We need to stop taking each other for

granted. That's another thing nobody tells you about marriage; sometimes it's good, sometimes it's bad, doesn't mean it's over. Perhaps this is as good or as bad as it gets? So, although our house stopped feeling like a home, I'm going to try to fix that, and I'm going to try and fix us. Even if that means counseling, or compromises, or perhaps some time away, just you and me . . . and Bob. Maybe all marriages have secrets, and maybe the only way to stay married is to keep them.

Your wife

xx

ADAM

"What does this mean?" I ask, holding the tiny drawer full of pennies in one hand and a broken GO AWAY I'M WRITING mug in the other. I may suffer from face blindness and the odd neurological glitch, but there is nothing wrong with my memory (most of the time). The desk is full of anniversary gifts my wife gave me over the years. "Are you in on all this?"

"What? No!" Amelia says.

I stare at her, searching for the truth, but I can't even see her face. Her features are swirling like a van Gogh painting and I feel dizzy just looking in her direction. Sometimes I can recognize people by the shape or color of their hair, or a distinctive pair of glasses. Sometimes I don't know if I know them at all.

"Then how do you explain this?" I say, turning back to the desk. "*You* arranged this little trip to Scotland; *you* drove us here—"

"I can't explain anything that has happened this weekend."

"Can't or won't? Did you already know that Henry Winter was dead?"

"I think you need to calm down. I didn't know anything. I still don't. Except that . . ."

"What?" I ask her.

"You said Henry delivered a new book in September, but now we know he died the year before."

"So?"

"So, what if someone else wrote it?" She shouts the question and I realize that I have been shouting too.

It's a ridiculous suggestion. The book has since been published all around the world. Does she seriously think that nobody—including his agent, his publishers, and army of fans—would have noticed if someone else had written a Henry Winter novel? But then I do the math and she's right, it doesn't add up.

"That isn't possible," I reply. The answer in my head is less decisive but I don't share that one with my wife.

Writers are a strange and unpredictable species. To be one requires patience, determination, sufficient self-motivation to work alone in the dark, and the self-belief to keep going when the shadows try to consume them. And they do try—I should know. The other thing all writers have in common is that they're kooky at best, crazy at worst. Would Henry fake his own death for some reason?

"We both saw someone let themselves into the chapel earlier. Remember? That's who we need to blame for all this. Not each other," Amelia says.

"What about the woman in the cottage?"

"The witch with the candles and the white rabbit? You said she was old . . ."

"I said she had gray hair. It isn't as though we've seen anyone else since we arrived."

"So, let's go back. Knock on her door again. Worst-case scenario, she casts a spell and turns us into white rabbits too," Amelia replies, sounding calmer than she should.

Maybe because she already knows what is going on here and this is all an act.

I'll always feel guilty about cheating on my wife, but Saint Amelia slept with someone she shouldn't have too. It's as if she

conveniently forgets that part of the story. But I can't. "Call me Pamela," the counselor, said we needed to move on, learn to put it behind us, but I'm still shocked by how easily my wife lies.

I wish I could see her face now, the way other people can. I wonder if she looks scared? Or does she look as composed as she sounds? And if so—given that we appear to be trapped and quite possibly in danger—why isn't she as afraid as I am? She seems to have forgotten all about her beloved dog. She's lying about *something*, and not knowing what scares me. A haunted marriage is just as terrifying as a haunted house.

"Come with me," I say, taking her hand—she's always complaining I don't hold it often enough.

Her face and voice might not give her away, but Amelia can't control her breathing. If she's genuinely stressed or scared, it's always the first thing to go.

We reach the old wooden spiral staircase leading to the first floor, and I point up at the gallery of black-and-white photos on the wall. It's been bothering me since we got here.

"Who are the people in these pictures, do you recognize any of their faces?" I ask.

I can tell that the portraits at the bottom of the stairs are of people dressed in Victorian clothes. The ones nearer the top look more recent. I can see that some of the subjects are adults, others are children, but—as usual—I can't see any of their faces.

Amelia shakes her head, so I start to pull her up the stairs.

"How about now? Anyone here look familiar?"

"You're scaring me, Adam," she says, and I can hear from her breathing that she's telling the truth. I'm about to apologize when she speaks again.

"Hang on, I think this photo is of Henry as a teenager . . . and the one below looks a bit like him too, but younger, with a man and woman. Parents, perhaps."

"Some kind of family tree maybe? Keep going," I say, not letting her go.

"I'm fairly sure most of these pictures *are* of Henry. I didn't notice until now, but then I didn't know what to look for. He's a lot younger than the face I see on book jackets and in the newspapers—all of which are so out of date."

Now I drop her hand.

I stare at the photos myself, trying to see what she sees, but it's pointless.

"Anyone else look familiar?" I ask, when Amelia stops abruptly at the top of the stairs. I notice her twisting the sapphire engagement ring round and round her finger.

"There are some pictures of a little girl too . . . hold on."

"What?"

"These pictures weren't here before. Do you remember? There were just three faded rectangular shapes with rusty nails sticking out of the wall. Someone has put them back." I'm about to ask if it was her, but bite my tongue. "I think this picture is of—"

I spot something over her shoulder before she finishes her sentence.

"One of the other doors is open," I interrupt, rushing toward it.

All of the doors on the landing were locked last night, except for the one leading to the bedroom that we slept in, and the one to the bell tower. But now another door is wide open, and I find myself standing inside a child's bedroom.

Everything is covered in dust like the rest of the chapel, but this room is also full of cobwebs. It smells musty, like it hasn't been aired for months. Maybe longer. The creepiest thing to catch my eye is the large doll's house in the middle of the room. It looks antique. It also looks remarkably like our London home—a double-fronted Victorian house. I'm unable to stop myself from opening the dusty doors, and when I see that the rooms inside are decorated in a similar way to our house, I start to feel sick. The same two carved wooden dolls are in every room, but they are not miniature replicas of Amelia and me. One is a doll-sized old man, wearing a tweed jacket and bow tie, the other is a little girl doll, dressed in

red. In every make-believe scene they are holding hands, and the old man is always smoking a pipe. When I take a closer look, I see that the pipes are really acorn cups and stalks.

"Have you seen this?" Amelia asks.

She is holding an old jack-in-the-box. I had one exactly like it myself as a child, and it terrified me. I don't understand the significance at first, until I see that the name Jack has been crossed out, so that now it says Adam-in-the-box instead.

My mother taught me the French name for these things when I was a little boy: *diable en boîte*, literally "boxed devil." So many unexpected things remind me of her. And whenever they do, I relive the night she died: the rain, the terrible sound of screeching car brakes, her red kimono flying in the air. The dog was mine. I begged her to let me have one, but then I didn't look after it. If thirteen-year-old me had walked the dog myself, like I promised to, she wouldn't have been killed walking along the pavement that night.

My fingers, seemingly independent of my mind, find the crank on the *Adam*-in-the-box and turn it. Slowly. The nostalgic tune plays and my mother's voice sings along inside my head.

> *My mother taught me how to sew,*
> *And how to thread the needle,*
> *Every time my finger slips,*
> *Pop! goes the weasel.*

Jack bursts out of the box and I jump, even though I knew what was coming. With its wild red hair, painted face, and spotty blue outfit, it looks terrifying, even more so than the one I remember as a child, because its eyes are missing.

I think I understand the not-so-subtle message, but what else am I *not* seeing?

As I turn to take in the rest of the bedroom, I notice that the wallpaper, curtains, pillows, and duvet are all covered in faded images of the same thing: robins. Then I see the dusty, freestanding,

child's blackboard in the corner of the room. The chalk words on it have faded, and were clearly written years ago, but I can still make them out:

I must not tell tales.
I must not tell tales.
I must not tell tales.

TIN

Word of the year:
metanoia *noun*. A transformative change of
heart. The journey of changing one's mind,
self, or way of life.

28th February 2018—our tenth anniversary

Dear Adam,
It isn't really our tenth anniversary. I'm writing this letter a
little late because of what happened.

I thought things were pretty good with us this year. I
thought we were happy. I was, and I thought you were too.
From the outside looking in, our marriage was definitely
pretty solid. But I was ~~blind stupid a gullible fool~~ wrong.
Nothing seems real now that I know the truth. I feel like I'm
trapped inside a snow globe; one more shake and I'll disappear completely.

For a long time, it has felt as though someone was

watching us. I can't quite explain the feeling, or put it into words, but I think we all know when we're being watched. Whether at work, or walking the dog, or just on the tube. You can feel it when someone else's eyes are staring in your direction for longer than they should. You always know. It's instinct.

Normally, when I get home from work, you're still in your writing shed. But the night before our tenth anniversary, I found you sitting in the lounge, in the dark, watching an old episode of *The Graham Norton Show* on the BBC iPlayer. Henry Winter is known for never giving interviews, but to celebrate the publication of his fiftieth novel in fifty years, he agreed to do one last year. We watched it together at the time. Graham Norton was as funny and charming as ever, but I remember feeling sick when he introduced Henry. An old man I barely recognized hobbled out onto the stage before taking a seat on the red sofa. The walking stick, with a silver rabbit's head handle, was a new addition to his tweed jacket and bow tie uniform. As was the smile on his face. It looked like it hurt.

I wish we'd never seen the interview, but we did, and last night I watched you watching it over and over and over again. The bit where Henry Winter mentioned you. I stood quietly in the hallway of our home, and watched while you rewound and played it seven times.

Graham leaned forward. "Now, tell me, just between us"—the audience laughed—"what do you really think about the TV and film adaptations of your books?"

The false smile vanished from Henry's heavily lined face.

"I don't own a television set, I've always preferred reading."

"But you must have seen them?" Graham persisted, taking a sip of his white wine.

"I've seen them. I can't say I like them much. But I was

persuaded to let the screenwriter have a go—his career was going nowhere before I said yes—and even if I don't like what he did to the books, a lot of other people do. So . . ."

Graham laughed. "Yikes, let's hope he isn't watching!"

But you were watching. So was I. I don't think you've spoken to Henry or written anything new since.

You blamed your agent for what Henry had said, and I felt awful—I like your agent, he's one of the good guys in what can sometimes be a bad business—but I still couldn't tell you the truth. I thought things with us were finally back on track, telling you that I was the reason Henry let you adapt his books in the first place didn't seem too bright an idea.

I don't know what made you sit in the dark, and watch an old clip of Henry putting you down. I don't know why you still care what he thinks. I noticed the half empty bottle of whiskey then—Henry's favorite brand—sitting next to your Bafta award. It's hard when the highlight of someone's career comes right at the beginning of it. Sometimes it's best to start small—give yourself room to grow.

I crept back out to the hall, slammed the front door, then ran straight up the stairs. "Just going to have a quick shower," I called, so that you would think I hadn't seen you. When I came down, the TV was off, the whiskey was gone, and the Bafta was back on the shelf. I wondered how long you had been pretending to be okay when really you were feeling broken. Putting on an act every night when I got home. Your job means that you spend a lot of time on your own. A little too much sometimes, maybe. I wanted to fix you, but wasn't sure how.

The next day—our anniversary—I decided to leave work early. I was determined to cheer you up and surprise you. Something felt wrong even as I walked up the garden path. The magnolia tree you planted in the middle of the lawn for our fifth anniversary, looked like it might be dying. I chose

to ignore what could have been a sign and let myself and Bob inside the house. Everything was still and silent, just like it always is when you're out in the writing shed, which you almost always are. There was a tin of baked beans on the kitchen table—I thought it must be some kind of joke, knowing that tin was the traditional gift for ten years of marriage. I smiled and headed straight upstairs to our bedroom. I planned to spend a bit of time grooming myself instead of abandoned dogs for a change, before surprising you.

But you surprised me instead.

You were still in bed.

With my friend from work.

She'd called in sick that morning. Now I knew why.

Everything stopped when I walked into the room. I don't just mean you, or her, or what you were doing. And I don't just mean that I stopped breathing—even though it felt like I did—it was as though time itself stood perfectly still, waiting for the pieces of my broken life to fall and see where they would land.

I just stood there, staring, unable to process what I was seeing.

She smiled. I'll always remember that. Then I remember you looking between the two of us. Your wife in the doorway and your whore in our bed.

"I thought it was you," you said, wrapping the sheet around yourself. When I didn't respond, you said it again. As if the words might sound less like lies if you said them a second time. "I thought it was you."

Just the thought of lying can make you blush, and your cheeks turned bright red.

I'm not proud of what I did next. I wish I had said something clever, but I've never been good at knowing what to say until long after an event, and even now I can't find the right words for what I saw that afternoon. So I didn't say anything,

but I did go to the garden shed, grab a shovel, then dig that bloody magnolia tree up and out of my once perfect front lawn. She left and you just watched in horror. The tree had grown bigger than me by then, but I dragged it through the front door and up the stairs, scratching the walls and leaving a trail of dirt and broken branches behind me. Then I threw it on the bed where you had slept with her, before tucking it in beneath the sheets, like a baby.

"I'll do whatever you want to fix this. Counseling? A holiday? We could go to Scotland, like we did for our honeymoon? Anything?" you said, as I packed a bag. But I don't think anything can fix us now. Do you?

Your wife

AMELIA

Adam still hasn't put the pieces of the puzzle together.

He stares at the little girl's bedroom where everything is covered in robins, looking like a lost child. Until I take his hand and lead him back out onto the landing. We stop at the top of the spiral stairs, and I point at the final framed photo on the wall.

"Who is it?" he asks, although I'm fairly sure he must know by now. Having face blindness can't stop someone from seeing the truth.

The grandfather clock in the bedroom starts chiming and we both jump . . . I thought it had stopped.

"It's you," I say. We study the image then: the expensive-looking suit he wore for the wedding, the confetti on his shoulders, the wedding dress, the rings, the happy smiles . . . and someone else in the shot. "Henry is in the background. We both know he wasn't invited, but the fact that he was there—standing on the street outside the registry office by the looks of it—along with seeing this picture on *his* wall of family portraits, suggests that he thought of you as much more than just a screenwriter who adapted his books."

Adam still doesn't understand.

This isn't going to be easy. But my husband needs to know the truth now, and I need to be the one to tell him.

"The woman in the wedding photo isn't me."

ADAM

"What do you mean?" I ask, staring at a picture of a bride and groom whose faces I can't see.

"It's a photo of your *first* wedding. When you married Robin."

We stand in silence at the top of the staircase. It feels as if we stay like that for a long time, while I try to process what Amelia has said.

"I don't understand—"

"I think you do," she says. "I think that even though you were married to Robin for ten years, she never told you that she was Henry Winter's daughter. I think she grew up here and that little girl's bedroom was hers."

I stare at my second wife for a long time, trying to see from her face whether this is some kind of prank. But the van Gogh swirls are back, and I grip the banister for balance.

"This is insane. That can't be true!"

Amelia shakes her head. "I know you can't see it, but these three photos on the wall—the ones that were missing yesterday—are all of your ex-wife. This is you and Robin getting married, with a photo-bomb from Henry." She points at the next picture. "*This* is Robin when she was younger, teenaged I'd guess, in a rowboat fishing on

Blackwater Loch. And this"—she nods toward the final frame—"is a little girl, who looks like Robin, sitting on Henry's lap and reading a book, while he smokes a pipe."

My mind is racing back and forth through time, and I speak my thoughts out loud.

"This can't be real. Henry didn't have children—"

"The headstone in the graveyard says different."

"Robin never wanted to talk about her family, especially her father. She said they were estranged—"

"I don't doubt it, but I'm guessing there's a reason why she never told you who he was."

I study the faces in the photos again, but even now that I know what to look for, they all look the same.

"I know you can't see it for yourself, so you're going to have to trust me," Amelia says. After seducing me, her best friend's husband, trusting *her* is something I've never been great at. "I'm telling you that these pictures are all of your ex-wife. The ones of her as a little girl look the spitting image of the ones of Henry as a little boy. The likeness is uncanny. They could be twins separated by forty years, or it might be time to accept that Robin *is* Henry's daughter."

Her words feel like a series of slaps, pinches, and punches. I can't get my head around it, but I'm starting to believe what Amelia is saying.

"I don't understand why either of them wouldn't have told me something as big as this," I say, hating the pathetic sound of my own voice. I might not be able to see beauty on the outside, but Robin was the most beautiful person on the inside. I could *feel* it, whenever she was in the same room. Everyone else knew it as soon as they met her too—she was just so good, and genuine, and *honest*. I can't imagine her lying to me about anything, let alone something as huge as this.

"Maybe there was a good reason why neither of them wanted you to know? Who did you meet first? How did the idea of you adapting Henry Winter's books come about?" Amelia asks.

I think back to that happy day, when Robin and I shared a crappy basement flat in Notting Hill. We had so little then, but far more than I have now. We were kindred spirits who survived difficult childhoods and were alone in the world until we found each other. Robin always believed in me and my work, no matter what. She believed in me when nobody else did, and was always there whenever I needed her. Always. Without ever wanting anything in return. I feel Amelia staring at me, waiting for an answer.

"My agent randomly called when I was out of work, saying that Henry Winter had invited me to meet him at his London flat," I say, one of my happiest memories obliterated as soon as I do.

"Is that normal?"

I don't answer at first. We both know it isn't. "Well, *his* agent died rather suddenly—"

"Of what?"

"I don't remember . . . only that it was a shock. His agent was quite young."

"Funny how people who came between you and Robin seem to die or disappear."

"What does that mean?"

"She didn't exactly have many friends."

She didn't need them. She had me, and rightly or wrongly, I was all she wanted. But I took it for granted.

"She didn't have a problem making friends," I say, aware that I am now defending my ex-wife. "Everyone liked Robin. She just rarely liked them back. She became quite friendly with October O'Brien when we were working together."

"October died. There is a drawer full of newspaper cuttings about her in the kitchen."

"You can't seriously think that . . . it was *suicide*. Robin was friends with *you*, too. She got you a job at Battersea when you were a volunteer, she was kind to you, trusted you—"

"This isn't about *me*. Might that unexpected meeting with an international best-selling author have taken place because you were

living with his daughter?" Amelia says, as though speaking my private fears out loud. "I guess for those ten years you were married to Robin, you were Henry Winter's son-in law. You just didn't know it."

"Bob," I whisper.

"What about him?"

"He was Robin's dog. She adopted him from Battersea, loved him like he was a child. If she has him then at least we know that he's safe."

"Do you really think she's behind all of this?" Amelia asks.

"Who else can it be? The most important question right now, is why are we here, and why now? If she wanted revenge, it's a long time to wait. So what *does* she want? Why trick us into coming to Scotland?"

"I don't know, she's your ex-wife."

"She's your ex-friend. You told me that when you won a weekend here, the email said we could only come *this* weekend. Is that right?" I ask.

She shrugs. "Yes. But why? What's so special about this weekend?"

"I don't know. What's the date?"

Amelia checks her phone. "Saturday the . . . twenty-ninth of February. It's a leap year, I hadn't even noticed. Does that mean something?"

"Yes," I say. "It's our wedding anniversary."

She looks confused. "We got married in September—"

"Not *ours*. It's the date I married Robin."

ROBIN

Robin remembers walking away from the house in London, the day she found Adam and Amelia in bed together. She remembers the magnolia tree, and she remembers taking off the sapphire engagement ring that had once belonged to Adam's mother, along with her wedding ring, and leaving them behind on the kitchen table. The rest is a blur at best. She grabbed her bag, a few of her favorite things, then got in her car and just drove. She didn't know what she was going to do, or where she was going to go, she just had to get far, far away from them, as fast as possible. Her biggest mistake was leaving Bob behind. The only people with no regrets are liars.

That was when Henry called. To tell her he was dying and to ask her to come home.

Robin hadn't spoken to her father for years, but a series of fallen stars seemed to align themselves that afternoon, to guide her back to the home she ran away from as a child. Truth be told, she had nowhere else to go.

Robin still remembers when Amelia first started volunteering at Battersea Dogs Home, and how she took pity on the mousy, lonely

creature, in the same way she took pity on all the abandoned animals that arrived there. She helped Amelia to get a job, and a life, became her friend, and in return the woman stole her husband. She looks so different now, with her blond hair, fancy clothes, and Robin's ex-husband on her arm. But, as awful as being betrayed by a friend is, it was Adam who Robin blamed at first. For everything.

Not anymore.

Now she blames them both, which is what this weekend is really about and why she tricked them into coming here.

Robin has experienced grief only three times in her life:

When she stopped trying to have a child of her own.

When her husband cheated on her.

And when her mother drowned in a claw-foot bath.

The whole world thought it was an accident, *but it wasn't*. Robin has always believed that Henry was responsible for her mother's death. That was why he really sent Robin away to boarding school, and why she ran away as soon as she was old enough to leave for good. He removed almost every trace of her mother from the Scottish chapel she had lovingly converted into a home. The bathtubs were the first to go. Her mother loved to cook, so Henry emptied almost every kitchen cupboard and drawer until there were only two of everything left; two plates, two sets of cutlery, two cups. *No* saucepans, *no* pots or pans, were left behind. The smell of cooking reminded him of his dead wife, so the old housekeeper would make big batches of meals at home instead, then fill the chapel freezer with them so they both didn't starve. Robin kept what she could of her mother's possessions, including two pairs of stork-shaped gold and silver embroidery scissors—her mother loved to sew, as well as cook—and hid them beneath her bed. She never believed that her mother's death was accidental. People who read and write crime novels and thrillers know there are an infinite number of ways to get away with murder. Robin suspects that it happens all the time.

It always felt as though her parents were performing a part in a play they would rather not have been cast in. Is disinterest a form

of neglect? Robin thinks so. But things were much worse after her mother died. Her world became very small and very lonely very fast. Henry thought throwing money at the problem would fix it, just like he always did, and it was why she never wanted a penny from him as an adult. She would rather sleep in a freezing cold cottage, with an outside toilet, than spend another night under his roof. His money was blood money in more ways than one.

Henry bought the fanciest doll's house Robin had ever seen when her mother died. Each room had the same two little figures inside it. One looked like Henry, the other was a miniature Robin. A happy toy family to replace their broken real one. He carved the dolls himself with his wood chisels, just like the statues outside the chapel, and all the Robin-shaped birds he had whittled over the years, while puffing on his pipe, or sipping a glass of scotch.

Nobody else knew what really happened to Robin's mother. Nobody suspected a thing. Henry even wrote about a man who killed his wife in the bathtub a few years later in his novel called *Drowning Your Sorrows*. It made Robin question whether all of his stories might be based on facts rather than fiction, and the thought terrified her. The book was a huge bestseller, everyone at her boarding school was talking about it, even the teachers.

It inspired Robin to write a story of her own. Her English tutor was so impressed, that—unknown to Robin—she sent a copy to Henry at the end of term, saying that a gift for storytelling clearly ran in the family. It was about a novelist who committed crimes in real life, then wrote about them in his books, always getting away with murder.

When Robin came home that Christmas, Henry barely spoke to her at all. He stayed locked inside his secret study with his beloved books. Just like always. One afternoon she found her dolls floating in the bathroom sink. They looked like they were drowning, just like her mother had in the claw-foot bath. When she woke up on Christmas morning, there were no gifts in the stocking that hung at the end of her bed. The only thing that had changed in the night

was that Robin's hair had been cut. There were two long blond plaits lying on the pillow where she had slept, and her mother's pretty stork scissors were on the bedside table.

Henry Winter didn't just write about monsters. He was one.

He made her write lines as punishment for writing that story at school:

> *I must not tell tales*
> *I must not tell tales.*
> *I must not tell tales.*

So Robin never wrote a word of fiction again.

Until Henry was dead.

After she buried him in the graveyard behind the chapel, Robin returned to the secret study that she had never been allowed to set foot inside as a child, and sat down at that antique desk. She took out her dead father's laptop. Remembering the password was easy: it was her name. She found Henry's uncompleted work in progress, and started reading. The idea sounded crazy inside her head at first. What other word was there to describe a woman who worked with dogs trying to finish a novel by an international best-selling author?

But that's what she did.

Robin deleted most of what Henry had written—she didn't think it was very good—and then replaced it with her own words. She wrote three drafts in three months, and when the book was finished, and she had edited it to the best of her ability, she felt as though the transition from her father's story to hers felt seamless. Then she typed the whole book out again—on Henry's typewriter, just the way he would have done. The real test would be sending it to his agent: if anyone could spot the difference, it would be him.

Robin already knew that Henry always wrapped his manuscripts in brown paper and tied them with string—she'd seen him do it often enough as a child—so she did the same, then drove the parcel to the post office.

Robin had barely left Blackwater since she arrived three months earlier. It seemed strange to her that the world outside the chapel's big wooden doors was the same as the one she had lived in before, when Robin's life had changed beyond recognition. There had been no reason to leave until then, and it was her first trip to Hollowgrove—the town closest to Blackwater Loch—for more than twenty years. But as Robin drove her old Land Rover, with the manuscript beside her on the passenger seat, she was still scared that someone might recognize her. They didn't. But Patty in the corner shop, recognized the brown paper parcel instead.

"Is that a new book by Mr. Winter?" she asked, chewing bubble gum between words, like she was a teenager, not a woman in her late fifties. Robin felt her cheeks turn red and couldn't answer. "It's okay if it's meant to be a secret, I can keep it," Patty lied. "It's just that's how he always posts them—tied up in string and what not."

Robin froze, still unable to speak. Patty's eyes narrowed.

"Are you the new housekeeper? Heard he fired the last one . . ."

"Yes," said Robin, without thinking it through.

Patty tapped the side of her nose with her index finger. "I see, pet. Probably told you not to tell anyone anything, didn't he? As if anyone around here cares whether he's written a new book. The only author I'll ever love is Marian Keyes, now there's a woman who knows how to write. Do I *look* like I have time to read the words of a madman? That's what Henry Winter is if you ask me— all the disturbing books he's written. You've my deepest sympathies working for an old miser like that. Don't you worry about a thing, Patty will post and keep all your secrets."

If only Patty had known how big Robin's secrets really were.

After that, the waiting was the hardest part.

Robin finally understood how nerve-racking it is for writers to send their work out into the world. In the days after she posted the manuscript, she kept the curtains drawn, ate frozen meals when she was hungry, slept when she was too tired—or drunk—to stay awake, and completely lost track of what day it was. When the

phone rang, she knew that she couldn't answer it. Anyone calling would be expecting to hear Henry's voice, including his agent, so she waited a while longer.

When a letter arrived from Henry's agent the following day, it took Robin a few hours and another bottle of wine to feel brave enough to open it.

When she finally did, she cried.

> Finished the novel in the early hours. It's your best yet!
> Will send to publishers today.

They were tears of joy, relief, and sorrow.

She wanted to tell someone, but Oscar the rabbit wasn't the best at conversation. She'd renamed him the first day they met, because Oscar was a boy rabbit not a girl, unknown to Henry. And Robin was *her* name. It was the only good thing her father ever gave her. She was so proud of that novel, but the truth, whether spoken or not, was still impossible to ignore. Henry's best book yet was really hers, but it would still be his name on the cover.

Robin tried to put the letter from Henry's agent into one of the desk drawers—she didn't want to look at it anymore—but the drawers were all too full. She pulled out the first few pages of what looked like an old manuscript, and was surprised to find her ex-husband's name printed on the front:

ROCK PAPER SCISSORS
By Adam Wright

Attached to it was a letter from Adam, dated several years ago:

> I know how very busy you are, but I always wondered whether this screenplay might work as a novel? I think that might be my best chance of getting it made. I'd be very grateful for your opinion. I do hope you enjoyed the latest

adaptation, your agent said that you did, and said he would pass on this letter for me. It was an honor to help bring your characters to life on screen. Any advice you can give me about my own would be gratefully received. It's always been my dream and I like to think some dreams do come true.

It made her so sad that Adam had trusted her father with his most beloved work. She knew that Henry probably hadn't even bothered to read it.

One of the few things that Robin took before she fled her home in London, was the box of anniversary letters she had secretly been writing to Adam every year. She still missed him—and Bob—every single day. She reread those letters that night, along with Adam's screenplay, and a new idea formed in her head. The idea seemed too crazy at first, but she realized that there was a way to rewrite her own life story, and give herself a happier ending than life had so far chosen to.

STEEL

T H A N K Y O U

Word of the year:
insouciant *adjective*. Free from worry, concern
or anxiety; carefree.

28th February 2019—what would have been our eleventh
anniversary

Dear Adam,
It isn't our eleventh anniversary of course, because we didn't
last that long. I now live in a thatched cottage in Scotland,
and you're in our London home. With her. But I still wanted
to write you a letter. I'll be keeping this one to myself, along
with all the other secret anniversary letters I wrote over the
years. I know it might sound crazy—especially now that
we're divorced—but I sat out by the loch and read them recently. All of them. My goodness, we had our up and downs,
but there were more good times than bad. More fond memories than sad ones. And I miss you.

Firstly, I wanted to say sorry for the lies. All of them. I grew up surrounded by books and fiction—it's hard not to when your father is a world-famous author. My mother was a writer too, but I never told you about her either. I don't expect you to understand, but I couldn't talk about them with you.

When we first met, I believed in you and your writing, but I was impatient, and I wanted your dreams to come true too quickly so that we could concentrate on ours. Having not spoken to Henry for years, I called him and asked him to let you adapt one of his novels. It was only ever meant to be one adaptation. I thought it would lead to success with your own screenplays, but by trying to help your career, I sometimes worry that I killed your dreams. Henry used you as a way to try and get close to me. He wasn't interested in me at all when I was a child. But I think his own mortality made him realize I could be useful as an adult—someone to look after his precious books when he was gone. My father cared about each of his novels far more than he ever cared about me.

These last two years have taught me a lot about myself. Now that I've left it "all" behind, I've realized how little I had. It's too easy to get blinded by man-made city lights, even though they could never shine as brightly as the stars in a cloudless sky, or white snow on a mountain, or sunbeams dancing on a loch. People confuse what they want with what they need, but I've realized now how different those things are. And how sometimes the things and people we think we need, are the ones we should stay away from. My hair is more gray than blond these days—I haven't visited a hairdresser since I left London, and it's grown very long. I wear it in plaits to avoid too many tangles and knots. I do miss our home, and us, and Bob, but I think the Scottish Highlands suit me. And I've realized I have more in common with my father than I used to admit, even to myself.

Henry liked his privacy so very much that he bought

everything in this valley, along with the old church and cottage, before I was born. The Scottish laird Henry purchased the land from had a few too many gambling debts, and just happened to be a fan of Henry's books, so sold it for a ridiculously small sum. Henry even bought the nearest pub a few years later, so that he could close it down. He just wanted peace and quiet and to be left alone. Completely alone.

The locals had been unimpressed by an outsider owning so much of the valley. There were petitions to stop Henry converting the church—even though nobody had used it for half a century—but he did it anyway. He was a man who always did what he wanted and got his own way. When local interference continued, he made up ghost stories about Blackwater Chapel, so that anyone who didn't already know to stay away, would. Why he wanted to live such a lonely life, hidden away from the world in self-isolation, used to baffle me. There are no shops, or libraries, or theaters, or people for miles, there is nothing here except the mountains and the sky and a loch full of salmon. The man didn't even eat fish. But now, I think I finally understand.

I have almost nothing but almost everything I need. My father's love of good wine meant that the crypt was crammed full of it, and his old housekeeper left a seemingly endless supply of homemade and hand-labeled meals in the freezer. Henry's personal library is stocked with all of my favorite books, and the ever-changing views here take my breath away every single day. But it can be hard to enjoy the good things in life when you don't have someone to share them with. I miss our words of the day and words of the year. I don't eat especially well—I'm a little too fond of tinned food these days—but I feel better than I ever did in London. Maybe it's the taste of fresh air in my lungs, or the long walks I take exploring the valley. Or maybe it's just feeling free to be me.

It can be hard to step out from a parent's shadow when you inherit their dreams. I often wrote stories as a child, but Henry's shoes were always too big to fill. Plus, he let me know from an early age that he didn't think I could write. I never thought I might be able to write an entire novel, but dreams can only come true if we dare to dream them in the first place. My self-confidence divorced me long before you did, but life taught me to be brave and to always try again. If you never give up on something you can't ever fail.

Whenever I weighed my father's words against my own, his seemed heavier, stronger, more permanent than the thoughts inside my head, which always seemed to come and go like the tide. Washing away my confidence. But castles made of sand never stand tall forever. I am free of his judgment now, and have realized the only person who forced me to live in his shadow, was me. I could have stepped out any time I wanted if I hadn't been so afraid of being seen.

Sometimes I sit in front of the loch when the sun is starting to set and pretend that you and Bob are here sitting next to me. I like to smoke Henry's pipe in the evening, and watch the salmon jumping across the water, before the moon rises in the sky to replace the sun. Then I listen to the sound of frogs singing, and watch the bats swoop and soar in the sky, until it gets so cold and dark, I have to head back to the cottage. I don't like to sleep in the chapel—too many unhappy memories haunt the rooms—but I have fallen in love with Blackwater Loch. This place never felt like home until I left it. I wish I could share it with you, along with all the secrets I was forced to keep. You promised to love me forever, but I wonder if you still think of me or miss me at all?

It's hard to picture Amelia in our old house in London, sleeping in my bed with my husband, walking my dog, cooking in my kitchen, working in my office at Battersea in the job I helped her to get. I still can't believe you gave her my

engagement ring. Or that she'd want to wear something that was once your mother's, and then mine. But stealing things that belong to other people seems to be a habit of hers. She's the kind of woman who expects something for nothing, and thinks the world owes her a debt. She was always reading magazines on her lunch breaks—never books—and liked to enter all the competitions inside them, or on the radio, or on daytime TV, hoping to win something for free. That's how I knew she'd never turn down a free weekend away. It was almost too easy to get you to come here.

I'm sure I'm not the first ex-wife to want revenge. I ~~sometimes imagined killing you both~~ try not to think about it. My personal variety of fury has always been surprisingly calm. I read and write instead. It's a loneliness coping mechanism that I developed as a little girl, when my father was always too busy working to notice me. It sounds daft now, but I never realized before how alike the two of you are. I seem to have spent a lifetime hiding inside stories: reading other people's when I was a child, and now writing my own.

There is one secret I want to share. I wrote a novel and now I am writing another. Dreams are like dresses in a shop window; they look pretty, but sometimes don't fit when you try them on. Some are too small, others are too big. Luckily, my mother taught me how to sew, and dreams can be adjusted to fit, just like dresses.

I think my new book is a good one and you're in it.

Rock Paper Scissors is all about choices. I've made mine, the time will come when you'll need to make yours. The only good thing about losing everything, is the freedom that comes from having nothing left to lose.

Your (ex) wife

AMELIA

People tend to think that the second wife is a bitch and the first is a victim, but that isn't always true.

I know how it looks. But ten years is a long time to be married, and theirs had run its course. I didn't used to think it was possible to be too kind—kindness is meant to be a good thing—but Robin was the variety of kind that invited people to walk all over her: her colleagues, her husband, me. In her mind, she befriended me out of pity when I started volunteering at Battersea Dogs Home. But the truth is she needed a friend more than I did; I've never met a lonelier woman.

Of course I was grateful when she helped me to get a full-time job, and of course I felt guilty about sleeping with her husband. But it wasn't some sordid affair. Their relationship was over long before I arrived on the scene, and Adam and I are married now. Instead of all of us being miserable. And she *was* unhappy—constantly complaining about her husband the big Hollywood screenwriter, while some of us were stuck dating life's rejects.

From the first time I met my husband, he was like an itch I couldn't resist scratching. I stayed on the sidelines for a long time,

watching, waiting, trying to do the right thing. I changed my hair, my clothes, even the way I speak, all for him. I tried to be who he needed me to be. Not for myself, but because I thought I could fix him, and I knew I could make him happier than he was with her. She didn't know how lucky she was, and two out of three happy endings are better than none.

Robin didn't exactly put up a fight. If anything, the divorce was surprisingly amicable given that they'd been married for a decade.

She left. He stayed. I moved in.

It was best for everyone and we were happy—Adam and I. We still are. Perhaps not as happy as we were, but I can fix that. This weekend was supposed to help, but I realize now that it was a big mistake. It doesn't matter. I'm sure dealing with his crazy ex will only bring Adam and I closer together again. And she *is* crazy. If I was in any doubt before, now I know for certain.

I tell myself that as we stand at the top of the staircase, looking at the photo of *their* wedding day on the wall. They are both smiling for the camera. As usual, I wonder what my husband sees. Does he see the face of someone he misses? Or is it just a blur he can't recognize? Does he think she is beautiful? Does he look at the picture and think they look good together? Does he wish they still were?

They must have been happy, too, in the beginning, just like us.

Changing love into hate is a much easier trick than turning water into wine.

It didn't seem to matter that Adam and I had very little in common when I first moved in to the house they used to share. He didn't seem to mind that I didn't love books and films as much as he did, and the sex was great for the first few months. I took better care of myself and my body than Robin ever did—I went to the gym and I made more of an effort with my appearance once I had someone to look pretty for. We did it in every room of the house that his ex-wife had so lovingly renovated—always my idea—an exorcism of the ghosts of their marriage. And, unlike so many couples, Adam and I never seemed to run out of conversation. His world fascinated

me—the trips to LA and the celebrities he got to meet at readings, it all sounded so . . . exciting. Adam liked talking about himself and his work just as much as I liked to listen, so it was a good match. We got married as soon as the divorce was finalized. It was a small affair, and very private. I didn't mind that it was just the two of us at the registry office that day, I didn't think we needed anyone else. I still don't.

If Robin really is behind all of this, and has been plotting some kind of revenge, then I'm considerably less scared than I was before. I'm smarter than her. A lot stronger too, mentally as well as physically. If this is her way of trying to win her husband back, it won't work. Nobody wants to be with a crazy woman, and I think it's safe to presume that's what she has become.

"We should just leave," I say.

"She slashed the tires."

"Then we'll walk to the next town, or hitch a ride if we see a car."

"Okay," Adam replies, without much conviction. It's as though he's gone into shock.

"Come on, help me grab our stuff."

I step back onto the landing, but open the wrong door by mistake—they were *all* locked when we arrived last night; the bell tower, the child's room—and now I see what must be the master bedroom—Henry's room. There is a large bed in the middle, as you might expect, but what I wouldn't have predicted and haven't seen in a bedroom before, are all the glass display cabinets covering each of the walls from floor to ceiling. Unlike in other parts of the house, these shelves aren't filled with books. Instead they are crammed full of little carved wooden birds. When I take a step closer, I realize they are all robins. There must be literally hundreds of them, all the same but different.

"This place just gets stranger and stranger. Let's go," I say again.

Adam follows me back out onto the landing, then into the bedroom where we slept last night. I wish that he hadn't. Robin's

presence is clearly visible in here too. There is a red silk kimono neatly arranged on top of the white sheets on the bed.

"What is this supposed to mean?" I say, but it is a stupid question, one which we both already know the answer to. The woman in the red kimono is what Adam has recurring nightmares about, caused by the memory of what happened to his mother. That's what she was wearing when she walked his dog late one night and was killed by a hit-and-run driver.

"Why would Robin do this?" he whispers.

"I don't know and I don't care. We need to leave, *now*."

"How?" he asks again.

"I told you already, we can walk if we have to . . ."

He looks away and I follow his stare. Three words have been written on the mirror above the dressing table, using red lipstick:

ROCK PAPER SCISSORS.

SILK

Word of the year:
redamancy *noun.* The act of loving the one
who loves you; a love returned in full.

29th February 2020—what would have been our twelfth anniversary

Dear Adam,
I've been writing you letters on our anniversary since we got
married, but this is the first one I'm going to let you read, and
I strongly suggest that you read it alone before sharing any of
its contents. The thought of finally being completely honest
feels good. The first thing I want you to know is that I never
stopped loving you, even when I didn't like you, even when
I hated you so much I wished you were dead. And I confess
that I did for a while. You hurt me very badly.

It is exactly twelve years since we got married, on a leap
year back in 2008. You must know by now that Henry Winter

was my father. There are so many reasons, good ones, why I never told you. He was there so often in our marriage, always lurking in the background, even on our wedding day. You just never recognized his face, the same way you didn't always recognize mine. But I lied to you only to protect you. My father didn't just write dark and disturbing books, he was a dark and dangerous man in real life.

I had a complicated relationship with my dad, especially after my mother died and he sent me away to boarding school. I knew you were a huge fan of his novels, but I never wanted what you and I had together to be contaminated by him: I wanted you to love me for me. I never wanted him to have any hold over me, or you, or us. But I did ask him to let you write a screenplay of one of his novels all those years ago. Having asked for his help, even just the once, it made me feel indebted to that monster in a way that I never, ever wanted to be. I don't expect you to understand, but please know how much I loved you to do that. Hindsight tends to be cruel rather than kind. Looking back now, perhaps if you had known who I really was, we would still be married and celebrating our twelfth anniversary. But there are so many things I could never tell you.

In public, Henry Winter was a brilliant writer of novels, but in real life he was a collection of unfinished sentences. He bullied my mother until she couldn't stand it anymore. When she died, he bullied me. As a child, he often made me feel as if I wasn't really there. As though I were invisible. The characters in his head were always too loud for him to hear anyone else. His lack of belief in me as a child led to a lifelong lack of belief in myself. His lack of interest made me feel as though I were of none to anyone. His lack of love meant that I was never fluent in affection, except with you. I sometimes think he would have kept me in a cage if he could, like his rabbit. And like my mother. Blackwater Chapel was her cage and I never wanted it to be mine.

Henry's books were his children, and I was nothing more than an unwanted distraction. He called me "the unhappy accident" on more than one occasion—normally when he'd had too much wine—even wrote it in a birthday card once.

> To the unhappy accident,
> Happy 10th Birthday!
> Henry

The card arrived two weeks after my birthday, and I was only nine that year. He never called himself Dad, so neither did I.

Nothing I did as a child was ever good enough. We are our parents' echoes and sometimes they don't like what they hear. I realized that the only way for me to have a life of my own was to remove my father from it. But Henry wasn't just exceptionally private, and a little peculiar, he was also very possessive. Of me. I felt like I was being watched my whole life, because I was. I left home when I was eighteen, changed my surname to what had been my mother's maiden name, and didn't come back until the day he called to say he was dying.

Everything I've done since I did for you, and for us.

I've written a novel, two now actually, both in Henry's name. Nobody else knows that he is dead, or needs to. Here's the pitch for the latest book:

Rock Paper Scissors is a story about a couple who have been married for ten years. Every anniversary they exchange traditional gifts—paper, copper, tin—and each year the wife writes her husband a letter that she never lets him read. A secret record of their marriage, warts and all. By their tenth anniversary, their relationship is in trouble. Sometimes a weekend away can be just what a couple needs to get them back on track, but things aren't what or who they seem.

Sound familiar?

It's a combination of your screenplay and the secret letters I have been writing to you every year since we got together. I've changed a few names, of course, and blended fiction with facts, but I think you'll like the result. I do. When Henry sends it to his agent, he'll include a letter to say that he wants you to start work on the screenplay straightaway. You'll finally get your own story on screen, just like we always dreamed.

But only if you end things with Amelia.

My plan isn't as crazy is it might sound. It could be good for you, and us. I miss us every day and wonder if you might, too? Do you remember that tiny basement studio we used to live in? Back when we were still learning whether we could live with or without each other. Some couples can't tell the difference. That's the version of you I miss most. And the version of us I wish we could find our way back to. We thought we had so little then, but we had it all, we were just too young and dumb to know it.

Sometimes we outgrow the dreams we had when we were younger, happy when they turn out to be too small, sad when they prove to be too big. Sometimes we find them again, realize that they were a perfect fit all along, and regret packing them away. I think this is our chance to start again and live the life we always dreamed of.

There are other things that you didn't know about Henry, aside from him being my father. He hired a private investigator for years to keep an eye on me, and you, and us.

A private investigator who knew that you were having an affair before I did.

Who knew things that I didn't know and that you still don't.

The private investigator is a man called Samuel Smith. He still thinks my father is alive—along with the rest of the

world—but aside from that huge miss, he seems pretty good at his job. Thorough. He sent weekly reports about us to my father for years—unknown to me—and they were both fascinating and sad to read. He didn't just follow us, he followed anyone we got close to. Including October O'Brien. And Amelia. He even sent my father pictures of our home, before and after I left it (I don't like what you've done with the place). Samuel Smith the private investigator knew more about us than we knew about each other. I thought for a long time about whether or not to share this information with you. It brings me no happiness to cause you pain, but like I said in the beginning, I love you. Always have, always will. Always always, not almost always, like we used to say. That is why I have to tell you the truth. All of it.

It was no coincidence that Amelia started working at Battersea, befriended me, and was always asking questions about you. You were always part of her plan. Your paths had crossed almost thirty years earlier, but you couldn't recognize her face. Samuel Smith found out more than he bargained for when you cheated on me. It's a question nobody ever wants to ask, or answer, but how well do you really know your wife?

Amelia Jones—as she was called before you married—has been lying to you since the moment you met. She lied to me too. Amelia has a criminal record and has been in and out of jail since she was a teenager. She lived in a series of foster homes growing up and was almost always in trouble. At one point, she was living on the same council estate as you. She even attended the same school for a few months, when you were both thirteen. That's when she progressed from shoplifting to joyriding. Amelia was suspected of stealing seven cars, before she was arrested on suspicion of causing death by dangerous driving. The police questioned her about a hit-and-run, but she was underage and her foster mother came

forward as an alibi—something the woman later confessed was a lie—and the cops couldn't make it stick.

The car they caught her in was the car that killed your mother. *what the fuck*

The only witness—you—couldn't pick her out in a police lineup, because you couldn't recognize the face of who was driving. But she knew you. *This is crazy.*

Amelia Jones moved to a new foster home, far away. She turned a new leaf and started again. Maybe she felt genuine remorse for what she had done? Maybe she felt guilty for getting away with it? Maybe that's why she followed you for years, and came up with a plan to get close to you, through me? Perhaps in some twisted way she was trying to make up for what she did. You'll have to ask her.

I know I lied to you about my father, but at least my lies were to protect you, and us. Nothing you think you know about Amelia is true. Your wife was to blame for your mother's death when you were a child, and I think it's only right that you know that, before making a decision. Don't believe me? Maybe try telling Amelia that you know the truth, but be careful, she is not the woman you think she is.

I know this will be hard to take in, let alone believe, but deep down, didn't you always feel as though something wasn't quite right about Amelia? The first time you met her, when she arrived uninvited at our home claiming to have had a bad date, you described her as an actress. It turns out your first impressions were right. I found the notebook by the bed where she writes down every detail of your nightmares. Did you ever wonder why she does that? I'm sure she said it was to try and help you remember the face of who killed your mother, but maybe it was to make sure you never did? It's no wonder she needs pills to help you sleep at night, the guilt she must feel would keep anyone awake. *Omg Amelia is crazy*

Knowing what you now know—and I have all the private

investigator emails and documents to prove it—do you still love her? Can you ever really trust her again? What happens next is up to you. It's a simple choice, like when we used to play rock paper scissors.

Option one—ROCK: You try to leave with the woman who killed your mother.

Option two—PAPER: You walk out of there alone and come find me and Bob in the cottage. We're waiting for you, and I want nothing more than for us all to be together again. I will move back to London, we can publish *Rock Paper Scissors* as a novel using Henry's name—nobody else ever needs to know—and then I promise you will finally get your own screenplay made. You won't need to adapt anyone else's work ever again and can spend the rest of your life writing your own stories.

Option three—SCISSORS: You don't want to know option three.

The choice is yours. I know what I'm asking you to decide sounds difficult. But it really is as easy as rock paper scissors if you can remember how to play.

Your Robin

xx

AMELIA

We're standing in the bedroom that has been made to look just like the one we share at home, the one I redecorated when Robin moved out. Except that now, things are even stranger than they were before. This is not at all how I hoped this weekend would go. I'd already decided to end the marriage if this trip did not go well—I'd spoken with a solicitor *and* a financial advisor, who suggested a life insurance policy might help me get what I deserved in a divorce settlement. I wanted to give things one last shot, but I'm starting to wish I'd just left. I've already found a flat to move in to—it's nice, with a view of the Thames—but I hoped it wouldn't come to that. I *hoped* this weekend might fix us. The estate agent is holding the flat for me until next week, says I can move in straightaway if I want, so I always knew that only one of us might be going back to the house that was only ever their home.

My whole miserable life keeps playing on a loop inside my mind recently, and I can't seem to find the off switch. I lie awake at night—despite the pills—longing to delete all the memories I wish I'd never made. All the mistakes. All the wrong turns. All the dead ends. I'm not making excuses, but I didn't have an easy childhood. I

know I'm not the only one, but those lonely years shaped who I am today. Tiny violins always sound loudest to those playing them. Being passed from one foster family to another, like unwanted goods, taught me never to get too comfortable, and never to trust anyone. Including myself. Every new home meant a new family, new school, new friends, so I'd try being a new version of me. But none of them were a perfect fit.

I've always been haunted by the death of my parents because it was my fault. If my mother wasn't pregnant with me, she wouldn't have been in the car and my father wouldn't have been driving her to the hospital when a truck smashed into them. If Adam hadn't met me his life would have turned out very differently too. We have so much in common, but we feel further apart than ever before. I watched Adam for years. His success—and the internet—made that easy. I've tried to be a good wife to him, but he still seems to see me as the bad penny and *her* as the lucky one. I've tried to make him happy. I've been trying to make amends for things that happened in the past for too long. I've become so many different versions of myself trying to please other people, that I no longer know who I am. I need to focus on the future now. Mine. Atonement is like that pot of gold at the end of the rainbow that nobody ever really finds.

"Why would Robin write 'rock paper scissors' in red lipstick on the mirror?" I ask, wondering if Adam's ex has a history of mental health issues that I am unaware of. I watch as he starts pacing the room, looking a little deranged himself. "Why would she trick us into coming to Scotland? Why would she keep her father's identity a secret for ten years and then not tell anyone when he died? And why would she steal our dog—"

Adam interrupts my questions. "Technically, Bob was her dog—"

"Exactly: *was* her dog, but then she just left. Disappeared without a word. You never even heard from her again after the magnolia tree incident, except through the solicitor—"

"Well, I imagine coming home early on our anniversary and

finding her husband in bed with her best friend was probably quite upsetting."

"Your marriage was over long before I came along."

"I never wanted to hurt her—"

"From the looks of things, I think that ship has sailed. *You* might want to hang around here reminiscing about your lovely first wife, but whoever Robin used to be, it seems pretty clear to me that she is now a full-time psycho. I think we can safely presume it was her face I saw looking in through the window last night. She must have been behind *all* the strange things that happened since we arrived, trying to scare us. She probably deliberately turned off the generator too, trying to freeze us to death—"

"I switched the generator off," Adam says.

His words make no sense at first, like he is speaking in tongues.

"What?"

He shrugs. "I just wanted to get back to London as soon as possible. I thought if the power went completely, you'd agree to go home."

The revelation winds me a bit, but I remind myself that Robin is the enemy, not Adam. I won't let her win. Whatever happens when we go back to London, it's more important than ever that Adam and I stay on the same team for now. It's us against her.

"You realize that Robin is probably who you saw in the thatched cottage down the lane? I bet she's still there now, and I think it's time we went and had it out with her. You might be scared of your ex-wife, but I'm not."

"I *am* scared," he says, and this is the least attracted I have ever been to my husband. A small part of me thinks I should leave them to it—they deserve each other.

"It's Robin, remember? Your sweet little first wife who couldn't kill a spider?"

"But if she's been living here all alone for the last couple of years . . . people can change."

"People. Never. Change."

We both experience a freeze-frame when we hear three booming bangs downstairs, so loud it feels like the whole chapel, and us, trembles.

"What was *that*?" I whisper.

Before he can answer, it happens again; the sound of knocking so loud, it's as though there must be a giant trying to get in those big gothic church doors. The look of fear on Adam's face transforms mine into anger. I am not afraid of *her*.

I leave the bedroom, run down the stairs and through the library lounge, knocking some books over in my hurry. Adrenaline is pumping through me, and despite all the strange goings-on of the last twenty-four hours, when I remember who I am dealing with, I'm now sure there must be a rational explanation for all of it. No ghosts, no witches, just a crazy ex-wife. I'm going to make her regret doing this to us.

I reach the boot room and see that the church bench is still blocking the door. I try to move it out of the way but it won't budge. Adam appears behind me, looking less like the man I married and more like the man I planned to leave.

"Help me," I say.

"Are you sure this is a good idea?"

"Do you have a better one?"

As we lift the heavy furniture out of the way, I remember how childlike my husband can be. The way he reverts to the boyhood version of himself whenever life gets too loud used to be endearing. It made me want to protect him. My fingerprints are all over his heartbreak, and I wanted to wipe it clean and start again. Now, I just wish he'd man up.

The chapel doors rattle as someone on the other side slowly knocks three times, again. The sound echoes all around us, and we both take a step back. The wall of tiny mirrors catches my eye, and I see multiple miniature versions of my husband's face reflected in them. It almost looks as though he is . . . smiling. When I check the

real version, standing right next to me, the smile has been replaced with a look of pure terror.

I'm losing my mind.

I hesitate before trying the door handle, and feel a small sense of relief when it is locked.

"Where is the key?" I ask, holding out my hand. I'm sure we both notice that it's shaking.

Adam takes the antique-looking iron key from his pocket and gives it to me, too scared to open the door himself. I try to slot it in the lock, but it won't go in. Something is blocking it from the other side. I try again but it won't budge, and I bang my fist on the wooden door in frustration. None of the stained-glass windows in the property open, and this is the only way in or out.

Then I see a shadow move beneath the door.

"She's out there. That crazy bitch has bloody locked us in."

I pound on the door when she doesn't reply, then properly lose my temper and call her all the names she deserves to be called.

Robin doesn't say a word, but I know she's still there. Her shadow doesn't move.

Then an envelope with Adam's name on it slides beneath the door.

ADAM

I pick up the envelope, and Amelia tries to snatch it from my hands.

"It's addressed to me," I say, holding it out of reach. Then I walk into the kitchen, slide into one of the old church pews beside the wooden table, and open the letter. There are several pages all penned by Robin. I might not be able to recognize faces, but I'd know her handwriting anywhere. Amelia sits down opposite. I try to keep my face neutral as I read, but the words don't make that easy.

How well do you really know your wife?

I lift the letter higher, so that she can't see it.

It was no coincidence that Amelia started working at Battersea . . .

When I reach the second page, my fingers start to tremble.

Your paths had crossed almost thirty years earlier, but you couldn't recognize her face.

"What does it say?" Amelia asks, reaching for my hand across the table.

I pull back. Don't answer.

The police questioned her about a hit-and-run . . .

I feel sick.

The car they caught her in was the car that killed your mother.

It's hard not to react when you read something like that about the woman you are married to. Amelia seems to sense that something is very wrong.

"What is it? What has she written?" she asks, leaning closer.

"Some of it is difficult to read," I reply. It isn't a lie.

When I get to the end, I fold the letter and put it in my pocket. Then I get up and walk over to one of the stained-glass windows. I can't look at Amelia's face now. I'm scared of what I might see.

I knew this affair was a mistake from the start, but sometimes small mistakes lead to bigger ones. Robin wasn't just my wife, she was the love of my life and my best friend. I didn't just break her heart when I cheated on her, I broke my own. The errors of judgment lined up like dominoes after that, each knocking the next one down. When people talk about falling in love, I think they are right, it is like falling and sometimes when we fall we can get very badly hurt. It was never really love with Amelia. It was a simple case of lust in love's clothing. Until I made matters even worse than they already were, by marrying a woman I had nothing in common with.

Maybe it was a midlife crisis? I remember feeling so down about my work. My career had stalled, I couldn't write and I felt . . . empty. My wife seemed just as disappointed with me as I was with myself. But this beautiful new stranger acted like the sun shone out of my middle-aged arse, and I fell for it. *She* came on to me, and I was too flattered and pathetic to say no. My ego had an affair and my mind was too muddled to know it should never have been anything more than that. It should never have happened at all.

It was Amelia who wanted to move in as soon as Robin moved out.

She found the engagement ring that Robin had left behind, and dropped endless hints about how much *she* wanted to wear it, even though it was never a perfect fit for her finger. Always too tight. She bullied me into signing the divorce papers as soon as they arrived, and she booked the registry office—the same one where Robin and

I got married of all places—for a quickie wedding without even telling me first. The woman delivered emotional blackmail like a conscientious postman. A second marriage was the ransom I should never have paid.

Something felt wrong, right from the start, but I thought I was doing what was best for everyone involved: cutting off the old loose threads that can cause a new relationship to unravel. I was too stupid or vain to pay attention to the alarm bells sounding inside my head. The ones we all hear when we're about to make a mistake, but sometimes pretend not to.

I never stopped loving Robin and I've never stopped missing her. I'd actually already spoken to my solicitor about my options if I wanted to leave Amelia. But this letter. The idea that she was in the car that killed my mother, then spent all these years spying on us, trying to get close to me . . . that can't be real. Surely Amelia isn't capable of that?

"Have you ever been in trouble with the police?" I ask, still staring out the window.

"What was in that letter, Adam?"

"Did you used to live on the same council estate as me as a teenager? Go to the same school?"

She doesn't answer and I feel sick.

The memory of that night comes back to haunt me, as it has so many times before. I remember the rain, almost as if it were a character in the story. As if it played a part, which I suppose it did. The sound of watery bullets hitting the tarmac is ingrained in my mind as a result. The road my mother was walking along was like a snaking black river, reflecting the night sky and the eerie glow of streetlights, like urban man-made stars. It all happened too fast and was over so soon. The horrifying screech of tires, my mother's scream, the awful thud of her body hitting the windscreen, and the sound of the car driving over the dog. The noise of the crash was the loudest thing I'd ever heard. It only lasted a few seconds, but seemed to play on repeat. Then there was only a terrible silence. It

was as though the horror I had seen turned the volume of my life down to zero.

I still can't look at Amelia. My mind is too busy filling in the blanks her words won't.

"Did you used to steal cars?" I ask her, in a voice that doesn't sound like my own.

Amelia doesn't reply, but her breathing is getting louder behind me. I hear her little sharp intakes of breath, as she stands and starts coming closer. I wish she wouldn't, but I turn to face her.

"Did you get arrested for death by dangerous driving when we were both thirteen?"

"I think you need to calm down," she wheezes, twisting my mother's ring round and round her finger. A nervous tic. A tell. I stare at the sapphire, twinkling in the dim light as if to taunt me. A small but beautiful blue rock. That ring should *never* have been on Amelia's hand.

"Did you go for a joyride in the rain one night?" I ask.

"We both need to stay calm and . . . talk."

She starts to sob and gasp at the same time, but I still can't look her in the eye. I just keep staring at the ring on her finger.

"Did the car mount the pavement?"

"Adam . . . please—"

"Did it crash into a woman wearing a red kimono while walking her dog? Did you leave her for dead and drive away?"

"Adam, I—"

"Did you think you'd get away with it forever?"

I look up and stare at Amelia's face. For the first time, it looks familiar to me. She takes the inhaler from her pocket, and starts to panic when she realizes that it is empty.

"Help me," she whispers.

"Were you the person in the car the night my mother was killed?" I ask, fighting back the tears in my eyes.

"I love . . . you."

"Was it you?" Amelia nods and starts crying too. "How could

you keep something like this from me? Why didn't you tell me who you were? This is . . . sick. *You're* sick. There's no other word for it. Everything about you, us, it's a . . . lie."

She can't breathe. I stare at her, no longer knowing what to do, or say, or how to react. This feels like one of my nightmares: it can't be real. Despite everything, my instinct is to help her. But then she speaks again, and I only want to do one thing: Shut. Her. Up.

"I'm . . . not the only one who . . . lied." I don't know what my face does when Amelia says this, but she takes a step back. "I'm sorry. I only ever . . . wanted to make you . . . happy," she whispers, gasping for air.

"Well, you didn't. I was *never* really happy with you."

Then I see Amelia's face clearly for the first time. And as soon as I do, it changes, darkens into something ugly and unfamiliar. Her eyes are suddenly wide and wild as they dart around the kitchen. It all happens so fast. Too fast. Her hand drops the inhaler, and reaches for the knife block instead. She's coming at me with a shiny blade. But then another face appears behind my wife, and I see another flash of metal, and this time it's a pair of extremely sharp-looking scissors.

SCISSORS

Word of the year:
schadenfreude *noun*. Pleasure, joy, or self-
satisfaction derived by someone from another
person's misfortune.

16th September 2020

Dear Adam,
It isn't our wedding anniversary, but it has been six months
since I came home, and I couldn't resist writing you a letter.
We've managed to put the past behind us, and we're a family
again: you, me, Bob, and Oscar, the house rabbit. Sometimes
when you set something free it comes back. Nobody knows
what happened in Scotland and nobody ever needs to.

It was hard at first, for both of us, returning to London to
find so many traces of her in our home. But it was nothing
that some bin bags, the local rubbish tip, and a lick of paint
couldn't solve. We've been returned to our factory settings,

and everything is back how it used to be. Almost. Working at Battersea Dogs Home seemed out of the question—too many reminders of all the things I would rather forget—but that's okay, I have a new job now: I'm a full-time writer.

Not that anyone knows, except you.

It's been a busy six months. *Rock Paper Scissors* is going to be published next year. It might not be my name on the cover, but it's my book, and it's hard not to feel anxious about people reading it. So much of our real lives have gone into this novel. The screen rights have already been sold—to a company you have always dreamed of working with—and there is a watertight clause in the contract stating that you will be the only screenwriter on this project. Henry signed the deal himself, or at least I did. Sometimes I think it's the fear of falling down that makes people trip up. We're not born afraid. When we're young, we don't hesitate to run, or climb, or jump, and we don't worry about getting hurt or fret about failure. Rejection and real life teach us to fear, but if you want something badly enough, you have to take the leap.

When the box of advance author copies arrived today, I cried. Tears of joy, mostly. I opened it using the vintage stork scissors I brought home from Scotland. I'd had them since I was a child, my mother bought two pairs—one for me and one for her. They were almost all I had left to remember her by, and they ~~looked good as new once they'd been in the dishwasher~~ made the experience extra special for me. I kept one pair and deliberately left the other set behind at Blackwater Chapel, because it's time to move on, and some things are best left in the past. Those scissors marked the end of an unpleasant ~~woman~~ chapter in our lives, and today they helped to reveal our new future, by opening a box of books. The novel has already been sold all over the world—twenty translations so far. I don't care whose name is on the cover, we know it's our story and that's all that matters to me.

Nobody needs to know that Henry Winter was my father. Or that he is dead.

Or what happened to your second wife.

It still upsets me that she was ever your wife at all. It made me so happy when you took off your wedding ring while we were still in Scotland and threw it in the loch, as though you wanted to leave the past behind us too. I tried to remove your mother's sapphire engagement ring from Amelia's lifeless hand before we left. Not because I wanted it back, but because she never deserved to wear it in the first place. It wouldn't come off her finger, no matter how hard I tried to twist or pull the damn thing, and it bothered me more than it should have. Some people are as stubborn in death as they are in life.

I'm not saying everything is perfect, there's no such thing. Marriage is hard work sometimes. It can also be heartbreaking, and sad, but any relationship worth having is worth fighting for. People have forgotten how to see the beauty in imperfection. I cherish what we have now, despite it being bloodied and a little torn around the edges. At least what we have is real.

We still have secrets, but not from each other anymore.

I always think it is best to look forward, never back. But if we hadn't got divorced, then next year would have been our thirteenth anniversary. The traditional gift is meant to be lace, and I already know what I'm going to give you. Although I'll be the one wearing a new wedding dress, it will be for you. Everything I do always has been.

Your Robin

xx

ADAM

Books can be mirrors for whoever holds them and people don't always like what they see.

The last six months have been good, and I feel as if my life is back on track. Robin is home again, and has redecorated every inch of our house; it's almost as though Amelia was never here. I'm so happy that Robin is back, so is Bob, I think we both needed her far more than I ever realized. I might not be able to see what she looks like on the outside, but my wife is a beautiful person *inside*. Where it matters. Nothing she could ever do will change the person I see when I look at her. *Rock Paper Scissors* is *finally* getting made, and even though the opening titles will say "based on the novel by Henry Winter" I can live with that. Dealing with difficult authors is so much easier when they are dead. It turns out my wife is just as good at writing thrilling horror stories as her father was. Perhaps it isn't surprising. The scariest haunted houses are always the ones in which you are the ghost.

I think there comes a point in everyone's life when you just have to do what you want to do. Chasing the dream becomes

involuntary, you have to, because we all know time is not infinite. And I've been chasing this for so long, didn't I deserve to catch up with my dreams eventually? I like to think so. I have the best job in the world, but writing is a hard way to make an easy living. If I thought I could be happy doing anything else, I would absolutely do that instead.

Despite everything, I'm sleeping better than ever before. My nightmares have stopped completely since we returned from Scotland, almost like I left the pain of my past behind. Perhaps because I finally have some sense of closure about what happened when I was a boy.

I still think about my mother and the way she died every day. And although the nightmares have stopped, the guilt has never gone away. It was my fault and nothing will ever change that. If I'd walked the dog myself—like my mother asked me to—she wouldn't have been out on the street that night, and the car wouldn't have hit her. But thirteen-year-old me was angry because he watched my mother do her hair, spray her perfume, paint her face, and wrap herself up in the red kimono like a free gift. She only wore it when a man was coming to stay the night at ours. She said they were *friends*, but the flat had paper-thin walls, and none of *my* friends made noises like that.

Different men stayed over a lot. I. Didn't. Like it. So when that evening's *friend* knocked on the door—another face I didn't recognize but was sure I'd never seen before—I stormed out. Thirteen-year-old me met a girl in the park that night, behind the tower block where I lived. We sat on the broken swings and shared a large bottle of warm cider. It was the first time I drank alcohol, the first time I smoked a cigarette, and the first time I kissed a girl. I was in no rush to go home. It made me wonder how many firsts a person can have before life only offers them seconds.

The girl tasted like smoke and bubble gum, and she said that I could do more than just kiss her if we could find somewhere to do

it. She taught me how to steal a car—she'd clearly done it before—then she taught me how to drive it behind a disused warehouse. She taught me how to do other things for the first time too in the backseat, we made noises of our own, and teenage me thought he was in love.

That's why I did what she said when she told me to drive around the estate. I remember the sound of her laughter, and the rain bouncing off the windscreen making it almost impossible to see. "Faster," she said, turning up the car radio. "*Faster!*" She put her hand on my crotch and I looked down. I took the corner *too* fast and we started to spin. When I looked up, I saw my mother.

And she saw me.

It all happened so fast: the sound of screeching brakes, the car mounting the pavement, my mother's red kimono flying in the air, the smash when her body hit the windscreen, and the thud of the wheels rolling over the dog. Then the silence.

I couldn't move at first.

But then the girl was screaming at me.

When I didn't respond, she pushed me out of the car, climbed into the driver's seat, and drove away. Some of the neighbors came out not long after that, they found me leaning over my mother, crying, and covered in her blood. Everyone presumed I'd been walking the dog with her when it happened.

I didn't even know the girl's name. And I'd never been able to recognize faces. When the police asked me to ID some pictures of a teenage girl they suspected of driving the stolen car, I genuinely couldn't help.

I thought I'd never see her again so it was a shock to discover we were married.

Do I feel bad about what happened to Amelia?

No.

Sadly, people die every day, even the good ones. And she wasn't

one of them. None of us know when we're checking out, life isn't that kind of hotel. I'm happy now. Happier than I thought I could be again. I just want to put everything behind me, and now I finally can. Sometimes a lie is the kindest truth you can tell a person, including yourself.

Adam was the one driving the car what??

SAM

Samuel Smith is not a happy man.

As a young boy, he was obsessed with horror and crime novels. He devoured books by Stephen King and Agatha Christie, and dreamed of being a detective one day. Becoming a private investigator was as close as he got. When Sam celebrated his fortieth birthday alone, drinking warm beer and eating cold pizza in his London flat, he made a confession to himself: this was not living the dream.

But the next day—when Sam was feeling rather worse for wear—an elderly man called. He asked for Sam's *professional* help to keep an eye on his estranged daughter. The old man was reluctant to tell him his name at first, but being a PI was a job that required facts, so Sam had to insist. Eventually, the caller confessed he was Henry Winter, and Sam's disappointing career suddenly became a lot more interesting.

He thought it must be joke, a belated birthday windup by a friend perhaps, but then remembered that he didn't have any. Reading books was how Sam spent most evenings. His favorites were the creepiest ones, and Henry Winter was the king of horror in Sam's eyes. He had been reading the author's stories since he was

a teenager. Once he had checked a few facts, and made sure it was the real Henry Winter who was asking for his help, Sam would have been happy to do the work for free.

But a man has got to eat.

It wasn't as though the elderly author was short of a bob or two: quite the opposite. But Sam still started to feel bad about how much he was charging him. Following Henry's daughter and keeping tabs on her husband was easy money.

Sam likes to think that he and Henry became friends over the years that followed, and in some ways they did. Sam even managed to persuade the old man to get a laptop, so that they could email from time to time. He would follow Robin or her husband twice a week or so—when they walked the dog, or on their way to work, or sometimes he just sat outside their house in Hampstead Village—just to keep track of things. Then he sent a monthly report Henry's way. But their exchanges weren't all work related. They often chatted about books, or politics, instead of Robin and Adam. Sam took great pride in the fact that Henry trusted and confided in him, even though they had never met.

They spoke at least once a month, so when he didn't hear from Henry for a while, Sam started to get a little concerned. First, the phone calls stopped and were never answered or returned, but back then Henry still replied to emails occasionally. He was surprisingly keen to see pictures of the dog all of a sudden, and wanted to know every detail when his daughter's home was redecorated after she moved out. Sam's long lens camera came in very handy on those occasions. But the author never used the same friendly tone he had before, and then all communication came to an abrupt end, along with his regular payments.

Sam had been keeping an eye on Henry's daughter for more than ten years, and it made him sad when his relationship with the author ended suddenly and with no explanation. He drank more beer, ate more pizza, and didn't buy the latest Henry Winter novel until the day *after* it came out, in protest. Sam had been a silent

part of the family since Robin married Adam. He was there when her husband started having an affair, and he felt a bit down himself when they got divorced. Digging around in the dirt of their marriage was easy work, but that wasn't the only reason why he did it for as long as he had. They were an interesting couple to keep tabs on: him with his writing, and her with a famous father, and a secret past. Sam had even grown rather attached to their dog, having watched Bob since he was a puppy. So he was genuinely sad when things went wrong for Mr. and Mrs. Wright.

When the daughter moved back in with her ex-husband a few months ago, after disappearing from the face of the planet for a couple of years, Sam decided to drive to Scotland and tell Henry about it in person. The author had always been painstakingly private and had refused to ever share his home address, but of course Sam knew where he lived. He might not have made it as a detective, but he still knew how to find out most things about most people.

Newspaper interviews with Henry Winter were rare, but Sam had kept one from a few years back. It was about where the author liked to write, and showed a picture of Henry in his study, sitting at an antique desk that once belonged to Agatha Christie. It didn't take long for Sam to find out which auction house the desk had come from. Or to bribe a delivery driver to give him the address where it had been sent.

Henry's Scottish hideaway was still harder to find than Sam could have imagined. The drive up from London was painfully long and slow, and without directions the postcode he'd been given proved close to useless. After driving around in circles looking for the mysterious—possibly nonexistent—Blackwater Chapel, and passing endless mountains and lochs that had all started to look the same, Sam went back on himself to Hollowgrove, the only town he had seen for miles.

There was only one shop, it was getting dark, and Sam spotted the woman putting up a CLOSED sign in the window as soon as

she saw him climbing out of his car. He knocked anyway, and she pulled a face that was even more unpleasant than the one she had been wearing before.

The woman opened the door and Sam noticed her name badge: PATTY.

She had a face like a carp and it was as red as her apron. Her beady eyes glared and she barked the word "what" at him with venomlike spit. She was clearly a woman who was good at making people feel bad. Sam resisted the urge to offer his condolences for Patty's sister, who he was sure had been murdered by a girl called Dorothy near a yellow brick road. But Patty's distinct lack of kindness turned out to be very helpful.

"Nobody has seen Henry Winter for a couple of years, and good riddance I say. He fired his old housekeeper with no notice—she was a friend of mine. The new housekeeper used to pop in now and then to get supplies—odd woman with a sweet tooth for baked beans and baby food—but even she stopped coming to town a few months ago. I don't know if I should tell you how to get to Blackwater Chapel. I don't want you coming back here and blaming me if something bad happens. That place isn't just haunted, it's cursed. Ask anyone."

Sam bought a bottle of overpriced whiskey—he didn't want to meet his friend empty-handed—and the old crow gave him directions anyway. When Sam gave her a ten-pound note to say thank you, she drew him a map.

Sam felt like a character in one of his favorite detective novels once he was back on the road. The phone calls from Henry ended around two years earlier—the same time the woman in the shop said the author stopped going into town. Sam didn't know anything about a housekeeper, old or new, Henry never mentioned them. The only person Henry ever really wanted to talk about was his daughter, Robin. Their estrangement still bothered Sam, because it clearly made the old author very sad indeed.

Robin was a difficult child. Her mother—a romance novelist

who Henry met at a literary festival back in the day—died when the girl was only eight years old. She drowned in the bath. Robin had two authors for parents, so it probably shouldn't have been a surprise that she struggled to separate fact from fiction. Henry said she was always making up stories, and it got her in trouble at boarding school as well as at home. She got suspended once, for telling girls in her dormitory tales about witches who whispered their victim's names three times before killing them. It was all just the result of an overactive imagination—which to be fair, she'd inherited—but when Henry tried to discipline her, Robin cut off her own hair with a pair of scissors one night, leaving two long blond plaits for him to find on her pillow.

Henry blamed grief, and himself, but nothing he did to try to help the child worked. She ran away from Blackwater Chapel too many times for him to count, and when she was eighteen, she ran away for good. Henry didn't know where she was for years, until Robin got in touch asking him to help her husband. Henry was fond of Adam from the start. He always sounded like he was smiling when he talked about the man Robin married. He didn't like the screen adaptations of his novels, but the fact he continued to agree to them was testament to how much he liked Adam. It was obvious that he grew to think of his secret son-in-law as the son he never had. He thought Adam had been a good influence on his daughter's life, and so long as she was happy, he was happy to stay out of it. That's all he wanted to know when he asked Sam to follow them.

Was she happy?

Robin was always fond of writing letters as a child, as well as making things up that got her into trouble. She wrote Henry one last letter before she ran away to London. It was a thank-you, as well as a goodbye. She said the only thing that he had ever given her that she truly loved was her name. Her mother had insisted they christen her Alexandra, but Henry never liked that, so always used the child's middle name instead, the one he had chosen: Robin. He

said she liked it so much because it made her feel like a bird, and birds can always fly away. When Robin flew, she never came back.

Sam kept one eye on the winding Highland roads—which were difficult enough to navigate even before it got dark. He also kept glancing down at the hand-drawn map the woman in the shop had given him, trying to make sense of it. He noticed that Patty had also scribbled down her phone number. Sam shuddered. Despite being lost in the desert for a long time when it came to the ladies, he'd rather die of thirst than drink at that well. When he turned off the main road, he saw that there had been a sign for Blackwater Loch all along. He'd driven past it several times earlier because, by the looks of it, the sign had been chopped down. Possibly with an axe. This was clearly a place someone didn't want people to find.

He drove along a little track, narrowly avoided hitting some sheep, and passed a small thatched cottage on the right. It looked abandoned. Sam was about to give up, had decided to maybe try and find a hotel for the night, but then his headlights illuminated the shape of an old white chapel in the distance.

Sam's fuel gauge was low but his hopes were high as he parked his thirdhand BMW outside. His optimism didn't last long. The chapel was in total darkness. He could already tell that nobody was home: the big old wooden doors weren't just closed; they were chained together with a padlock. Henry clearly wasn't there, and from the thick cobwebs covering the doors, it appeared he hadn't been for some time.

Upset at the thought of a wasted journey, and not quite ready to give up, Sam grabbed his torch from the boot of the car and went for a walk around the chapel. He hoped he might find another way in, but despite endless stained-glass windows there were no other doors. He did stumble across several wooden statues in the dark though. The eerie-looking rabbits and owls carved from ancient tree stumps, were so well hidden by shadows, that Sam walked right into the first one and automatically apologized before taking a step back. Their ghoulish, gouged eyes made him shiver. But then

he felt a strange surge of relief—Henry had talked to him about how much he loved to carve wood, he found it calming after a long day plotting to kill people—and Sam knew that he was at least in the right place.

Then he found the cemetery at the back of the chapel.

The granite headstones blended in with the rest of the pitch-black scenery at first, but when Sam got closer, his torchlight revealed that most were seriously old. So much so they were either leaning at angles, falling apart, or covered in moss. But not all of them were ancient or impossible to read. The newest one, which stood out from its crumbling neighbors in the distance, and couldn't have been more than a year or two old, grabbed his attention. He headed in that direction, but tripped over an unexpected mound of dirt and dropped his torch. Sam was pretty hard to scare—he'd read all of Henry Winter's novels twice—but even he had a dose of the heebie-jeebies as he crawled on his hands and knees, in a graveyard, late at night, trying to retrieve his torch. The heap of dirt suggested that someone had been recently buried there, and the grass hadn't quite had enough time to grow over the uneven soil. There was no marker, no name, and it reminded him of a pauper's grave. But then he noticed something sticking out of the ground . . . an old inhaler.

Sam felt uneasy all of a sudden, and the shopkeeper's warning about the chapel being cursed returned to haunt his thoughts. Then he heard someone whisper his name three times in the shadows just behind him.

Samuel. Samuel. Samuel.

But when he spun around, there was nobody there.

It must have just been the wind. Fear and imagination can lead the brightest of people down dark paths. No wonder a child growing up here imagined so many awful and twisted tales confusing fact and fiction, he thought, remembering all the stories that Henry said Robin had made up. He was going to ask the old man about that again as soon as he tracked him down. He had spotted a small

police station in Hollowgrove, and made a mental note to stop there on the way back, hoping they might know where his friend was living now. Somebody must. World-famous authors don't just disappear. Besides, Henry had a new book called *Rock Paper Scissors* coming out next year. Sam knew because he had already pre-ordered it.

He picked himself and the torch up off the muddy ground, and walked over to the newest-looking headstone in the cemetery. He had to read what was engraved on it several times before his brain could begin to process the words.

HENRY WINTER

~~FATHER~~ KILLER OF ONE, AUTHOR OF MANY.

He didn't believe at first that Henry was dead.

There was a tiny glass box on the grave, the kind someone might keep trinkets inside. Sam shone his torch on it, and hesitated before bending down to take a closer look. When he did, he saw that the box contained three items. A sapphire ring, a paper crane, and a small pair of vintage scissors designed to look like a stork. It was the ring that caught his eye, not just because of the sparkling blue rock, but because it was still attached to what appeared to be a human finger. The wind picked up then, and Sam thought he heard someone whisper his name again, three times. He didn't believe in ghosts, but he ran to his car as fast as he could and didn't look back.

ACKNOWLEDGMENTS

Huge thanks as always to Jonny Geller and Kari Stuart, not just for being the best agents in the known universe, but also for being two of the best, wisest, and kindest human beings I am lucky enough to know. Huge thanks also to Kate Cooper and Nadia Mokdad for selling my stories around the world, and to Josie Freedman and Luke Speed for the screen adaptations of my novels. Thank you to all the lovely people at Curtis Brown and ICM, with special thanks to Viola Hayden and Ciara Finan.

Thank you to the wonderful team at Flatiron Books, especially my editor, Christine Kopprasch. I am quite superstitious when it comes to writing, and I don't tell anyone anything about my books until I have written them. Not even my dog, and I love him the best. I had wanted to write about face blindness for a long time, so imagine my surprise when my agent sent Christine this book, and she revealed that she had the condition. Thank you, Christine, for your genuine love of books, your persistent kindness, and for making this book so much better than it was. Extra-special thanks to Donna Noetzel, Lisa Amoroso, and Rhys Davies for the beautiful cover and illustrations in this novel. Thank you to Cicely Aspinall and the

team at HarperCollins in the UK, and to all my other publishers around the world for taking such good care of my books.

Thank you to Scotland for inspiring so much of this story. If there is a more beautiful place on Earth, I have yet to find it. All of my books have been partly written and/or edited in the Scottish Highlands, and my visits grow longer each year. Special thanks to the face in the window of the property I rented during the "Beast from the East" snowstorms of 2018, and the converted chapel where I had the idea for this novel. I remember every single thing about the day this story happened inside my head.

Thank you to Daniel, for being my first reader, best friend, and the best lockdown partner a girl could wish for. For all of those reasons and so many more, this book is for you.

Thank you to the booksellers, librarians, journalists, book reviewers, book bloggers, and bookstagramers who have been so kind about my novels, and to everyone else who has helped put my books into the hands of readers. My final and biggest thanks is to all of you. Your beautiful pictures of the books and kind words always mean the world to me, but even more so this year. When I look back at 2020, I know it was the kindness of readers that kept me writing during the darkest of times. I'm forever grateful for your support, and I hope you continue to enjoy my stories.

PLEASE NOTE: In order to provide reading groups with the most informed and thought-provoking questions possible, it is necessary to reveal important aspects of the plot of this novel—as well as the ending. If you have not finished reading *Rock Paper Scissors* by Alice Feeney, we respectfully suggest that you may want to wait before reviewing this guide.

Rock Paper Scissors

DISCUSSION QUESTIONS

1. "Marriages don't fail, people do" (p. 2). It's hard to know who to trust in this marriage thriller, as both Adam and Amelia are unreliable narrators at times. Whose side were you on at the start of the book, Adam's or Amelia's? Did you change your mind?

2. "My husband doesn't recognize my face" (p. 1) is the opening line of the novel. Adam has a neurological glitch called prosopagnosia, which means he cannot see distinguishing features on faces, including his own. Had you heard of prosopagnosia (face blindness) before reading *Rock Paper Scissors*? How much of a part did Adam's condition play in the plot, and what about it did you find interesting?

3. *Rock Paper Scissors* features letters written to Adam by his wife on their anniversary each year, letters she has never let him read until now. Each one begins with a "word of the year." There's a fair bit of "hornswoggling" (p. 110) and the odd "biblioklept" (p. 60); they aren't always "chuffed" (p. 159) to be with each other, and the "shenanigans" (p. 32) that the couple got up to in the past tell us a lot about their present. Which was your favorite word of the year and why?

4. "Maybe all marriages have secrets, and maybe the only way to stay married is to keep them" (p. 226). Adam's wife believes this to be true, but do you? Can we ever really know everything there is to know about another person, even someone we love?

5. Adam is highly superstitious; he salutes magpies and would never walk under a ladder. Are you superstitious about anything? Adam also carries an old paper crane and a lucky penny in his wallet at all times. Do you believe in luck? Is there something sentimental you would feel lost without?

6. Henry Winter, the elderly novelist in the book, has chosen to live in a converted chapel in a beautiful but very remote corner of the Scottish Highlands. Why do you think some people need to be alone, while others surround themselves with friends and family?

7. "We are our parents' echoes and sometimes they don't like what they hear" (p. 262). All of the main characters in this novel have been haunted by their parents in one way or another. Why do you think none of them were quite able to move on with their lives and put the past behind them? Would things have been different if they had?

8. What was your favorite twist in the book?

9. Let's talk about Robin. What were your first impressions of this character? Did your opinion of her change while you were reading?

10. If you were one of the characters in this book, with whom would you most relate and why?

11. All of the illustrations at the start of each chapter in this novel were bespoke. Have you ever seen drawings in a psychological thriller before? Did you like them? Did you have a favorite?

12. Have you read any of Alice Feeney's other novels (*Sometimes I Lie, I Know Who You Are, His & Hers, Daisy Darker*)? If so, which of her books did you enjoy best and why?

13. *Rock Paper Scissors* is being made into a TV series for Netflix by the producer of *The Crown* and *Behind Her Eyes*. What is it about the book that you think might make it work on-screen? Is it the setting, the characters, or the plot?

14. Were you worried about Bob the dog? (Alice Feeney says she is owned by her black Labrador!)

15. It wouldn't be right if we didn't end with a quick game of rock paper scissors! Talk about how the game plays a part in the book, then play a quick round with whomever you're with right now. Even if it's just *your* dog (if that's the case, you really ought to win!).

Read on for a sneak peek at
Alice Feeney's new novel

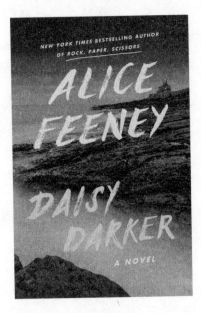

Available Fall 2022

I was born with a broken heart.

The day I arrived into this lonely little world was also the first time I died. Nobody spotted the heart condition back then. Things weren't as sophisticated in 1975 as they might be now, and my blue coloring was blamed on my traumatic birth. I was a breech baby, to complicate matters further. The weary doctor told my father to choose between me or my mother, explaining apologetically, and with just a hint of impatience, that he could only save one of us. My father, after a brief hesitation he would spend the rest of his life paying for, chose his wife. But the midwife persuaded me to breathe— against all their odds and my better judgment—and a hospital room full of strangers smiled when I started to cry. Everyone except for my mother. She wouldn't even look at me.

My mother had wanted a son. She already had two daughters when I was born, and chose to name us all after flowers. My eldest sister is called Rose, which turned out to be strangely appropriate as she is beautiful but not without thorns. Next to arrive, but still four years ahead of me, was Lily. The middle child in our floral family is pale, and pretty, and poisonous to some. My mother refused to name me at all for a while, but when the time came, I was christened Daisy. She is a woman who only ever has a plan A, so none of us

were given the contingency of a middle name. There were plenty of other—better—options, but she chose to name me after a flower that often gets picked, trampled on, or made into chains. A mother's least favorite child always knows that's what they are.

It's funny how people grow into the names they are given. As though a few letters arranged in a certain order can predict a person's future happiness or sorrow. Knowing a person's name isn't the same as knowing a person, but names are the first impression we all judge and are judged by. Daisy Darker was the name life gave me, and I suppose I did grow into it.

The second time I died was exactly five years after I was born. My heart completely stopped on my fifth birthday, perhaps in protest, when I demanded too much of it by trying to swim to America. I wanted to run away, but was better at swimming, so hoped to reach New York by lunchtime with a bit of backstroke. I didn't even make it out of Blacksand Bay and—technically—died trying. That might have been the end of me were it not for the semideflated orange armbands that kept me afloat, and my ten-year-old sister, Rose. She swam out to save me, dragged me back to shore, and brought me back to life with an enthusiastic performance of CPR that left me with two cracked ribs. She'd recently earned her first aid badge in Brownies. Sometimes I suspect she regretted it. Saving me, I mean. She loved that badge.

My life was never the same after I died a second time, because that's when everyone knew for sure what I think they already suspected: that I was broken.

The cast of doctors my mother took me to see when I was five all delivered the same lines, with the same faces, as though they had rehearsed from the same sad little script. They all agreed that I wouldn't live beyond the age of fifteen. There were years of tests to prove how few years I had left. My condition was unusual, and those doctors found me fascinating. Some traveled from other countries just to watch my open-heart surgeries; it made me feel like a superstar and a freak at the same time. Life didn't break my heart, despite

trying. The irregular ticking time bomb inside my chest was planted before birth—a rare congenital glitch.

Me living longer than life had planned required a daily cocktail of beta blockers, serotonin inhibitors, synthetic steroids, and hormones to keep me, and my heart, ticking. If that all sounds like hard work and high maintenance, that's because it was, especially when I was only five years old. But children are more resilient than adults. They're far better at making the most of what they have, and spend less time worrying about what they haven't. Technically, I'd already died eight times before I was thirteen, and if I'd been a cat, I would have been concerned. But I was a little girl, and I had bigger things than death to worry about.

Twenty-nine years after my traumatic arrival, I'm very grateful to have had more time than anyone predicted. I think knowing you might die sooner rather than later does make a person live life differently. Death is a life-changing deadline, and I'm forever in debt to everyone who helped me outstay my welcome. I do my best to pay it forward. I try to be kind to others, as well as to myself, and rarely sweat the small stuff these days. I might not have much in terms of material possessions, but that sort of thing never really mattered to me. All in all, I think I'm pretty lucky. I'm still here, I have a niece whom I adore spending time with, and I'm proud of my work volunteering at a care home for the elderly. Like my favorite resident says every time she sees me: the secret to having it all is knowing that you already do.

Sometimes people think I'm younger than my years. I've been accused of still dressing like a child on more than one occasion— my mother has never approved of my choice in clothes—but I like wearing dungaree dresses and retro T-shirts. I'd rather wear my long black hair in intricate braids than get it cut, and I'm clueless when it comes to makeup. I think I look good, considering all the bad things that have happened to me. The only visual proof of my condition is carved down the middle of my chest in the form of a faded pink scar. People used to stare if I wore something that revealed it:

bathing suits, V-neck sweaters, or summer dresses. I never blamed them. I stare at it too, sometimes; the mechanics of my prolonged existence fascinate me. That pink line is the only external evidence that I was born a little bit broken. Every couple of years during my slightly dysfunctional childhood, doctors would take turns opening me up again, having a look inside, and doing a few repairs. I'm like an old car that probably shouldn't still be on the road, but has been well looked after. Though not always and not by everyone.

Families are like fingerprints; no two are the same, and they tend to leave their mark. The tapestry of my family has always had a few too many loose threads. It was a little frayed around the edges long before I arrived, and if you look closely enough, you might even spot a few holes. Some people aren't capable of seeing the beauty in imperfection, but I always loved my nana, my parents, and my sisters. Regardless of how they felt about me, and despite what happened.

My nana is the only person in my family who loved me unconditionally. So much so, she wrote a book about me, or at least about a little girl with the same name. If mine sounds familiar, that is why. *Daisy Darker's Little Secret* is a bestselling children's book, which my nana wrote and illustrated. It can be found in almost every bookstore around the world, often nestled between *The Gruffalo* and *The Very Hungry Caterpillar*. Nana said she chose to borrow my name for the story so that—one way or another—I could live forever. It was a kind thing to do, even if my parents and sisters didn't think so at the time. I suspect they wanted to live forever too, but they settled for living off the book's royalties instead.

Nana had more money than she knew what to do with after writing that book, not that you'd know it to look at her. She has always been a generous woman when it comes to charity and strangers, but not with herself or her family. She believes that having too much makes people want too little, and has always hesitated when asked for handouts. But that might be about to change. Many years ago, long before I was born, a palm reader at a fair in Land's End told my nana that she wouldn't live beyond the age of eighty. She's

never forgotten it. Even her agent knows not to expect any more books. So tomorrow isn't just Halloween, or Nana's eightieth birthday. *She* thinks it's her last, and *they* think they might finally get their hands on her money. My family haven't all been in the same place at the same time for over a decade, not even for my sister's wedding, but when Nana invited them to Seaglass one last time, they all agreed to come.

Her home on the Cornish coast was the setting for my happiest childhood memories. And my saddest. It was where my sisters and I spent every Christmas and Easter, as well as the long summer holidays after my parents got divorced. I'm not the only one with a broken heart in my family. I don't know whether my parents, or my sisters, or even Nana's agent take the palm reading about her imminent death seriously, but I do. Because sometimes the strangest things can predict a person's future. Take me and my name for example. A children's book called *Daisy Darker's Little Secret* changed my family forever and was a premonition of sorts. Because I do have a secret, and I think it's time I shared it.

2

October 30, 2004, 4 p.m.

Seeing Seaglass again steals my breath away.

It normally takes at least five hours to drive from London to Cornwall, slightly less by train. But I've always enjoyed swapping the hustle and bustle of the city for a network of twisted memories and country lanes. I prefer a simpler, slower, quieter way of living, and London is inherently loud. Navigating my way back here has often felt like time travel, but my journey today has been quicker than expected and relatively pain-free. Which is good, because I wanted to get here first. Before the others.

I'm pleased to see that nothing much has changed since my last visit. The stone Victorian house with its Gothic turrets and turquoise tiled roof appears to have been built from the same granite rocks it sits on. Pieces of blue-green glass still decorate some of the exterior walls, sparkling in the sunlight and gifting Seaglass its name. The mini mansion rises out of the crashing waves that surround it, perched upon its own tiny private island, just off the Cornish coast. Like a lot of things in life, it's hard to find if you don't know where to look. Hidden by crumbling cliffs and unmarked footpaths, in a small cove known locally as Blacksand Bay, it's very much off the beaten track. This is not the Cornwall you see on postcards. But aside

from the access issues, there are plenty of other reasons why people tend to stay away.

My nana inherited Seaglass from her mother—who allegedly won it from a drunken duke in a card game. The story goes that he was an infamous bon viveur, who built the eccentric building in the 1800s to entertain his wealthy friends. But he couldn't hold his liquor, and after losing his "summer palace" to a *woman*, he drowned his sorrows and himself in the ocean. Regardless of its tragic past, this place is as much a part of our family as I am. Nana has lived here since she was born. But despite never wanting to live anywhere else, and making a small fortune writing children's books, she has never invested much on home improvements. As a result, Seaglass is literally falling into the sea and, like me, it probably won't be around much longer.

The tiny island it was built on almost two hundred years ago has slowly eroded over time. Being exposed to the full force of the Atlantic Ocean and enduring centuries of wind and rain has taken its toll. The house is swollen with secrets and damp. But despite its flaking paint, creaking floors, and ancient furnishings, Seaglass has always felt more like home to me than anywhere else. I'm the only one who still visits regularly; divorced parents, busy lives, and siblings with so little in common it's hard to believe we're related have made family gatherings a rather rare occurrence. So this week-end will be special in more ways than one. Pity fades with age, hate is lost and found, but guilt can last a lifetime.

The journey here felt so solitary and final. The road leads to a hidden track on top of the cliff that soon comes to an abrupt dead end. From there, the only two options to get down to Blacksand Bay are a three-hundred-foot fall to certain death or a steep, rocky path to the sandy dunes below. The path has almost completely crumbled away in places, so it's best to watch your step. Despite all the years I have been coming here, to me, Blacksand Bay is still the most beautiful place in the world.

The late-afternoon sun is already low in the hazy blue sky, and

the sound of the sea is like an old familiar soundtrack, one I have missed listening to. There is nothing and nobody else for miles. All I can see is the sand, and the ocean, and the sky. And Seaglass, perched on its ancient stone foundations in the distance, waves crashing against the rocks it was built on.

Having safely reached the bottom of the cliff, I remove my shoes and enjoy the sensation of sand between my toes. It feels like coming home. I ignore the rusty old wheelbarrow, left here to help us transport ourselves and our things to the house; I travel light these days. People rarely need the things they think they need in order to be happy. I start the long walk across the natural sandy causeway that joins Seaglass's tidal island to the mainland. The house is only accessible when the tide is out, and is completely cut off from the rest of the world at all other times. Nana always preferred books to people, and by living in such an inaccessible place, her wish to be left alone with them was mostly granted and almost guaranteed.

The invisible shipwrecks of my life are scattered all over this secluded bay with its infamous black sand. They are a sad reminder of all the journeys I was too scared to make. Everyone's life has uncharted waters—the places and people you didn't quite manage to find—but when you feel as though you never will, it's a special kind of sorrow. The unexplored oceans of our hearts and minds are normally the result of a lack of time and trust in the dreams we dreamed as children. But adults forget how to believe that their dreams might still come true.

I want to stop and savor the smell of the ocean, enjoy the feel of the warm afternoon sun on my face and the westerly wind in my hair, but time is a luxury I can no longer afford. I didn't have very much of it to spend in the first place. So I hurry on, despite the damp sand clinging to the soles of my feet as though trying to stop me in my tracks, and the seagulls that soar and squawk above my head as if trying to warn me away. The sound of their cries translates into words I don't want to hear inside my head:

Go back. Go back. Go back.

I ignore all the signs that seem to suggest that this visit is a bad idea, and walk a little faster. I want to arrive earlier than the rest of them to see the place as it exists in my memories, before they spoil things. I wonder if other people look forward to seeing their families but dread it at the same time the way I always seem to. It will be fine once I'm there. That's what I tell myself. Though even the thought feels like a lie.

The windchimes that hang in the decrepit porch try to welcome me home, with a melancholy melody conducted by the breeze. I made them for my nana one Christmas when I was a child—having collected all the smooth, round pieces of blue and green glass I could find on the beach. She pretended to like the gift, and the seaglass windchimes have been here ever since. The lies we tell for love are the lightest shade of white. There is a giant pumpkin on the doorstep, with an elaborate scary face carved into it for Halloween; Nana does always like to decorate the house at this time of year. Before I can reach the large weathered wooden door, it bursts open with the usual welcoming party.

Poppins, an elderly Old English sheepdog, is my nana's most trusted companion and best friend. The dog bounds in my direction, a giant bouncing ball of gray and white fur, panting as if she is smiling and wagging her tail. I say hello, make a fuss of her, and admire the two little plaits and pink bows keeping her long hair out of her big brown eyes. I follow the dog's stare as she turns back to look at the house. In the doorway stands Nana, five foot nothing and radiating glee. Her halo of wild white curls frame her pretty, petite face, which has been weathered by wine and age. She's dressed from head to toe in pink and purple—her favorite colors—including pink shoes with purple laces. Some people might see an eccentric old lady, or the famous children's author: Beatrice Darker. But I just see my nana.

She smiles in my direction. "Come on inside, before it starts to rain."

I'm about to correct her about the weather—I *remember* feeling the sun on my face only a moment ago—but when I look up, I see

that the picture-perfect blue sky above Seaglass has now darkened to a palette of muddy gray. I shiver and realize that it's much colder than I'd noticed before, too. It does seem as though a storm is on the way. Nana has a habit of knowing what is coming before everybody else. So I do as she says—like always—and follow her and Poppins inside.

"Why don't you just relax for a while, before the rest of the family joins us?" Nana says, disappearing into the kitchen, leaving me—and the dog—in the hallway. Something smells delicious. "Are you hungry?" she calls. "Do you want a snack while we wait?" I can hear the clattering of ancient pots and pans, but I know Nana hates people bothering her when she's cooking.

"I'm fine, thanks," I reply. Poppins gives me a disapproving look—she is never one to turn down food—and trots out to the kitchen, no doubt hoping to find a snack of her own.

I confess that a hug might have been nice, but Nana and I are both a little out of practice when it comes to affection. I expect she is feeling just as anxious as I am about this family reunion, and we all deal with anxiety in different ways. You can see fear on the surface of some people, while others learn to hide their worries inside themselves, out of sight but not out of mind.

The first thing I notice—as always—is the clocks. It's impossible not to. The hallway is full of eighty of them, all different colors, shapes and sizes, and all ticking. A wall full of time. There is one for every year of Nana's life, and each one was carefully chosen by her, as a reminder to herself and the world that her time is her own. The clocks scared me as a child. I could hear them from my bedroom— *tick tock, tick tock, tick tock*—as though relentlessly whispering that my own time was running out.

The bad feeling I have about this weekend returns, but I don't know why.

I follow my unanswered questions farther into Seaglass, hoping to find answers inside, and I'm instantly filled with a curious collection of memories and regrets. Transported back in time by the

familiar sights and smells of the place, a delicious mix of nostalgia and salty air. The diffused scent of the ocean loiters in every corner of the old house, as though each brick and beam has been saturated by the sea.

Nothing has changed in the years I have known this place. The whitewashed walls and wooden floors look just as they did when my sisters and I were children—a little worn out maybe, by the leftover love and loss they have housed. As I breathe it all in, I can still picture us as the people we used to be, before life changed us into the people we are now, just like the sea effortlessly reshapes the sand. I can understand why Nana never wanted to live anywhere else. If this place were mine, I'd never leave it behind either.

I wonder again why she has really invited the whole family here for her birthday when I know she doesn't love or even like them all. Tying up loose ends, perhaps? Sometimes love and hate get tangled, and there is no way to unpick the knot of feelings we feel. Asking questions of others often makes me ask questions of myself. If I had the chance to iron out the creases in my life before it ended, which ones would I choose to smooth over? Which points and pleats would I most want to unfold so they could no longer dent the picture of the person I wished to be remembered as? Personally, I think that some wrinkles and stains on the fabric of our lives are there for a reason. A blank canvas might sound appealing, but it isn't very interesting to look at.

I head up the creaky stairs, leaving the ticking clocks behind me. Each room I pass contains the ghosts of memories from all the days and weeks and years I have walked along this hallway. Voices from my past trespass in my present, whispering through the cracks in the windows and floorboards, disguised as the sound of the sea. I can picture us running through here as children, giddy on ocean air, playing, hiding, hurting one another. That's what my sisters and I were best at. We learned young. Childhood is a race to find out who you really are, before you become the person you are going to be. Not everybody wins.

I step inside the bedroom that was always mine—the smallest in the house. It is still decorated the way it was when I was a girl, with white bedroom furniture—more shabby than chic—and old, peeling wallpaper, covered in a fading pattern of daisies. Nana is a woman who only says and does things once, and she never replaces something unless it is broken. She always used to put flowers in our bedrooms when we came to stay as children, but I notice that the vase in my room is empty. There is a silver dish filled with potpourri instead, a pretty mix of pine cones, dried petals, and tiny seashells. I spot a copy of *Daisy Darker's Little Secret* on the bookshelf, and seeing it reminds me of my own secret. The one I never wanted to share. I lock it away again for now, back inside the box in my head where I have been keeping it.

The ocean continues to serenade my unsettled thoughts, as though trying to silence them with the relentless *shh* of the sea. I find the sound soothing. I can hear the waves crashing on the rocks below, and my bedroom window is stained with the resulting spray, droplets running down the glass like tears as if the house itself were crying. I peer out and the sea stares back: cold, infinite, and unforgiving. Darker than before.

Part of me still worries that I was wrong to come, but it didn't feel right to stay away.

The rest of my family will be here soon. I'll be able to watch them walk across the sandy causeway one by one as they arrive. It's been such a long time since we've all been together. I wonder whether all families have as many secrets as we do. When the tide comes in, we'll be cut off from the rest of the world for eight hours. When the tide goes back out, I doubt we'll ever all be together again.

ABOUT THE AUTHOR

Alice Feeney is a *New York Times* million-copy best-selling author. Her books have been translated into over twenty-five languages and optioned for major screen adaptations, including *Rock Paper Scissors*, which is being made into a TV series by the producer of *The Crown*. Alice was a BBC journalist for fifteen years and now lives in Devon with her family.

Think you know the person you married? Think again...

Things have been wrong with Mr. and Mrs. Wright for a long time. Every anniversary the couple exchange traditional gifts and Adam's wife writes him a letter she never lets him read. Until now.

Self-confessed workaholic Adam Wright has face blindness. He can't even recognize his own wife. And Amelia is sick of feeling unseen.

When Adam and Amelia win a weekend away to Scotland, it might be just what their marriage needs. This weekend may make or break their marriage, but they didn't randomly win this trip. One of them is lying, and someone doesn't want them to live happily ever after.

Ten years of marriage. Ten years of secrets. And an anniversary they will never forget.

PRAISE FOR *ROCK PAPER SCISSORS*

"Entertaining and grippingly suspenseful on every page."
—*DEADLY PLEASURES*

"Chilling and clever, with a twist so sharp you'll get whiplash. *Rock Paper Scissors* is the kind of blistering, one-sit read that Alice Feeney is just so incredibly good at."
—CHRIS WHITAKER, bestselling author of *We Begin at the End*

"[A] disturbingly twisty domestic thriller."
—*PARADE*

ALICE FEENEY is the *New York Times* bestselling author of *Sometimes I Lie*, *I Know Who You Are*, *His & Hers*, *Rock Paper Scissors*, and *Daisy Darker*. *Rock Paper Scissors* has been optioned for Netflix by *The Crown* producer Suzanne Mackie's Orchid Pictures.

© Brian Grant

Cover design by Lisa Amoroso
Cover photographs: winter trees © Federico Tardito/Alamy; church © Arnd Wiegmann/Reuters

US $17.99 / CAN $23.99
ISBN 978-1-250-26612-5

FLATIRON BOOKS
WWW.FLATIRONBOOKS.COM

PRINTED IN THE UNITED STATES OF AMERICA

51799 >

9 781250 266125